Mys.
CRE

Creeth, E. H.
(Edmund H.)

Deerlover

$15.95

DATE		

97472

deerlover

deerlover

E. H. Creeth

A FOUL PLAY PRESS BOOK

The Countryman Press
Woodstock, Vermont

AUTHOR'S NOTE

This is a work of fiction, although the central question it addresses—the rights of animals—is a real one. The characters, situations, and sequences are fictional, and—to date—any resemblance to actual events or the experience of persons living or dead is coincidental.

First Edition
Copyright © 1987 by E. H. Creeth

Library of Congress Cataloging-in-Publication Data
Creeth, E. H. (Edmund H.)
   Deerlover.
   "A Foul Play Press book."
   I. Title.
PS3533.R35D4   1987   813'.54   87-8824
ISBN 0-88150-094-1

The lyrics on pages 41 and 42 are from
"Help Me Make it Through the Night"
Words and Music by
Kris Kristofferson
Copyright © 1970 by Comine Music Corporation
Nashville, Tennessee 37203
All Rights Reserved   Used by Permission

Book design by Wladislaw Finne
Yarmouth, Maine

Photocomposition by NK Graphics
Keene, New Hampshire

Printed in the United States of America
by Arcata Graphics

A Foul Play Press Book
The Countryman Press

To my wife Susan,
For her devotion to animals

That day, Pwyll, Prince of Dyved, who thought he was going out to hunt, was in reality going out to be hunted, and by no beast or man of earth.

—The Welsh *Mabinogian*

NOVEMBER

15

i

With his slightest movement forward or to the side, or
even when he eased his body sideways without taking
a step (so as not to crunch the dry leaves underfoot),
the trunks of maple and of birch shifted a little in his
view into new but always impenetrable relationships.
Never could he quite see around or through them,
through their subtly shifting patterns of verticality. And
the scattering of young pines held out their light green
sprays at eye-level against this gray-white background
to further baffle his sight. Yet Robinson did not mind
this dense north-woods cover. In fact he preferred it.
The time was just after dawn on the first day of the
season.

He took one step at a time, stopping to listen and
stare all around before taking another. Like any good
hunter he moved, though necessarily at a sharp angle,
as much as he could against the slight drift of the air
in this dense forest. He never stepped on a twig to
crack it. But if he did make some accidental sound
above the inevitable sound of the leaves as his foot
pressed them, if, say, the butt of the scoped .308 slung
on his back bumped a tree, he froze a full minute to
let the woods quiet themselves. His binoculars clung
to his chest just under his chin on a rubber strap so
that they would not swing and hit against him. His
khaki pants and red hunting jacket were of wool because wool, though it did not keep out dampness so
well as poplin or the synthetic fabrics, made no clothing
noise of its own or when rubbed against brush. The
red would appear to color-blind deer as a moderate
gray among grays, suspicious only in its blocky shape
and strange movements.

Ahead of him the ground rose gradually, and at the top of a slight ridge gray sand bared itself here and there, and beyond lay a long depression running east and west, a longitudinal swale filled with water and criss-crossed by the black trunks of fallen trees, balsam and buttonwood, their roots betrayed and loosened by the gathering water. He looked for tracks in the sand but found none and stepped down, crossing on a mossy log, arms spread to keep his balance above the water, then leaning against a slim birch on the far side. Here at last he could see far to east and west, but nothing moved. He wanted a smoke to calm his nerves. The chronic terror was beginning to edge in.

He drew a cigarette and placed it in his mouth. He had taught himself to rub the match almost silently against the side of the matchbox and yet with enough friction to ignite. He lit the cigarette, inhaled deeply, and began to feel better. By instinct he watched the drift of the smoke, just perceptibly to his left, westward, confirming the wind direction. He had experienced nothing to make him think deer feared the smell of tobacco smoke in any case. It might be that they liked it. Even that it might attract them. The tame deer in the park near his home came to him when he smoked at the barricade. When no attendant was watching, he gave them cigarettes which they ate with obvious pleasure. They let him stroke their moist black muzzles.

Now he half expected to catch a glimpse of the pair of hunters he had followed into these woods. The sight of them, leaving their blue pick-up and stalking into the cover of the trees, had inspired him to try his own luck here. In their blaze orange jump suits, holding their long-barreled deer rifles in both hands, they seemed to be a couple of true sportsmen who knew what they were doing. Blaze orange was said to be the most easily visible color to the human eye. State hunting regulations required every hunter to wear one item of clothing in this color. Robinson had a silly looking hat that he kept stuffed in his pocket.

He had pulled over and parked well off the shoulder behind some scrub fifty yards beyond their truck and angled in to intercept them. Now he was not so sure of their capability. The relationship of wind direction and light was wrong here. A hunter would have to shoot into the light, rendering himself visible, his target shadowed. Make your prey look into the light. You are a blur and he is illuminated. And though there was water that might attract deer, the forest seemed too thick for them. They liked areas where woods edged off into plowed fields or meadows or lumbered sections. There they could stand and feed on shoots or the leavings of a farm operation and still reach instant cover when alarmed. He had not known what to expect in here. All hunting sites were strange to him. He never hunted in the same place twice.

Seeing no speck of bright orange down the gully eastward, he decided the hunters were still ahead of him. He had moved too slowly to catch up. Gazing ahead, he picked out an inverted beer can dropped over a poplar sapling. It looked faded by the elements. It had probably been there all year. It would help mark the way out.

He touched the tip of his cigarette into the brown water at his feet and left the extinguished butt on the fallen trunk where he stood. He climbed out of the boggy dip. Instantly at the top of the ridge his senses came alert. In a patch of the gray sand were deer tracks—a single heavy animal walking eastward. And droppings, large and well formed and, he thought, fresh, though it was hard to be sure since the nighttime dew, not yet dispelled, might give them that appearance. A buck he thought, a single big buck who might indeed bed down in this dense wood where few hunters would try to penetrate. Does usually moved in groups of three or four, and in mid-November would still have their spring-born fawns with them. Soon they would chase them off or run away from them and become, themselves, available to the rut, but not quite yet. Bucks were loners. There was no family life among deer. A single set of large, deep tracks almost certainly meant a buck.

He bent to examine the spoor more closely. The droppings were steaming, though ever so slightly. He froze in the awkward posture in which he found himself, the .308 askew on his back, its sling almost ready to slip off his lowered shoulder, his hands and arms motionless before him. Without moving his head in the slightest, he raised his eyes.

The buck stood not more than twelve yards away along the low ridge beside the gully where, he supposed, it had come to drink before bedding down for the day. The left side of the animal was mainly toward him but aimed a little away, the head on the broad neck turned back in his direction, the left ear with its inner lining of white raised and cocked toward him, the soft brown eye directly on him. Rarely, except maybe in very deep country, did one stumble like this upon a mature buck, or even have the chance to see one, the whole animal. Last season, out hunting every day, peering into deep woods and scanning across fields with his binoculars, he'd glimpsed only two, the first by the black gleam of its nose through cover under the tips of antlers, the other, identifiable by its solid stance and boxy shape (as against the triangular impression of a distant doe) far across harvested land before a stand of cedar. Evidently this deer, though aware of some presence, had not distinguished him. Nothing was more terrifying to a wild animal in this environment than the human face. Robinson had brought along his webbed head mask. It was in his pocket with the cap. He had not put it on because it interfered with his vision when using the scope and glasses. Too late now.

Presumably he merged somewhat with the trunks and branches near him or with the baffle of growth behind him. The deer, smelling nothing suspicious in the east wind, did not distinguish him as human. Its tail, darker brown against the brown gray of the body, was down, showing that it was not yet alarmed, only curious. This moment could not last. It must be relished and remembered. The rack, with its nine points, reached high above the ears, the antlers spreading wide at mid-height then curving in toward each other like a pair of cupped bony hands. The deer's outline had a reddish edging, the effect of the filtered light of dawn upon its short hair. The fine coat was trimmed here and there with white, the white of the rump, the backs of the front legs and the inner sides of the hind legs. Beside the deer's rear feet rose a patch of late-surviving yellow flowers.

Then the deer shook its head, snorted and pawed the ground once, bounded into the woods, the tail raised now, displaying its white backing and waving left and right over the bouncing rump like a flag of alarm.

Robinson followed, not hurrying but moving less cautiously than before. The buck was out of sight far ahead of him. For a half mile the woods were interrupted now and then by the long gullies, which were less and less wet. Beyond the last of these came a grassy clearing that he thought at first was an abandoned road or a fire break, for it ran straight east and west as far as he could see. But it was a break cut for power lines. They hung hardly more than a hand's reach high at the bottom of their sag from poles perhaps a hundred yards apart. He did not step into the clearing, of course, but climbed up to and made his way along the side to where a fallen log jutted into it. He worked his way out behind this and raised his head. Far down the cleared strip to the east the two hunters stood in plain sight.

He pulled the binoculars up for a closer look. They were apparently not talking, knowing enough at least to keep quiet, but were gesticulating to each other excitedly. One pointed into the woods on the far side of the break toward an opening about half way between them and Robinson. They must have seen the buck run across where it had to expose itself to reach safety, surprising them by its sudden appearance and going too fast—because it was running from Robinson—to allow a shot. Very likely they had reconnoitered the area the day before, without their guns, and found the pallet of matted grass where the buck slept, or even come upon the animal itself. Their strategy had been to return and shoot the buck when, at dawn, it had to enter the cleared strip to get home, for it could not go around it. They'd be ready, and each would have a shot. But the deer, frightened by Robinson, had not entered cautiously but bounded across. Now they might wait an hour and try the sneak approach. To shoot a buck off-guard and bedded down on its home territory was one of the surest satisfactions possible in the hunt. Or they might return at dusk and try the reverse of their original strategy when the buck went out to forage and to drink. There might be no water on his side of the clearing. They might break the law just a little and use a lantern just after dark.

Robinson watched the hunters only a few seconds. He shifted slightly to glass along the far woods from where they stood towards himself and then even more carefully and slowly examined the side of the opening toward which the men had seemed to point. It was unlikely that the animal was within sight. It had crossed downwind of the hunters and might have scented them. It should be in the impenetrable center of its sanctuary, if there was sanctuary. Yet there might be other hunters on the other side, or perhaps a farm and plowed fields. And, after all, the breeze in his face was slight, almost imperceptible. The men were three hundred yards away. Their scent might not yet have carried this far down the canyon cut in the woods. They were keeping silent. They were invisible from anywhere inside the entrance to the opening. The running deer might not have seen them.

Inch by inch he examined the outer perimeter of the woods along the clearing, trying to see into them, with the power of the binoculars, testing whether a narrow line of sight allowed by the chance disposition of trees showed anything horizontal, whether the patch of whiteness behind a network of twigs was the chin of the deer, whether a pair of straight saplings were in fact its legs.

On the first sweep, nothing. But on the second, coming back toward the way cut out for the poles, he thought he saw, many feet back and radically broken up, the curve of a buttock. There was no other such shape to be seen in the woods. When he shifted his position along the log trying for a better view it disappeared. But when he moved back again the few inches and looked, it was still there. He laid the glasses against his chest, slid down the decline beside him so as to be out of sight, and unslung the rifle. Then he resumed his prone position, resting the back of his left hand with the rifle on it on the log for steadiness, the sling looped tight around his upper arm for further bracing. He jiggled his body to get more comfortable, pelvis not so low that his back was strained, elbows weighted evenly, spread legs supported by both his knees and the toes of his boots.

The hunters had separated. One had gone from view, the other remained, deer rifle resting on its butt beside him, his back to Robinson. What was their strategy now that the first had failed? It must be that the missing hunter would circle round behind, getting the deer between them, and scare it into the open, where either or both men would have a shot at it, a running shot maybe, but a possible one. That must be the plan, though Robinson wished he had seen which way the absent hunter had gone. A two-man drive was a shaky proposition at best. The deer could double back behind one driver. Such a drive was dangerous too. The stander might in his excitement fire into the woods and kill the driver.

There wouldn't be very much time. Sweat beaded on his forehead. He sighted toward the spot on the perimeter. The scope was set at 1X, no magnification but better light collection than with the unaided eye. He could not discern the shape. With the thumb and forefinger of his right hand he turned the ring to 4X. The woods leaped toward him. Yes, he thought he saw again the curve that could only be of flesh. If so, the buck must feel itself surrounded and was relying on motionlessness, the only defense remaining. He couldn't be certain. It didn't matter now.

He shifted his aim and felt the leather tighten about his bent arm. It was not a perfect situation: though the sun had not risen above the treetops, he was indeed firing into light. He turned the ring to 9X. The rifle was sighted for 200 yards and this was farther. Against the gentle wind, he would aim two inches high. He held his breath, suddenly aware of the pleasant freshness of this place and the chirping of distant birds. He diminished the wobble at 9X to almost nothing, just the slightest rhythmic motion from his pulse, and squeezed the trigger of the .308.

He saw what he saw through the scope even before he felt the jolt of the recoil against his right shoulder. In spite of that jolt the crosshairs never left their mark, the left shoulder just below and inside the shoulder bone. The body of the hunter kicked up, spun all the way around and dropped face forward out of sight behind the tall grass.

Robinson rolled himself down the declivity beside him, the rifle held close going under him and under him again as he rolled, till he reached the bottom and lay motionless and sweating. He worked the bolt action, ramming a new load into the chamber. He picked up the hot brass shell from the leafy bed beside him and stuffed it into the face mask in his pocket. Then he rose, slung the rifle over his shoulder, and stalked back in the direction of the highway and his car, just another deer hunter on the prowl.

But he muttered his motto to himself: *Caveat venator.*

ii

He'd made it a practice never to investigate his kill. To walk out to the body and attach the tag issued with his hunting license would have style and propaganda value. If caught at the scene, he could pretend to be an ordinary hunter come upon the accident who wanted to help. But the risk in human contact was too great. Once connected with a death, he'd have to cease his work, waste the rest of the season. If the victim were only wounded, so much the better to stay away.

Amidst the shifting maple and birch, the identical swampy dips, he lost his sense of direction for a few moments, disoriented even though he knew the swamps always ran east and west. The first trace of panic—he must not linger in this area—then he saw the beer can on the poplar sapling, fifty yards to his right, and he knew where he was and headed with relief for the car.

As he was emerging into the brush beside the highway, letting himself relax a little after this successful beginning of the season, he walked right into the other hunter. Incredibly, there he was in his damn blaze orange, trudging toward him, carrying something in each hand, a deer antler held downward in each hand. He had not cut round to get behind the deer at all. He had returned to the pick-up to get the antlers.

The man didn't have his rifle. He must have left it with his partner. Robinson braced himself to fake a friendly exchange. Now was the time he should be wearing the mask of webbing. This man, who would return and find his partner shot, might recall his face. It was difficult to think clearly.

"Howdy," the man said. "Any luck?"

"No—"

"Heard a shot."

"So did I."

The man nodded. He seemed relieved. He was taller than Robinson, handsome, tanned or dark-complected, crew cut.

"My brother and I have a good buck cornered in there," he said. "I was afraid you'd got him."

"No—" Try a little convincing humor. "Sorry to say."

His *brother*.

"We thought we'd try to rattle him out with these."
He knocked the antlers together.

Robinson had read of this technique as part of his research, but had never seen it used. A hunter would bang a pair of antlers together, trying to simulate the sound of two bucks clashing for the right to the territory. Any buck within earshot would be drawn by the sound, seeking to hold the territory if it was his, or to gain it if he had none. So deep was this drive that a buck would approach even when he saw the hunter with the antlers. Approach to be shot.

"Good luck," said Robinson. "I've had it with here. Too much cover, woods too thick."

"Same to you. See you around." Robinson hoped not.

"Cooper's the name. Fred Cooper."

"Smith, " said Robinson stupidly, cursing himself. Better have something fancy to go with it. "Gerard Smith."

"See you, Gerry."

And Cooper trudged past him into the woods, carrying the antlers he would not rattle today.

iii

Robinson, sweating again, pushed through the brush onto cut grass near the pavement. With an effort of will he refrained from looking back. If the other man turned too, Robinson would look suspicious, and the man would remember. And, curse it, he had, blazoned on his back, the required back tag, white sticky paper half the size of a car license plate with his number on it, registered in Lansing. The hunter, even if he looked back, would not memorize the number, would he? Having no reason yet to be suspicious?

An impulse came over him simply to spin and shoot the man in the back, leaving no witness. No, better to follow him in and do it. He was unarmed. But that was not Robinson's style, and impulsiveness was danger-ous, and anyway now the moment was past.

He reached his car, the Vega in faded red, five years old, as nondescript as a car could be. From where the hunter had re-entered the woods he might glimpse the car but not the out-of-state plates. At his truck he could have seen everything but had no reason to notice. Robinson would get quickly away from here and try to think.

iv

He'd arrived very late the night before at Grayling. He could, of course, being retired and financially inde-pendent, have driven up a few days in advance of the start of the season and rested in the comfort of the motel, going out when he felt like it to scout promising territory. But he wanted to be in the log-jam of hunters driving up the Interstate the night of the fourteenth, bumper to bumper sometimes, glancing and gesturing across the lanes at each other, especially in the long bottleneck before the Zilwaukee Bridge across the Sag-inaw River, to be amidst them, in a sense one of them. Soon after that, the huge billboard of the WILLIAMS GUN SIGHT CO. Silhouettes of deer, antlered bucks in the crosshairs. "Everything for the Sportsman." This, too, served to strengthen his resolve.

V

Robinson got control of his nerves and calmed down driving the fifty miles back to the Howard Johnson's near Grayling. After all, the man Cooper, eager to rejoin his brother, had not looked closely at his face. He might not connect the man leaving the woods with the shooting of his brother at all. Even if he did, he could not be certain nor could he prove anything. The .308 bullet had to have gone clear through its target and vanished in the woods. It could never be found and matched to his rifle. A bullet of that energy would run the whole length of a deer, shot, as they often were, bounding away, in the rump. He had seen the ruined animals in the packing houses with others jaw-wounded, paunch-shot, leg-shattered. They had suffered hours or days till proudly claimed by whoever came upon them, dying or dead.

Above all, his safety lay in numbers. He was indistinguishable from 700,000 armed men who would invade the woods and fields this season, maybe 200,000 this prime morning. Oh, and though he'd not chanced to cross paths with any deer on the drive to Grayling, he knew that at the terrible dawn, even as Cooper perished, elsewhere the terrified animals were fleeing onto the highways in bafflement, many smashed into by cars, even careening into the sides of cars.

No personal link existed to connect him with his prey, no motive in any sense understood by the law.

Nonetheless, after breakfast he packed his few things and drove away south on the Interstate. His room had been serviced already. He did not check out. He'd reserved for two nights. He mussed up the bed and left the key on the bureau. He always tried to leave a confusing and irrational track, should anyone try to figure the pattern of his movements. He had reserved some rooms in advance, having had to sleep in his car a few nights last season, but planned to function, usually, at least fifty miles away, sometimes two hundred, so that there was no correlation between his bedroom and his kill. He had time. He liked to drive, to reflect and think as he did so. This season he might reserve rental cars in Bay City, go down by bus, leaving the Vega at some irrelevant spot, driving back up, so that his own car could not be associated with the episodes. He was not certain the plan would work out in practice.

He turned left on State 23 to Au Gres, at the southwest corner of the rifle-hunting precincts, on the north shore of Saginaw Bay. The Community Calendar, raised large in bands of redwood, clinched his decision. The letters proclaimed only: Welcome Hunters.

At Lutz's Motel he secured the last available room, parked the Vega twenty-five yards away from it, carried in the suitcase containing his clothes, records, maps, charts, and clippings. He changed into casual clothes and drove on to the first roadhouse down the highway, a half mile from the motel. Town and Country. It was about 6:00. The place was full of hunters, many with their flourescent caps and back-tags, laughing, talking in rough and manly fashion.

"Naw, they can't hear that good. No better'n you or me even with those tall ears." No available seat at the bar nor empty table. He overheard this while standing just inside the door.

"Lots o' times I heard one when he didn't hear me. And later I hung him up on my meat pole."

He was standing there, awkward, by the door when to his surprise a girl approached him from a table in the back corner of the room behind the pool table. He had an impression that she had been sitting there with a man in a loud sports jacket, but now the table was unoccupied.

"Will you join me?" She looked at him frankly but he thought sadly too, as if she would prefer not to be doing this. She was very young and fresh, not quite pretty, too fleshy in face, hips, thighs, a little too round-faced, faint whitish vertical scar over her right eye, thick straight hair black instead of the expected blonde.

She reminded him of someone, not Laura, some secretary from the old days in the school office. Once or twice a year since Laura died he'd gone to prostitutes, as well as having one-night relationships with women he'd approached in bars, even in the supermarket. After these years, loyalty to Laura was no longer an issue. She would have said that too.

He followed the girl back to her table at some distance to get a look at her body as she moved. But then he hurried round and held her chair for her and that made her smile.

"A gentleman," she said. "I don't get a lot of that. Are you always a gentleman?"

"Yes." To his knowledge this was so.

He asked whether she would mind if he had something to eat as well as a drink. Tonight he would allow himself the crab salad. No, she didn't mind, but the time would have to go on the meter. "It's only forty an hour," she said. "Or fraction thereof. Flat rate, anything you like. Has to be at your place—motel, camper." She smiled a second time. "Recreational vehicle. Whatever. I'd like a daiquiri."

"Can they make one here?" His voice was high, shaky, not because of her. He'd have some Scotch and get over it.

"Since yesterday I've had several. Buy me a salad? I'm on a diet. Ever hear of a hooker on a diet?"

vi

At his room, ushering her in, he looked quickly around. He had expected to return alone. Maps, charts, clippings might be lying in sight. He'd put everything like that in the half-open top drawer of the bureau. As he pushed it in the realization struck him that though he was afraid it was not of her and what she might see and deduce, nor of Cooper and the law.

He did not want sex now, or not yet, but someone to talk to him, just someone to say something to him. He'd told her so in the bar. This morning he had slain a man's brother.

"I can't make a daiquiri," was all he said now. "Will you sip some Scotch?" He took the bottle from his suitcase on the luggage rack, his hand trembling.

She said she would, with lots of water and some ice. There was an ice machine at the end of the row of rooms on this level. She knew because she had been at the motel last evening and this afternoon.

He took the plastic ice bucket down to the machine, leaving her with the evidence in the bureau drawer.

"You don't like your line of work very much, do you?" He had fixed her weak drink in one of the two fat waxed-paper-wrapped glasses in the bathroom, drinking his own Scotch neat.

"So what"? she said. "Reluctance adds to my attractiveness. You hunters are big on reluctance." She gulped from her drink, glanced down at herself. "Well, what now? Aren't you going to ask how a nice girl like me . . ."

"No, damn it." Her spiritedness was an annoyance, not what he needed.

"I'm how he makes his living. Rod, the man you saw me with." She spoke as if it were a recital. "Me and three other girls. Me especially. He's our manager." She paused. "He's also my husband. Because a wife can't testify against her husband."

"Do me a favor and forget about Rod."

She bristled then, standing with one hand tracing lines on the top of the cheap bureau.

"Look, mister. Make up your mind. First you say you'll pay me to talk, which is kind of kinky to begin with. Now you start adding conditions. As far as I'm concerned you can just pay for my time so far. We'll call it quits."

He knew that, before this, a true professional would have presumed that he doubted his manhood. She'd ask, "Do you have a problem? I can help you with it." She'd call him "my darling," feel about with her fingers, kissing, unbuttoning his shirt. Coming on strong, but in fact eager to get the thing over with, get out with the money, hoping for a tip she could keep for herself. She'd have asked already for the basic rate, cash in hand in advance.

"Easy," he told her. "I'll pay what I said. I just wanted to hear about you, is all."

"Jealous, huh?"

He smiled up at her from where he sat on the one armchair. Damn, she had spunk. "Tell me some more about Rod," he said.

Rod had this string of four girls. He drove them from

city to city in his station wagon. They worked out of Miami, mainly the conventions there and up north. They'd just come from the Republican Convention in Detroit for the two-week season in northern Michigan. This was a regular circuit for hookers, like the patterns of migratory birds. If he didn't mind her saying so, she liked this part of the circuit the least. "I suppose you came here to hunt."

"Yes."

"You seem different from most hunters. They're a rough bunch, I can tell you. I'll take a delegate in Miami or Detroit any day. Up here, everybody's on his worst behavior, getting away from wife and kiddies, proving what a big man he is—I'm sorry. I shouldn't talk to a paying customer that way. Like I said, I don't often talk with customers at all."

"That's all right," he said. "I take it as a compliment."

He was a little drunk. He felt a dangerous impulse to confide in her. It was good to have even this meaningless contact against the general loneliness and terror. He must be cautious, keep her talking about herself.

"Actually," he said, aware of the slurring of his voice, "you're different from most hookers, too. We're not your typical hunter and hooker, are we?"

"I take that as a compliment," she said.

"Why don't you leave Rod and do something else? Are you a punching bag?"

"Why don't you stop shooting helpless animals?"

He looked across at her for a long time.

"I apologize again," she said. "You asked a serious question. I'll give you a serious answer. Because I'm afraid of him. When I've tried, he's caught me and beat me. He pushes me onto the floor and kicks me. You'll see if you like, you'll see the bruises. They add to my attractiveness too, like my reluctance. I make more than his other girls, who enjoy their work. Hunters, sorry..."

"Go on."

"Hunters see the marks. Rod makes sure the marks are where you will notice them. Sometimes the hunters add a few bruises of their own. Then they pay more. That's what I was thinking about when I asked if you were always a gentleman. There don't seem to be very many. Mostly, hunters are animals. Rod's an animal." She shrugged.

"That's a funny thing to say."

She looked at him, puzzled, not getting the point. He sat partly facing her on the armchair. She'd chosen the corner of the sofa, beside the bureau, probably supposing he'd come over and begin to maul her. Her hand rested on the arm of it. He leaned forward and placed his own hand on hers. Her knees were innocently together, though the pink skirt was too short, or too hiked up. The hand was cool.

"*Deer* are animals," he said.

"*Did you ever think*", Laura was saying, "*about how words we have for bad behavior refer to animals, when animals are never cruel, only people are?*"

They were at breakfast on the screened porch of the house they had bought for their retirement. Outside, goldfinches crowded for the thistle seed in her feeders.

"*They kill other animals, sometimes,*" he said.

"*They do because they must, to live,*" she answered. "*That's Nature's fault, not theirs—if there is any fault.*"

"*What should we say then,*" he'd asked. "*Instead of brutal, bestial, animal?*"

"*I don't know.*" *She sighed.* "*Maybe human.*"

"Are you falling asleep?" It was the prostitute's voice. He raised his eyes to hers and squeezed her hand.

"No. Almost, maybe. You made me remember

something. But I want to tell you. A wife—" He could only speak with failing enunciation. Drink helped, and sleep. This morning he had killed a man. "A wife cannot be made to testify against her husband. But she can do it if she wants to."

"Is that right?" She looked back at him, then took a sip of her watery drink. He nodded. "That's very interesting. Thank you. That will help. He conned me. He's awfully convincing. But, you know, the law won't help people like me. I can't go to a policeman and say, 'Help me.' What I do is against the law. It only protects law-abiding citizens like you."

NOVEMBER
16

i

He woke up from a bad dream with a start and pushed himself violently to a sitting position in the double bed. The pictures of the dream fled from consciousness. It must have been worse than usual. Something about a monster with plastic skin that crackled. But the images were lost.

Where was he? Beside him in the unfamiliar room his trousers had been folded on a chair and his shirt placed neatly over them. He remembered his stalk of yesterday morning, and Cooper, and bringing the girl here . . . He pulled up his legs and swung round to sit on the side of the bed. His head hurt. He was naked.

Groggily he reached for the pants and felt in the pocket where he'd stuffed his gold money-clip. It was there, evidently as fat as before. She had slid a piece of folded paper into it. He pulled out the note and opened it. The motel stationery.

11:00 P.M.

You passed out, strange man. (I don't know your name.) I had to leave on account of Rod. I have taken $80 for the same reason. You're not bad, for a hunter, and if you should want to hire me again before you go home that's OK. Between regulars I'm usually at the bar where we met. My name is Phyllis.

He began to count the folded bills. The hundreds were all there and the fifties. He counted the twenties. She had taken forty dollars for herself. Crazy to have passed out like that with a thousand dollars in his pants pocket. She could have taken it all. Was there a way, maybe, to accommodate his schedule so that he might become one of her regulars?

He could not reconstruct much of their last hour or so together. The whisky had blacked it out, blacked out reality first and then the nightmare. Good for whisky.

ii

After breakfast in a roomful of husky hunters, Robinson drove westward toward Tittabawassee State Forest. Soon tamarack swamps developed to left and right, but gradually the ground dried and they were replaced by stands of birch and beech. All along, the ground was yellow with fallen leaves.

Driving allowed him to think. He wondered again whether Laura would approve. No, she was herself too deer-like, too gentle. Yet that did not mean his course of action was wrong for him, being what and where he was. And it had all begun in moments with her, had grown out of those.

Cooper took his first step toward death near Grayling when Robinson and Laura watched the film about the encroachment of African farmers on the Serengeti. They cultivated grazing areas of wild animals on the rim of the plain, forcing them back. The farmers like poor farmers anywhere had no perspective, no idea of the integrity of gazelle or wildebeest, creatures which were just a nuisance to them. They had only the mentality of an earlier and ignorant century. How could they understand the new truth of the last quarter of the twentieth century? Robinson and Laura confessed to each other that in their hearts they cared nothing whatever about the farmers and their families, whether they thrived or famished. What difference did they make as against the irreplaceable Serengeti? What was the conceivable justification for filling in such a place with another spread of unnecessary scratch farms? Let these people get welfare in the cities. Let them not be fruitful nor multiply. Let them perish, if need be—"It's terrible to say that," Laura said, "but it's the way I *feel*."

Gradually, after her death, he'd developed a more sophisticated view of the loss of the Serengeti. He wished that he might consult with Laura about it, get her opinion. If the Serengeti vanished, whose, after all, was the loss? Mankind's only, when you came to think about it. How much did that matter after the passing of the ridiculous fiction that they were lords of the earth? Not at all. And if the gazelles, even the elephants, perished altogether, became extinct, when you thought about it hard, that was only a human loss, of no consequence. It was only the cruelty to what still lived that mattered, the living animals, the anxiety and pain and grief. What was extinct felt nothing, mattered nothing.

On successive nights, trying to drown his mind in television, he'd seen on PBS the films about the gorillas in the highlands of West Africa and the dolphins in Japanese fishing waters.

The gorillas were shy and gentle things. Shots of small groups of them, playing, grooming each other, suckling their young, tourist group in the foreground watching. One gorilla especially, named Micki by the tour guide, communing with her, crossing easily the gap between species.

Micki dead, burial service by the naturalist. Shot in the heart, head and hands severed.

On the news the very next evening a clip presented by the dispassionate newsman about Japanese fishermen who had driven a thousand dolphins into shallow water. They were clubbing them to death because they interfered with the tuna fishing. He and Laura had spoken of dolphins and of whales. Each, as a species, had adapted to the land and then decided to leave it, for the cool waters were a better place. A great and wise decision. Explorers of far-away star systems, Laura said, if they found advanced life would not find advanced technology but something like dolphins, intelligent as men, individualized, rich in sensitivities, playful, utterly non-human, without capacity for malice or cruelty. Her notepaper showed a block print of a whale, and inside was printed in child-like lettering, "Harmony Among All Creatures."

He had brought the reversible camouflage suit along in the back seat with his rifle. He would wear it brown-side out for contrast with the yellow ground cover here. On the site, later, he could quickly pull out the sand-colored insides to blend with it and become invisible, or to seem to be somebody else.

Once Laura had come home distraught, and when he asked what was wrong she said two of the Lohr men had driven up with a big snapping turtle in their truck while she was visiting Mrs. Lohr. They went out to look. The turtle was boxed in with concrete blocks in the bed of the truck. The Lohrs had seen it beside the road and caught it. "It was so fierce," she told him. "So brave and dignified. I felt as if it had rights that were being violated. I know it sounds dumb, but I wanted to save it, to offer them money to let it go. Of course I couldn't—" The Lohrs were an old-time family out there in the country where the Jays had retired. They would think she was odd. He'd said he'd see what he could do and drove the car, new then, back to the Lohrs, money in his pocket. He already had the .38 in the glove compartment. He wondered what would have happened then and there if they had laughed and refused his money. But the turtle was already broken out of its shell and thrown into boiling water for soup.

Always she praised the dignity of animals, even above their innocence, the dignity they reached after the sweet playfulness of their childhoods. Animal meant a living thing with an individual soul, unlike a plant or an insect. She belonged to societies to save the whales, the dolphins, the baby seals. The Association for the Protection of Fur-bearing Animals. GRA: The Group for the Rights of Animals. Many others. She wrote letters to Congress. Helped boycott tuna. She tried to get Robinson to picket supermarkets. He knew all this was useless. "But we've got to do *something*," she said.

The seals, fortunately, he had never seen on film, only an innocent face sketched on a wall poster. There was a limit, maybe, to the horrible images his mind could tolerate. He never let himself even start to think about vivisection.

He pulled over and stopped the car. He slid over to the passenger side and got out with the camo suit and tugged it on. The suit looked like brown workmen's coveralls padded out. It was polyester, warm and virtually weightless.

Back in the car, he accelerated rapidly, making the rear wheel spin on the shoulder then dig into pavement. The shift knob was embossed with an elephant. He liked to feel it pressed against his palm. In the waiting room, while Laura was dying, a film came on the TV about an English warden hired to protect elephants on the plains of Tsavo. One old poacher responsible for the killing of 150,000 elephants. Chief of an ancient tribe reduced now to a deadly handful. They used poisoned darts, developed in prehistory, which pierced the skin, about the ears where it was thin. The elephants always died, but not before weeks and sometimes months. The warden shot dozens of elephants to end their agony. He seemed to be doing almost nothing else. Sequence after sequence of the deaths of these elephants. As the bullet impacts, nerve endings shattering within, synapses splaying, the whole animal shudders through its length, flaps like a huge sack in the wind, deflates and sags, tilting on its feet for the slow sideways crash to earth, lifts once as the resilient flesh buoys up in reaction and then collapses, shapeless on the bones.

A whole field of tusks recovered by the warden, laid out in rows, acres and acres of them.

Someone rose and switched channels to "I Love Lucy." Robinson endured this irrelevancy for a moment and then turned the set back. "We must watch this" he said. The people seated round him muttered to each other but did not interfere. They took him for a madman. He ignored them.

Apparently the warden had caught the tribe of poachers in the act. Their chief, who had directed them in the killing of 150,000 elephants, turned out to be a man much older than the warden had expected and rather quiet and articulate. The elephants would be exterminated, yes. The insatiable lust for ivory on the part of civilized men of infinite wealth in lands he could not conceive of was responsible. It was their fault.

"No!" cried Robinson to the poacher on the screen, gripping the arms of his chair, half rising. "No. It is your fault!"

The image of the rear of a car flashed into consciousness, just ahead, almost under his hood, and he yanked the wheel to the left. The Vega squealed past the rear corner of the car and Robinson slowed and steadied it. He found himself driving beside a row of hunters' cars and trucks pulled over on the right side of his lane, engines idling. The line turned into a clearing where stood some kind of lodge, probably a ranger's station. Robinson stopped beside the last car still actually on the roadway and rolled down his right window. The driver looked across at him in his brown polyester, rolled his window down halfway.

"What's going on?"

"Got to register to hunt in state forest," the man said. "Conservation Officers." He waved behind him. "Get in line, fella. Good hunting."

"Thank you," said Robinson.

He made a U-turn and cruised slowly back across from the waiting cars, maybe twenty of them. There must have been many more before these for the good hunting just after dawn. The material sent him by the state hadn't mentioned registration. His name would be on the day's list with maybe a hundred fifty others. If anything odd happened here they could check the list. He'd no longer be one of the day's hundred thousand, a man who might be any of them, anywhere —

He pulled around behind the camper that was now last in line. He'd waste a half hour of good time but he wanted to register, for an alibi, part of the razzle-dazzle. He'd hunt elsewhere. He sat and waited. The engine of the Vega muttered softly. It was weeks after Laura's death before he could read anything. When he picked up a *New York Times* he saw in the obituaries "Lover of Elephants Dies." The warden had been transferred to a desk job in Nairobi a year ago and had died yesterday. His wife said he had done his job in Tsavo too well. Hence his removal. Poaching was on the rise. There were kick-backs to the government. The former middlemen were now operating directly with helicopters and machine guns to kill elephants. It was cheaper, however, to poison their waterholes.

Oh to have been in that warden's place, Robinson had thought. He'd had the terrible little tribe in his custody, caught with their damned tiny arrows. He could have stood suddenly apart from his astounded bearers and shot them all, on film taken by a staggering cameraman, shot them one after the other with his elephant gun and set an example and gotten world coverage and really made some difference. What did career or life itself, doomed anyway, matter against that golden chance? How could he claim he loved elephants and yet not have done that?

Once when he'd brought her mail to the hospital it included a bleeding heart appeal for the baby seals. There were photographs. Men with clubs maybe, the little seals, their heads raised against the northern sky. She held the flyer up before her, her thin arm bruised from within by the disease, veins bulging. "Oh, I could kill them," she said.

She hadn't looked across to where he sat, into his eyes. Maybe that was just as well.

The film itself had closed wih sequences of elephants examining delicately and lovingly with the tips of their trunks the bodies and skeletons of others of their kind. One elephant lifted from a pile of bones a single tusk and held it upright as if trying by contemplating it to understand—though being what it was it could not— that somehow ivory was the reason for all this death. The fate of Cooper was sealed then, in effect, as Robinson watched the elephant loop its trunk around and lift and stroke the severed tusk.

iii

After registering at Tittabawassee, Robinson drove back to Au Gres the same way he had come, and then north along a country road that soon turned to gravel. He'd always had good luck driving like this into *terra incognita*. The Au Gres River criss-crossed the road, and once he parked by a stone bridge and walked with his rifle up the eastern bank. He felt a sense of oppression here, almost of evil, as if he were walking up the Congo. The water was sluggish, greenish-yellow. An occasional large tree lay fallen clear across it, and he noted that at least one had been sawed, felled he presumed to block canoe traffic by summer tourists. The owners of the cleared land ranging away from this bank wanted privacy, or secrecy. On the opposite bank tall, leaf-stripped ashes loomed from a brown swamp, forbidding and impenetrable. Ahead something grayish-brown was spread on brush directly facing the river. He moved closer. It was a deerskin stretched to dry, and beyond it was another and then another. They had not been placed there today or yesterday, they were too seasoned. He touched the suede inner side of the skin with his thumb, near the ragged edge, pressed his fingers into the short fur opposite. This deer had been killed before the season, poached by the owners of the land on which it lived, probably by .22 shorts fired to the head at close range, not damaging the hide, inaudible to authorities cruising the roads. He looked for the other remains of deer but found none. The killings had been elsewhere. He looked across the river. It would be easy to stake a blind there and wait for someone to come and check the hides. Later, he decided. That would be an inefficient use of his time. He crossed the river on one of the fallen logs and walked back to the bridge along the west bank.

He drove farther north into a vast acreage of stubble fields. The glacier-planed expanse of land gave him a sense of the curvature of the earth. The woods to his right were low, seemingly an inch tall above the fields, diminished by distance. He saw no way to reach them. On his left, two hundred yards across stubble corn-fields, stood a stand of huge evergreens closely planted as a windbreak, but planted long ago. Such a place was possibly the daylight haven of a buck. He stopped beside the access road and considered. The area was not posted, but on the other hand no cars were parked anywhere in sight. It was the sort of place where the farm owners would know to hunt, but even they would have to come in by car or truck. He decided to let the stand of pines wait, try it maybe on his way home near dusk.

Still farther north, the tall swamp-forest of the local ash closed in on the road from both sides. Now and then a couple of cars, or a group of three, were parked on the shoulder. He considered these but passed them all, driving more slowly up the bleak corridor.

Ahead, pulled over to the left but facing north, a single car. Since there was no brush for cover, he sim-ply pulled in behind it. A new white Mustang. He got out of his car, bent and reached in the back for the .308, slung it over his shoulder, pushed his door shut silently, not locking it. He still wore the camo suit he had intended for Tittabawassee, brown-side out for contrast against the yellow ground cover of larch and birch leaves he had expected to hunt on there. Nor-mally a hunter would reverse the suit here, exposing the sandy yellow slashed with orange for contrast with dark brown woods like these. The brown would render him almost invisible. The foolish orange cap remained stuffed in the right-hand pocket under the face mask. Remembering his unexpected meeting with Cooper, he took out the mask and pulled it over his head, adjusting the eye-holes as best he could.

The Mustang came from a dealer in Ann Arbor. He

peered in the window on the driver's side, then tried both doors. They were locked. The foot-space on the passenger side was half filled with gear—a khaki backpack, a folded sleeping bag or set of blankets, some paperback books, some yellow and red tape cassettes. Popular music. One of the books read on the cover *Field Guide*. He could not read the smaller print.

He crossed the roadside gully into the woods, looking to left and right for tracks. None. The ground was too hard. But just into the swamp in a patch of mud before the fallen leaves began some ten yards north of where the car was, he found a pair of tracks going in. He was fairly sure there was only the single man, as he had expected from the clutter in the passenger space in the car. He entered the forest, following the direction of those tracks, though on the bed of large damp leaves already blackening with decay and muffling all sound of footsteps he found no others. The direction took him slightly north of west, just into the quiet north breeze he had felt out on the highway.

This was not deer country at all. What was the fellow doing in here? It was too boggy and obstructed. These trees loved water, but here there was too much of it and many had fallen across his way or lodged at crazy angles against trees still standing. He had continually to climb over, or stoop or even crawl under, to make any progress. Often he stopped to listen, hearing nothing but the very distant sound of water moving and of frogs and water birds. The river, possibly a pond too, a half mile ahead. Then a burst of sound and motion at his very feet, a mad flurry of wings and wind. He leapt back, heart pounding. He'd not realized he was so jittery. Only a brace of pheasants whose nest he'd nearly walked into. Their young should be gone by now. Nonetheless he backtracked and circled the area widely. Maybe the man was hunting pheasant, had a shotgun. It was all the same to him what the man was hunting.

He was down on all fours crawling under a huge fallen ash, fighting with the branches of it, his rifle and sling catching in them as he tried to move, back toward the direction the hunter had taken, when he heard the nearby crack of a rifle, no shotgun, and in the same instant splinters broke down stinging his face. The bullet had grazed the log just above and ahead of him. By instinct he hurled himself sideways from the place, yanked the .308 over into his arms, and rolled over and over it into some brush. But he was too exposed. Ahead lay a clump of scrub trees such as a rabbit might seek refuge in from dogs. He braced himself up, raised up his haunches, took a deep breath and plunged out, scurrying for it. *Crack.* The whirr of the slug just behind him, whacking into wood. He was hidden, pulled himself in a little to make sure, tried to think. The law? No. But maybe Cooper. He'd followed him all this way waiting for the appropriate revenge. Better not to call out. Hey, what the hell are you doing? Try to save himself with his human voice.

Yet there was another reason than fear that kept him silent. This was his unanticipated chance to play the animal himself, prey, victim. To be what he sought to save. Know what it felt like. To die like a deer, taken for a deer, would not be so bad. What better end for him? He tried to subsume himself into wild animal. What were these bulky ugly monsters around him? Their incomprehensible movements? Why the terror they inspired? What were they doing when they came with their hideous noises and their smells? How to account for them from any experience? It was good to have the chance to feel this way.

And yet in the end he could not. He was human and he had a mission. He had to use his brain to save himself. Most probably no one was seeking to kill him. The idiot Michigander he'd followed thought he was a deer. Just in case, he did not call out but listened, listened with all the intensity human ears allowed him, heard nothing, could not, footsteps on the mushy leaves. Yet somehow sensed the killer was closer, or rose and ran merely out of jitteriness, the sense that staying anywhere too long was dangerous. The third shot whanged into a tree just before him, and he fell spread-eagled over his rifle on the ground because instinct told him he was hunted not as a man but as a deer. He could fake out this hunter. Play dead. He listened with an absolute intensity, cheek against the cold leaves, eyes squeezed shut. At last there was an unidentifiable sound, nothing more than clothing rustling as when a man raised his arm, but very close. It bothered Robinson that the hunter was near enough to see him clearly and yet did not cry out in dismay or rush up to check how badly he was wounded. Was he then simply standing there, preparing to deliver the *coup de grace*? He tried to feel the exact lay of the rifle under him, to calculate how in one smooth motion, he might roll over and get it in his hands and fire. No matter, really, whether it was Cooper or the bungling hunter from Ann Arbor with his huge gun, a .44 say, probably with a magnum charge. His own rifle was cocked and ready. He'd worked the bolt upon entering the woods. He'd have the advantage of surprise. He braced.

"My God," a voice said.

Robinson raised himself onto his elbows and for a moment looked down at the mat of dank leaves he lay on and smiled into them. Then he rolled over and sat up with the rifle in his lap and looked through the

eye holes in the webbing at the incompetent from Ann
Arbor. A kid with gray pants and a phosphorescent
orange jacket and glasses, big round lenses with black
rims. What a sight. Robinson decided not to kill him.
He got up. The boy seemed stunned.

"You're a rotten shot," Robinson said. The boy
looked down shamefacedly at the heavy rifle he still
cradled. Iron sights. Imagine his peering through them
with those reading glasses.

"I don't know what to say," he said, looking up. "I
thought it . . . thought you were a stag. I'm terribly
sorry. Are you really all right?"

"Fortunately."

"I didn't think there was anybody in here. There
wasn't any car. Where did you come from?"

"You shot at movement," Robinson said, shaking
his head.

"Well, yes. It . . . you were something large and the
right shape. I couldn't think what else . . ." Quickly he
added, "And you haven't got the orange." He indicated his own jacket.

"There are no deer in here," Robinson said. "You'd
better get back to college before you kill somebody."

"Look, I'm awfully sorry. If there's anything . . ."
He approached. Hell, he was going to shake hands or
something. "Tell you the truth, it's my first time out. I
borrowed my father's gun, you know. I wanted to impress him. With a trophy, you know. And my girl friend,"
he added lamely.

The facelessness and anonymity of the mask were
having their effect on him. The kid must wonder why
Robinson did not remove it.

"Your first time," he said from behind the mask.
"On account of your father and girl friend. Make it the
last time and I'll let you off without telling the county

sheriff you damn near killed me. Swear you won't try hunting again."

"All right," the boy said, a little too quickly, scared now, maybe, not of what he had almost done but of Robinson. Best to keep him frightened and get rid of him that way.

"Swear," said Robinson, hefting his rifle, "by whatever in hell's holy to you. And then get out of here."

The boy backed away. "All right, I swear."

"You swear what?"

"I swear I won't hunt deer again. On . . . on my mother's grave."

He backed still further away as if he were afraid to turn his back on Robinson. Then he did turn and walked jaggedly toward the highway. Robinson watched him, the orange jacket bouncing under and over fallen trees. He followed slowly. It was still not too late to change his mind. The boy was the son of a hunter and would hunt. His children would. The body would be another object lesson, as good a part of the campaign as any other. It was safe for Robinson in this place.

But he hesitated a little too long and let the boy reach the shoulder and the cars. He could see him only intermittently through the tangle of trees. The boy seemed to look a long time at Robinson's car. Then he walked over to his own. Here Robinson had a better view of him. He unlocked the door, threw in the glasses, and slipped inside. He burned rubber making a U-turn and raced southward down the highway. So the glasses were fake.

The damn kid had been lying all the time.

iv

Easing slowly down the bump-ridden road back toward Au Gres, Robinson tried to assess his situation this unusual day and to decide what to do with the rest of it. For some reason he felt a tenseness coming on, first in his wrists, then a shakiness in the arms. It was hard to reflect. He tried to relax by gazing across the farmland that was now widening around him as the black swamps receded. Well, he had experienced directly what it was to be victim instead of assassin. That had helped and steadied him, despite this momentary case of nerves. Yet if he did not act this afternoon this would be the first day of his two-season campaign he'd failed to put a human death into the eternal register of things and so diminish the killing.

At the stand of dense, tall pines were parked an old pick-up and a camper. At least two men were in there, probably more. Hunters, whether they were the owners of this land or not. He slowed, hesitated, lacked the nerve to join them, in that piney darkness. He drove on, retracing his route rather than exploring, and when the road, improving in smoothness, began to interlace with the river, he decided also not to rig some makeshift blind on the west bank of it and wait for someone to come check the ragged hides. Later, not today. He was coming unglued, not because of Cooper or the law or the kid or anything else but the general terror of being here or anywhere else on the curvature of this small planet.

He lit his first smoke of the day and tuned to soft music on the radio. These things helped. He'd stay glued. He wanted some whisky. He wanted to be with Phyllis again.

At his room in Lutz's Motel he showered and shaved, sipping Scotch with ice and feeling better all the time. Outside it was not quite dusk. The perfect time to make the day count after all, but he couldn't force himself to do it. He felt guilty and irresponsible at this inability to give his luck one more chance. He dressed in casual clothes and bought a paper and drove to the Town and Country.

He took a window booth, ordered Scotch and the crab salad. He looked around for Phyllis. No sign of her, nor of any sportily dressed young man he might guess to be her manager-husband—Rod? Dick? He'd forgotten the name. Nor of any girl likely to be one of her associates in prostitution. He sipped Scotch, waiting for the salad. He put a quarter in the jukebox outlet at the table and punched the number for a song he had heard driving back to Au Gres. Still she did not come in. Maybe the law was present. More likely there was group sexual entertainment going on at the VFW hall or somewhere. He'd base himself here another day or two and try again. His selection was playing now. He'd missed the beginning of it, thinking of Phyllis—

> *Yesterday is dead and gone,*
> *And tomorrow's out of sight.*
> *And it's sad to be alone . . .*

Funny he should care about seeing her anyway. She was plain, bland. Intelligent, yes, alert, not stupid. Stupidity, like cruelty, occurred only in people. Come to think of it, he was bland himself, wasn't he? Everyone had always said so. Mild. Mild-mannered, his colleagues had called him, smiling. She was in reality a prostitute and he—not merely a hunter but a hunter of hunters. Something in common. Yet she was a victim also, victim of men.

I don't care who's right or wrong . . .

The waitress brought the salad and a second drink. Scotch and a few cigarettes were making him feel better.

Let the devil take tomorrow . . .

Where was she? He'd spread out his paper, turned toward the room to catch more favorably the light of sunset from the window beside him but not seeing, thinking of her. On the right side of the front page in a rectangular frame was a pencil sketch of a man's face staring head-on out of the paper. One of those police composites that never looked like anybody. Robinson wondered what rapist or child-molester was being sought. Maybe a suspect in Atlanta. He glanced at the caption. THE DEER LOVER? There was a momentary hiatus before the thought could take form: this was *himself*. He looked up over the paper at the crowded noisy room then quickly turned his face toward the wall and window. Anyone here could see him, recognize him. Should he get up and leave, stay out of public places?

But as he looked again at the drawing he began to calm down. It bore very little resemblance to the subject. After all, he had not recognized himself in it. Who else could from this? Fred Cooper hadn't any reason to look at him closely. The hair was cropped while Robinson's, though it lay close to his head when combed back as he always kept it, was if anything rather stringy. Also it was faded and yellowish, while the pencil sketch gave an impression of blackness. The eyes and mouth were also wrong, too simian and somehow malevolent. His face was flatter, blander, rounder. The chin, a little too weak, was a good likeness, true. But on the whole he didn't have to worry about being recognized on sight. Other hunters in this room looked more like the man in the sketch than he did.

He began to read the accompanying article. Harold Cooper, 34, of Detroit had been found that morning, in the woods near Grayling, shot in suspicious circumstances. The body had been found by Cooper's brother Frederick, who'd immediately reported the matter at the office of the county sheriff. Just before discovering the body, Frederick Cooper had seen an armed hunter leaving the area, and assisted the authorities in making the composite sketch. It was requested that the man who talked with Frederick Cooper—if he were indeed not responsible for the shooting—would come forward to help in the investigation. The whole area was being searched for evidence, and hunters were advised to avoid it. Four other hunters had been shot during the day (the related story was on an inside page of the paper) but these shootings were accounted for as accidents. What made the case especially alarming was the similarity to the series of unexplained shootings in Michigan last season together with the fact that this occurred on the morning of the first day of the season. Some journalists last year had begun to speculate about a single, hypothetical killer responsible for them all, though the police were not convinced of any link. Some had called this psychopath The Nature Nut, some The Deer Lover. Was he back on the scene? Would there be other such shootings?

Not today, thought Robinson.

The rest of the article, continued on another page, dealt with matters of no interest to Robinson—details of Cooper's life, his profession (the moving business), the arrangements—but he read it all to be sure there was no description of the Vega. Either Fred had not noticed it, though it was in plain view when he was at the pick-up getting the antlers, or the police were with-holding the information. He'd have to think what to do. He could neither abandon the car nor sell it because that would call attention to it. He'd have to keep using it for travel between motels but rent a car whenever he could when he was hunting.

The waitress came by and he ordered another drink. The situation was not so bad after all. His risk was greater, but so was the excitement that distracted him from the general terror. His mission was now on the front page of a metro paper. Think how many hunters, thousands maybe, that alone would discourage, and not only around Grayling. He should have realized earlier the possibilities in such publicity, in increasing and manipulating it. Magnify his impact enormously. He should have done it last season, written to the papers, verified the hypothesis of the lone psychopath. Why not write now, sign himself The Deer Lover? No, Deerlover. Predict, say, that he would strike in a certain county next day and then do it? He'd have to think it out, the dangers. The pay-off could be enormous.

He looked around the room. At a table near his booth one hunter was telling another how to field-dress a deer and get it out of the backwoods without having to drag the whole carcass.

"Just butcher it, put quarters in bags and carry it out. Head or antlers same way. If there's only one of you, take half and come back next morning. Keeps OK these cold nights if you flush it out right. Don't forget to take in bags, canvas or gunny sacks, not plastic."

"Butcher it?"

"Nothin' to it. But you got to treat it rough, not fool around."

"Butcher it . . . I don't know . . ." This younger man looked squeamish, callow. Robinson leaned back and watched his face while the other, whose back was to him, spoke.

"First thing you got to do is grab its prick."

"If it's a stag!" This was the boy's attempt at manly humor.

"Yeah. Otherwise use your imagination. Cut around it and back, deep. Muscles and tubes go right back to the asshole. Get all that loose from the bone space in there. Then cut frontwards to open up where the guts and stomach are. You'll hit the muscle under his lungs."

Robinson felt all this within himself, muscle, tube, and nerve. He felt in this new way his physical kinship to all other animals.

"Now you got to stand over the damn thing, get all its legs sticking up, get your hunting knife in both hands and rip right up through its throat. You got to break all them ribs apart, off either side of the breast bone. Then you roll it on its side. Feet downhill if there's a slope. Cut loose and yank out everything in there. Lungs, heart, liver, kidneys, prick, bladder, asshole. That junk'll sour the meat. Hang what's left on a tree branch by the antlers. All the blood flushes out the bottom. Cut it in quarters. Hack off the antlers or the whole head, whichever. Cart it out."

Robinson drove to his motel, carefully, against his drunkenness. He heard Laura's voice in his head. We must stop eating animals. And her golden rule: Do unto animals as they would have you do unto them.

Falling asleep, he remembered about Micki the gorilla. The head was to be stuffed by a taxidermist for a wall trophy, of course. The two hands, the great black hands, were made into ashtrays.

Next morning he drove up around the Huron shore to Alpena and killed a man before breakfast.

NOVEMBER

17

i

On the drive back from Alpena he pulled into a motel of the old-fashioned sort, two rows of separate cabins, seven or eight miles south of Au Gres. Run by the family, probably, losers, a forlorn Vacancy sign on a stick beside the highway. In the car he took out and studied his green appointment book. For tomorrow and for the nineteenth he had a reservation at a lodge in the Upper Peninsula, not prepaid and under the name of Fenimore. The twentieth was open: he'd improvise something on his way south from the U.P. The twenty-first was his last night at Lutz's. He'd bring Phyllis there if he could. Twenty-second and twenty-third were open. He'd pencilled in "Missaukee" for those days. He wanted one foray into private property, probably on the twenty-fourth. To close the season in some luxury—at least according to the literature he'd sent for and the prices—he'd reserved a cottage at The Homestead in Glen Arbor, on the upper western shore of Lake Michigan. So he could stay here the nights of the twenty-fourth, twenty-fifth (Thanksgiving), and the twenty-sixth.

From Glen Arbor he could reconnoiter the Dunes area and easily reach up to the Leelanau Peninsula, the little finger of the hand of Michigan, to the north, and also drop down to the Traverse area, maybe even a few miles south to an establishment he had read about called The Whitetail Hunter. It was closed until bow-and-arrow season resumed, but its owner, a young man named Corbett, would be there making his preparations. He guided groups of two or three hunters into remote areas of state-owned land where, in summer and fall, he had researched the haunts and pathways of trophy whitetails. The hunters waited behind piles of straw bales or in raised blinds provided by Corbett until the deer came within a twenty-yard range, foraging where they had always foraged. This was like the Texas situation, and Robinson might not be able to function, but he was thinking about it.

He booked a cabin with double bed for the nights of the twenty-fourth through the twenty-sixth. Paying cash in advance, tugging folded bills from the gold money clip Laura had given him (engraved R.J.), he gave a new false name, Richard Johnson. He hoped for one successful expedition in this area after yesterday's failure. It seemed best not to establish any unnecessary correlation, however approximate and obscure, between slain hunters and the name Robinson Jay.

The shrivelled little woman behind the desk, eyes wide at the sight of so much cash, raised no question when he said that Mrs. Johnson might join him there, at least over Thanksgiving, though she did not hunt. He hoped to bring Phyllis. Risky to have her with him so much and be so long in the same area. But if he struck, all but the one time, far away, that should be all right. Out of sheer instinct not to bed down too often in the same spot, he'd move here from Lutz's under the different name, seedy though the place was. Yet as he returned to his car, he thought it not so bad, just 40s instead of 80s. He'd stayed in such places with his parents. The double row of cabins led away to a grove of trees beyond which was presumably beach, and then rose the horizon defined by the bluish sunlit area of Saginaw Bay.

He drove slowly back to Au Gres. He'd take a late-morning nap, the day's work already done and his schedule mapped-out except for the twenty-second and twenty-third. He'd try Missaukee County. He'd never been there and the charts in *Michigan Outdoorsman* for last year showed it with a buck kill of "2.00 and over" per square mile and a hunter presence for the season of "20.00 and over," both very high. Feature articles in all the hunting magazines last summer stressed prowling for your trophy buck in back country, whither the buck had withdrawn to save his life and grow the rack. Whither, in other words, the wisdom of terror had led, to where most hunters never penetrated. Sixty percent of hunters ventured no farther than two hundred yards from a highway, thirty percent less than a mile. These statistics of distance applied to Robinson himself. It would be well to vary his *modus operandi* and at the same time lend a helping hand to those older animals in deep country.

Missaukee, judging from the topographic map he'd purchased by mail from the DNR, was promising territory. There were remoter regions in the U.P. but few hunters. Anyway, he'd suffered a rough, although successful night up there last season. In northeastern Missaukee, the usual grid of county roads evaporated in square miles of tree-lined marsh and swamps linked by streams. He might even rent a canoe. He could put his finger on the very spot (unless opportunity presented itself earlier) where he and the stately animals who hid there and some veteran hunter stalking one would converge as if by destiny.

At the Party Store to replenish his supply of Scotch, he glanced by habit up and down the stretch of highway that ran through Au Gres for State Police, Cooper's blue pick-up, the white Mustang of the kid who had nearly killed him. His eye caught a projecting sign a block away that read HARDWARE and underneath in smaller letters, SPORTING GOODS. Out of curiosity he walked over. In the window, black and wicked amidst a display of hunting clothes, hung a steel bow.

Two curved pieces like the leaf-springs of a car were riveted to a thick center piece of about the same length wrought to form a handgrip. There were three strings, not one. Not really strings but eighth-inch black cords, strung according to some complex principle over three-inch pulleys mounted inside the bow tips. Then he saw that the cords were of one continuous length looped around these pulleys, the arrangement designed to maximize the thrust delivered to the arrow. The price tag was twisted wrong but he could read it by pressing his head against the glass: $75.00.

Inside, he looked about. The equipment was inferior to his own. The proprietor, husky and porcine, at length emerged from the obscure back region of the store. Robinson asked to heft the bow, and the man fetched it from the window display. Apparently it was the only one in stock.

Robinson took the grip in his left hand. The bow was heavy as he expected. He extended his arm and curved the first two fingers of his other hand about the nearest of the three strings. His left arm trembled from the effort.

The man laughed. "Takes practice. Or you can brace against something."

Robinson laid the back of his left hand against the cash register beside him, still holding up the weight. The bow was steady.

"Can I draw it?"

"Yeah, but don't dry-shoot it. Wrecks the rigging. Just ease it back."

Robinson could not fully draw the string. The limbs of the bow bent inward toward each other as the com-pounding action worked, the other two strings remaining stretched between the pulleys. Beyond, out among the pots and pans in his line of sight, he imagined, from the article he had studied, the face and figure of Corbett.

"It's fifty pounds pull. Take you awhile to get used to it."

"What about arrows?"

"Yeah. They don't come cheap. But you can re-use 'em. Yank 'em out and use 'em again, not like bullets. And you can get new broadheads for 'em or new blades."

The man produced a plastic sheaf holding four arrows. They were of aluminum, maybe thirty inches long, with hard plastic feathers parabolic in shape. The man showed how these were slanted to make the arrow spin and go true. Robinson removed the plastic cover from the point of one arrow. Three pieces of leaf-shaped razor set around a stainless core. He touched a honed edge with the tip of his finger. The label stitched into the quiver read Easton Heartslicer.

It was $60.00 for the sheaf of arrows. He bought them and the bow.

ii

At the motel, after an omelette for lunch, Robinson took his nap. There was nothing to be done now about the stand of pines four miles north scheduled for tomorrow. He needed some Scotch to get off to sleep, and when he awoke around 2:00 he could not remember any dreams. A bad sign. Sleepers always dreamed, and if the dream was gone it had probably been bad. Maybe, he thought with a smile, back in Aurora he should see a psychiatrist and talk out his problem.

He decided to spend the rest of the afternoon practicing with the bow. He walked the mile down to the bayshore. He needed the exercise, and it might be wise to let people see him with the bow and no rifle, think he was a bow hunter. There had been bow-and-arrow-only season in October and would be another through December. But now bow-and-arrow hunting was still legal. In fact, a man with a firearm license was allowed to kill a second buck with his bow after killing the first with his rifle. He chose the beach over the lots behind the motel or some spot in the woods because he wanted to see far behind his target. Also, he liked to look out over the water. Saginaw Bay was only twenty miles across. Yet it defined the horizon. You couldn't see the other side. There was no other side. Here on the beach he was looking off the edge of the world.

His target was a box from behind the IGA market, stuffed with dried grass that he'd pulled from the beach-side. He pressed it against a steep bluff of sand and stood facing it with his back to the water. He'd chosen the box because it had on each side in dull red the representation of a tomato, its former contents. Corbett required hitting a target of such size at twenty yards. He did not want the deer he had tracked all year to suffer, or die unclaimed, because of incompetence. He made his clients pass a shooting test before he took them out, checked their equipment, felt the sharpness of their arrows. Robinson, too, did not wish any unnecessary suffering, any mere wounding or lingering.

He tried a kneeling position, arm extended on his left knee, but he couldn't get his head down to sight properly. He squatted cross-legged in the moist sand and tried again. This was better. With the bow straight-armed across his left knee, at full draw the base of his right thumb pressed his cheek just under the eye. He repeated the action with an arrow, laying it in the angle between his gloved knuckle and the bow grip, the bow tilted slightly to the right. He hauled back till a blade on the broadhead just touched his knuckle. The plastic fletching was a blur just before and under his eye and he could sight clearly along the shaft. He trembled. He'd have to learn to pull the fifty pounds more easily. He eased off, relaxed, tried again, this time getting his back into it as well as arm and shoulder muscles. Eye, arrow, and the tomato target were in one line. To-morrow he'd go into the IGA and buy a couple of the tomatoes. See them splatter when he connected.

But there was a problem with the release. He re-membered, suddenly, the same problem in childhood play with bow and arrow sets. If he held the string as now with the two curved fingers, the nock of the arrow between them, there was no way to let go cleanly. When he straightened the fingers the string would be held back slightly, and it would be impossible not to pull a little to one side. His solution in childhood had been to squeeze the nock between thumb and forefin-ger. He eased off and tried that. He couldn't hold tightly enough to get the full draw. He went back to the other hold, sighted, clumsily released. The mechanism of the bow made a surprising racket, a kind of whirring thump. Sound travelled faster than arrows. Was there a micro-second of warning for the animal in that? Sure enough, he'd pulled left a little so that the arrow hit near the right corner of the box. It had driven in up to the feathering, which was slightly damaged, and the blades had gone into the sand and lost part of their edge already.

iii

He arrived early at the Town and Country, a little after five. He sipped Scotch for a long time, watching the more or less local news on TV—Bay City, Saginaw, Flint—he didn't know. The sound of the big color set over the bar was turned down, inaudible over the hubbub in the tavern. He only wished to see whether the story of Deerlover, maybe also the composite drawing of himself, had made it to TV. Or the killing this morning in Alpena—which was like a dream now. Apparently not. Nothing in this afternoon's *News* either. At seven the bartender switched off the picture and Robinson ordered the crab salad from the leather-skirted waitress. He had to make himself eat well, resist the temptation to drink his meals. The pine glade set for tomorrow worried him. He must keep in good health. His arm and back hurt, but it was a good hurt, from stretching and using new muscles this afternoon.

Watching the TV news caused him to think, as he had after the first shock of seeing the composite, of the value of publicity to his mission. His purpose, after all, was not to take out a series of individual hunters. What mattered was reducing deer hunting in the state. If he announced his existence, if the reality of Deerlover were made public knowledge on the media, state and national, he, one man, could become a major deterrent to whitetail hunting in Michigan. No need to announce, after all, that his habit was to fell only one man per day. Best keep that information to himself. Let accidents by shoot-and-run hunters be attributed to him.

That way he could be in effect all over the north, dismay who knew how many of those 700,000?

Against that he had to weigh the risk factor. Once he announced himself, the decision would be irreversible. No more easy kills like this morning. Evidently the authorities had not convinced themselves of any link between last season's seemingly random deaths and Cooper's. There was only the newspaper speculation. The bullets from his .308 went through his hunters with so many excess foot pounds of energy that they vanished into an oblivion of field or forest. Almost certainly, no ballistics check was possible, even if some suspicious investigator thought of trying one. The existence of Deerlover could not be verified unless—to multiply his effect—he verified it himself and somehow proved it. Then all the resources of the law would be bent on apprehending him. There were computers now, sophisticated means of processing information that he didn't know. The benefits, he thought, outweighed the risk, but he must do nothing he would want to back away from.

After eating, he gazed about the large room where he had met Phyllis. There were empty tables and booths now, though not many. He let himself imagine that yesterday's paper was responsible for the diminution of hunters. Very few women, of course. A redhead in a bright red dress at a table in a far recess of the room next to the row of pinball machines. She was with a man in a flashy sportcoat, his back partly to Robinson. He thought it might be Rod. They must have come in while Robinson was lost in thought.

He took his glass and walked back to their table.

"Excuse me," he said to the man. "May I join you?"

"What for?"

Maybe he had the wrong man. He sat down anyway.

"I'm looking for a young lady named Phyllis."

A laugh. "Phyllis ain't no lady." Rod, though having revealed his identity immediately, said nothing more but studied Robinson, assessing him. He had on a pink shirt and a wide tie the same cream color as his jacket. He seemed young, around thirty, cropped hair and a face that could have been handsome if not too angular in jaw and forehead and sharp in the eyes.

At last Rod made up his mind. "Phyllis ain't coming tonight. She's under the weather. Fix you up with something better." He did not take his eyes from Robinson's. "A redhead. She'll give you a better time anyway. Guarantee you. She's into more stuff."

Robinson too did not glance at the redhead seated with them. He just remembered her appearance. She would be taller than Phyllis, longer-legged, more sensual, active. Was it a natural red or a henna? He could find out.

"I like Phyllis," he said, nonetheless.

Rod considered. "Pay extra?"

"Yes."

"Double."

"Yes."

"Double is eighty."

"All right."

"OK. I know where you are. I'll deliver her. Your credit is pretty good, but I want the first hour in advance, the rest right afterwards. If you don't have it—"

Robinson pulled out four twenties from the gold clip.

"You'll get it," he said. "Business is business. Gentleman's agreement. And I'll want her again. But don't threaten me with consequences. I have consequences too."

Rod did not understand.

"Yeah," he said. "I'll deliver her. You bring her back

here when you're finished. Before two. Eighty an hour.
She's not in good shape, like I said. Anything you want,
sure— But no rough stuff tonight. Know what I mean?''

iv

As soon as he was in his room he showered and changed
into fresh clothes: tan cotton pants and a white shirt
opened at the neck. She'd had some sort of bad time
last night and he wanted to look as unthreatening as
possible. He slipped on worn slippers that Laura had
given him. They were leather, but purchased long ago.
No point in throwing them away.

He went out to fill the plastic bucket with ice and
then, while he waited, quietly tidied the room. He stuffed
his dirty clothes into the plastic bag in the closet and
closed the door. The green appointment book was in
the inside pocket of the jacket. His maps and schedules
and clippings were still in the top bureau drawer. Only
these things linked him to the psychopath. Nothing to
be gained by hiding them better, locking them somewhere. He had to have them with him, and if it came
to a search they'd be found no matter where. He looked
round the room. The black bow stood hunchbacked
in its corner. It would frighten her. He put it in the
closet. The .308 shone dully where it lay in velvet in
its case on the desk, black of barrel and scope, grainy
brown of the stock. It had a terrible beauty. He closed
the top on it. A magazine from one of Laura's sub-
scriptions lay on the small square table by the armchair.
He carried such things with him to harden his resolve.
It was harmless, he'd leave it. It showed a raccoon with

its leg in a trap. He lit a cigarette and sat in the armchair facing the bed, waiting, seeing nothing, thinking nothing.

When he responded to the light tapping on his door she stood there close, her head and frizzy hair silhouetted against the glare of the parking-lot lights. At the far extreme of the lot a big blue station wagon slipped along and out onto the highway. Rod had let her out here and watched until she had crossed and Robinson had opened the door for her. He asked her in. She had on a short dress, too short. A prostitute's dress, of some shiny material, goldish, cinched at the waist with a gold belt, no coat to warm her in the chill walk across the lot. She held a skimpy matching purse, a little frayed. What was in a prostitute's purse? He looked into her face, pale, drawn, but not bruised as he'd half expected. The vertical line of scar tissue from the old cut over her right eye. The pink lipstick, he thought, covered white lips. Her large brown eyes caught his for an instant and then dropped.

"Thank you. I'm glad to be with you. Shall we?" She glanced toward the bed, still neatly made. "Do you want me to...do anything?" Her voice broke.

"Sit down," he said, offering the armchair. "I think you could use a drink. I just wanted to see you again. My name is Robinson."

She nodded. "I'm not ready for any more strangers. Maybe a weak Scotch like you made before. I'm not much of a drinker. But tonight—" She sat down, knees close together, hands on them. "Oh God, I've had a bitch of a time."

He fixed her drink with only a dribble of water and two ice cubes; regular Scotch on ice for himself. She took a sip, then a deeper sip, and shuddered. "Oh God, that's what I needed. Thank you."

"I tried to contact you last night, Phyllis. I'm sorry but I couldn't. Tonight I waited two hours at the T.and C. until Rod showed up. I'd like to see more of you."

"You've seen everything."

He smiled sadly at her for this bitterness. "Maybe. But I blacked out and forgot. If there was a way to make appointments...I'll be travelling around the state, hunting, but I could check back here, next couple of weeks."

"Reserve me?"

"Yes. You said you had regulars."

"See my manager. But no, don't do that. Just kidding. He doesn't like it when men get fond of me personally for myself. It's happened a couple of times." She paused, remembering, he supposed, those times. "He's dangerous."

An irrational idea crossed his mind, quickly faded. Out of the question now and after the season too. They could not be together without her discovering the truth.

"I pretended I didn't want to come here," she said. "For some reason he was insisting." She didn't know about the double rate. "So I kept protesting, saying I couldn't work tonight. So he brought me."

"Does he hunt?"

She raised her face to his, puzzled. Something in his voice, maybe? No. For her the question was a non-sequitur.

But then she smiled and shook her head. "He knows Forty-second Street, not the outdoors. He'd be a babe in the woods. But he has guns. He goes crazy sometimes." She added: "I'm scared to death of him."

"I know."

They sat quietly for a few moments. He was thoughtful. Though he could not be with her, he could help her escape from Rod, get her away and finance her. There was nothing in it for him but danger. Human suffering was not his province.

"Take me to bed?"

He rose, dimmed the floorlamp, pulled back the bedclothes. She was standing, fumbling with the tab of the zipper at the back of her neck. He touched her hands and guided them to her sides. He unclasped and removed the belt, crouched before her and reached up the pathetic skirt of her dress to her flanks and pulled down her panties. They lay about her ankles, figure-eight, upon the tinsel high-heeled shoes. She stepped out of them and he lifted her onto the bed, twinges of muscular pain from the bow practice, laying her with her head below the pillows. He removed her shoes and massaged each foot. He raised her knees. He asked her to lift herself, and when she did he drew the skirt up over her bosom, smoothing it there and under her, exposing her. He took one of the pillows and placed it under the small of her back. It was too soft, and he replaced it with a rough bolster from the couch. He slipped out of his trousers and underpants. He knelt below her, bent and kissed twice, three times, the tri-angle of brown curls so often ravaged by hunter and conventioneer. Then, upright on his knees and haunches, he prodded and began to enter her. He held back, prolonging. She shook her head, "Just go on without me. But take off your shirt. I like to look." He knew there was an irony lost on him here but unbuttoned the white shirt and tossed it aside. At his ejaculation there was not only the local sensual ecstasy, the re-action through his whole nervous system, but a flowing away of tension such as he could not remember. To-ward the end there had been some savaging, but when he fell forward upon her and laid his head beside hers, she laced her arms around him and whispered that he was different. Again, there was an irony, but something real as well.

She took her things into the bathroom and restored herself while he dressed.

When she came out she said he must take her home. The meter was running. She was costing him a fortune. She had something to give him that he might look at afterwards.

He told her of Rod's instructions to return her to the T. and C. She looked downcast. She fell back in the armchair facing the bed. This meant of course that Rod might send her out on another trick tonight.

"Let me see what you have," he said.

From the tiny purse she took out a piece of folded newsprint. He stared. She had the composite sketch of Deerlover. She'd recognized him in it. But it was just print with a little grainy photo in the upper corner, no drawing. She handed it across to him where he sat on the chair belonging to the desk.

It was from yesterday's *News* that had featured him on the front page, a back-page column called CINDI MAYER, whose photo was in the corner, subtitled "Drunks in the Woods." A diatribe against hunters, asking, he gathered from a glance at the first sentences, why any decent man would want to go out into Nature in the name of sport, take a friend or son, while Nature was invaded by thousands of drunks with rifles. Something about crossfire. It was like what he'd been thinking of before, the credit for the accidents.

"Don't get mad," she was saying. "I just happened to see it. Just something to think about. Read it later if you want. I just can't figure how a half-way decent guy like you goes out hunting deer."

"I'm not a drunk," he said. But then he recalled

their last time together when he passed out. She smiled. She remembered too. "Not usually. Never in the woods."

"But why?" She meant why did he hunt. "Forget it. It's none of my business. Take me to the damn T. and C." She primped up her hair, took her purse, started to rise, brave, businesslike, steadied maybe by having been with him.

"No, no. Stay awhile," he said. "It's hard to explain." It interested him to try to think like a deer hunter, and he could keep her with him until it might be too late tonight for her to have to accept another trick. At least he could do that for her.

He tried to explain about the sharpening of the senses, the new alertness after the lassitude of summer, how being out there with the basics, out of all civilization (except of course the latest in rifles and a pile of other gear produced by modern technology) renewed a man, got him ready for winter. It sounded convincing. There was an element of truth in it for himself. More truthfully he added: "And there's the solitude. I don't knock around much with other hunters."

In fact he was alone most days of his life, in Aurora, at the house, except for the cats and the two dogs. He most loved the cats. The dogs were too humanized. Mrs. Hibbard was reliable. He had enormously overpaid her to stay at the house with the animals again this season. Yet he wanted to be home to protect them. You did what you could where you were. They must be allowed to live out, in quiet and in dignity, their little lives.

Phyllis was staring at him, trying to understand.

"You could take photographs, not shoot them," she said.

"Oh, that's not the same. Not the same excitement

of the stalk, the kill, you know. I guess it's primitive. Fundamental. My forebears went out to hunt in order to live. I have to re-enact that. They brought home the venison."

She actually laughed, settled back in the chair. "At the same time *my* forebears were developing the oldest profession. Or Rod's forebears."

"Probably. Stay, Phyllis. I can afford the meter. Maybe you can—"

He broke off. He'd been going to say that maybe she could convince him to stop hunting, but something was wrong. At first he knew it only by instinct. Then, without turning his head from her, he shifted his eyes to the drapes behind her. They were open half an inch, and the slit of light from the parking lot had suddenly been cut off. Some one was standing there watching them. The drapes themselves from that light showed the faintest outline of the shadow of a man's shoulders. Cooper? The .38 was outside in the glove compartment of the Vega. And with Phyllis here— He turned casually away toward the closed case holding the rifle.

"What is it?" she asked.

"Don't turn. Act naturally. OK?"

"OK."

"Somebody's watching us through the window behind you."

She was silent for a moment, then whispered, "I think it's Rod. He's suspicious like I told you. He's checked up on me before. I've been here a long time and he's suspicious. Do you have a plastic basin or something like that here?"

"Just the ice bucket." It was on the desk beside the rifle case with their glasses and the Scotch bottle.

She rose and took the bucket into the bathroom. He bent and freshened his drink and took a sip, not looking toward the window. She was doing something to placate Rod, if it was Rod. She didn't realize the other men it might be. He heard her dump the ice into the bathroom basin, run some water.

She came back with the bucket half filled with warm water, steaming slightly. She held the little cake of motel soap. She bent and put these things on the floor by his chair. "I forgot a towel," she said, and went and brought one from the bathroom. "Now, if you stand and face the window and pretend you don't see anything, I'll practice my profession."

He realized what she was going to do and stood up for her, glancing blankly toward the drapes as if he saw nothing. The shadow was virtually indistinguishable, the darkened crack between the drapes narrower than he had thought.

She knelt before him, her back to the shadowed drapes, and unbuckled his belt and slipped his trousers down to the floor, then his underwear, face to his slack member. He stepped out of these clothes and she tossed them onto the bed. Cupping up water with her hands, she first washed him with the soap then rinsed and dried him.

"Sit down, Robinson, and we'll convince Rod and he'll go away and maybe you'll be able to reserve me."

She worked her fingers under and around. He had not thought he could respond so soon after but felt the quick pleasure at the nerve endings, the renewed pressure of the blood. She looked up at him.

"Is he still here?"

"Yes." It was true. He put his hand down into the thick dark hair and lightly massaged her scalp. "You don't have to really do this. It will look the same."

"I don't mind."

He lifted her round, wan face in his hands and looked down into it, the brown eyes shut now, the mouth in its pink lipstick slightly open. He touched the whitish scar on her forehead. Then she bent her head and began to work him with lips and tongue. Experiencing this, he kept his eyes on the motionless shadow on the drapes. If it was not Rod's, he was caught literally, as the phrase went, with his pants down, this girl kneeling between his knees. But it was Rod. Or it was a chance voyeur. Suddenly she stopped, except for the slightest continuing motion of her fingers under and around. She wanted, he thought, to say something.

"Slow and easy," she whispered, a little breathless. "I want to tell you about last night. In between, I'll tell you. OK?"

"Phyllis . . ."

"There were two men, but just one of me to go around." He felt her light breath against him as she whispered. "It was awful." For a few moments she continued fellating him. "They kept on their scratchy, bulgy hunting suits the whole time," she said then. "I was in my birthday suit of course. They kept coming at me different ways. They had a lot of imagination. Oh—" Again she resumed the action for a little. He was coming close to climax, trying to hold back, not so as to prolong this, but to postpone the hitherto unexperienced intolerable intimacy. She stopped again. "Is he still there?"

"Yes." But even as he spoke, the shadow on the drapes widened and faded as the voyeur, Rod or another, withdrew. Then suddenly the slit of light reappeared. He was gone. She couldn't see this behind her. "No," he said. "No, he just left. I guess it's OK."

She still whispered, not shifting position, as if nothing had changed: "They made me crawl for them, on all fours. I crawled backwards to them, to one of them or the other. They were so damn rough and big. I even wished I was back in fucking Miami, Detroit. They never really hurt me but I was scared shitless all the time.

They yelled instructions. Then I'd get near enough, bump up against the filthy suit . . ."

She bent her head. The prostitutes he'd visited after Laura's death offered what they called half and half, apparently standard procedure. It began this way to arouse him, concluded with straight intercourse. But Phyllis was not pulling back, turning away, was apparently intent upon an intimacy, an embarrassment he could not allow, could not and held back till he must yield to it so that the release when it came was a cataclysm, an education in sensuality.

"My God," he said, despite himself, believing in no God.

She sat in the armchair while he pulled on his underwear and slacks from the bed.

"I've had experience," she said. And then: "Sorry. I don't mean to be bitter." She stood and smoothed her skirt. "When you told me Rod was gone and so I didn't need to, well, then I wanted to."

"Look," he said, sitting on the bed. "I can't like they say take you away from all this, like what happened last night. I have responsibilities. But I can help you escape. I can finance you. Rod's gone. He's not suspicious. I can give you five hundred dollars right now. I'll drive you down to Bay City tonight and you can stay there and catch a Greyhound tomorrow to wherever you want where you have relatives or just anyplace you'd like to be. He'll never trace you, and you'll be out of it. I'll fix it so you can contact me and I'll send you more money if you need it, until you get a decent job. Pay me back whenever or never. It doesn't matter. Anyway, that was worth a fortune."

"You have responsibilities? Here?" She sat chin in hand, trying to comprehend him, the mystery of him.

"Yes."

"Sorry to be nosy. You're supposed to return me to the T. and C. when you're through with me. If you don't, he'll come after you."

"I'll be away a few days. I don't need to come back to this motel. I'll stay with you at a motel in Bay City tonight. He'll never find me. Even if he did . . ."

"You're crazy, you know that?"

"Please let me help you."

"Thanks, but no. Look. I'll tell him you were rough with me, that you hurt me in ways that don't show. He'll like that. He'll be glad to rent me to you again when you get back. The only time I ran away from him he found me. He's a devil. He'd find me again. I don't know how but he would. He took me to a house where there were some strange people as witnesses and a woman friend of his hurt me, almost killed me. I paid the doctor with my—you know—what I just did. He was a proctologist. I'm too scared. It's OK, now. Take me to the T. and C."

Why, he wondered, did there have to be so much fear?

As he was putting his wool jacket around her for the short walk to the Vega, she chanced to see the magazine cover of the raccoon with its right paw in the trap. She picked up the magazine, and he looked at it over her shoulder. The raccoon was expressionless as such an animal must be. Yet the whole photograph radiated pain. It was somehow drained and pale and white, which was the color of pain. He imagined using his knife, or gnawing off his own right arm to escape it. Legions of French trappers had opened up this region to humankind.

"Why do you have this on your table, Robinson, when your responsibility is to hunt?"

He grabbed her arm and took her to the car and

returned her to the Town and County and paid Rod $340.00 in cash, reserving her for the twenty-fourth and twenty-sixth. Not available for Thanksgiving, no way, said Rod. She winced at this news and dropped her eyes. Robinson himself had decided against having her the twenty-first. That crowded things too much. He'd need his rest that night. First things first.

NOVEMBER

18

At breakfast across the highway he pulled Phyllis' newspaper clipping from the breast pocket of his sports coat and read it. Tired last night from the long day and the intensity of the night, he had forgotten it. It was a satirical description of the social life of hunters: their macho ethic, their joyful abandonment of wives and girl friends for a few days, their camaraderie in the bars up north, the likelihood of heart attacks for those whose lives were otherwise sedentary, their drunken lurchings through the peaceful woods and fields, the danger to sober men hunting with friends and relatives. Nothing, except by implication, about the carnage they sought to perpetrate. Still, Cindi Mayer was a possible avenue. He studied the picture at the upper left-hand corner of the clipping. Thirtyish and gaunt. But the clip was small, an inch by an inch and a half and coarse-grained. She might be pretty.

He spent the rest of the morning at bow practice on the beach, re-considering from different angles the huge idea of involving the media: the leverage against the risks. The practice was better. The physicality of it helped him to think. He was learning to be comfortable in the different positions,—squatting, standing, even kneeling—whether staying free or leaning his bow hand against a trunk or stump. At twenty paces, he often hit one of the ripe tomatoes he had purchased. He still could not resolve the problem of getting a clean release. If he held the string and nock of the practice arrow in the curve of his first and second fingers, the release was sloppy, and the arrow lost drive and tended to veer to the right. If he used thumb against bent forefinger, he could not pull the fifty pounds. Of course there were solutions to this problem in the literature. He should have read articles on bow hunting during all those free months between seasons, sent for the manufacturers' catalogues. Now the best he could do was to consult the proprietors of local sporting good stores.

After lunch and the deep sleep of an afternoon nap— an indulgence to rest himself for the commitment of this evening—Robinson took out his lined yellow legal pad, sat at the desk in his room and wrote the letter.

11/18

Cindi Mayer:

I am writing to you because of your column in yes-terday's News. I think you may be sympathetic. I am the person pictured and referred to on the front page of that issue as the Deer Lover. It is quite true that I shot fifteen hunters in this area last firearm season. I intend to do better this season and have already started, although I failed because of mishaps on Tuesday, the second day. I shot the man Cooper on the morning of the 15th near Grayling and an anonymous heavy-built hunter in olive drab camouflage at the end of a corn-field outside Alpena yesterday soon after dawn. (It was necessary to shoot him twice.) On my way south and west I shall attempt a kill at dusk in or near a stand of planted pine four miles north of Au Gres. I shall post this letter in the mailbox outside the post office in the town first. The mail is picked up from the box at 6:00 P.M. daily. I mention these details to establish my cre-dentials and my credibility with you. I plan to com-municate regularly during the season. You will know my letters from those of possible cranks by the paper and the handwriting.

I do not consider myself a psychopath. My motive

*is sane and timely: to reduce the hunting of deer as
effectively and quickly as one man can.*

I look like any other hunter.

*If you will publish or describe this note, men in-
tending to hunt will know that I exist, and may reflect
that any stranger in the woods anywhere in Michigan
might be me.*

—*Deerlover*

Immediately after dropping the envelope into the
mailbox, Robinson realized that he should not have
made the reference to mishaps on Tuesday. That was
a clue to his identity. He must be more careful.

This evening no vehicles were parked at the end of
the access road cutting across the harvested cornfields
to the stand of planted pine. Robinson drove in anyway. He was committed by his letter to Cindi Mayer
to try to function in this place. From the equipment
spread on the backseat of the Vega he took only the
.308, shouldered it, slammed the door behind him. In
the woods, the atmosphere was immediately strange
and cool. He realized that no deer would come here.
The pines, planted simultaneously sixty or eighty years
ago on some triangular pattern at twenty-foot intervals,
had grown simultaneously to a trunk diameter of maybe
a foot, a height of maybe sixty feet, blended up there,
and shaded out under a canopy of evergreen anything
else that might have taken root and tried for the life-
giving light. So on this carpeting of generations of brown

needles and cones lay no acorns beloved of the deer, there were no sprouts or saplings for them to nibble. There were mushrooms, inedible to deer. The pines had shaded out their own offspring as well as any foreign intrusion. And between these discrete and distanced trunks there was no cover in any sense that deer would appreciate. Yet on Tuesday there had been cars out there at the end of the road, and a truck—hunters, he assumed, and so he traversed these pine woods hoping for game.

He could not tell how far north and south the stand extended, a mile or more, but after a minute or so he perceived in the bright light of the falling sun the western extremity of the stand and soon reached it. Wild brush grew to a man's height, and at its edge he found a dilapidated split-rail fence, thence a broad field left fallow for at least a year, more probably two, for it was interspersed with weeds and saplings a yard high, and along its far extremity ran another fence of the same character. To his right, north, there seemed to be more brush and then woods whose character he could not ascertain. He should have brought his binoculars. Near the woods a group of sheep were grazing. All the ewes faced away from him toward the woods, occasionally raising their heads to gaze into them. Farm animals often looked toward deer or toward people. He heard, or intuited that he heard, a sound behind him and to the north. He flattened into the brush and worked the bolt action of the .308. He lay and waited, easing his left elbow under the rifle, jiggling his legs apart for stability. Through the brush and pine trunks ahead he saw a flash of luminescent orange then nothing, but the hunter would soon come into view more directly across from him. He waited, changing his position slightly for a shot eastward at the point where the man would be nearest and most visible. Then indeed the man in orange stepped into sight, neck to ankles in the hunting suit, not stained as they usually were but brand new, brilliantly contrasted against the natural brown of the tree trunks and pine-needle bed of the grove. No chance of his being shot here by accident.

Robinson picked him up in the scope, no-power at this short range. But then he hesitated. The man had been clumping along, making no effort to be stealthy. He had a rifle, but he held it with his left hand about the barrel midway, the arm extended so that the butt bumped along on the ground. And he was not a man but a boy. Robinson turned the ring to 4X, not for a better shot but for a better look. The boy had stopped, exactly in the best target area. Up close, he looked dispirited, disconsolate. Robinson thought about the letter posted to the *News*. Its commitment could be met here and now by a simple squeeze of the trigger. The impact, through the media, would be multiplied far beyond this simple deterrent. The child was undoubtedly a hunter. What difference did age make? The child was the father of the man, who would hunt season after season. And yet suddenly Robinson knew that he would not pull the trigger. In the scope the boy's face showed pale and freckled, worried, miserable. Robinson rose, strode out to the brush, pretended to have just caught sight of this child.

"Hello," he called.

"Hello." Tentatively.

"Look, this isn't a good place to hunt today."

"I figured that. I, I just wanted to give it a try."

"I don't mean the territory, though it's hopeless. I mean the maniac that's out here shooting hunters."

"Maniac?"

"Some bleeding heart that goes out shooting hunters to save the deers. Heard about him?"

"No."

Robinson watched. There was something in the boy's eyes. "Crazy, huh? If you don't know, you don't know that he wrote the papers that he's going to strike right here, north of Au Gres, today. Tonight. That's why I said it wasn't a good place to be hunting."

"Well, thanks. Thank you."

"You—excuse me for asking—but you aren't him, are you young man?"

"God no. More power to him! I wish—" He stopped, maybe by a thought unutterable to him.

"You don't like hunting?"

"Hate it."

"Then why—"

"It's obvious, isn't it?" It wasn't. But the boy gestured towards the woods northward.

"Your father?"

"Stepfather. He's trying to make a man out of me. Hasn't succeeded so far. I haven't killed anything yet. There's deer up there. We saw them, but they spooked. He's going to scare them this way, through the woods or down the field. I'm supposed to bag one, hide there in the weeds and shoot one way or the other, whichever they come."

"Are you a good shot?"

"Last time we did this, yesterday, I missed. He gave me hell."

This answer, Robinson thought, might be evasive.

"Whichever way they come, if the Deerlover doesn't bag you first."

"He can have me. Or him for that matter." Bitterly.

"Listen: OK. Look, I believe you. You aren't him. Now I'm going to tell you something *you* may not believe but had damn well better."

"I've got to get into position, to shoot."

"No, forget that. Listen, I'm not what I look like. I'm Peterson, FBI." Insanely, he pulled a card out his breast pocket, flashed it in the kid's direction. It was a credit card.

"You're putting me on."

"I'm not putting you on. I'm trying to save your goddamn life. The guy's *here*. He'll shoot you, or me on sight. What you've got to do is hightail it out of here and let me handle things. If your stepfather shows up I'll explain. I've got to try to get the two of you the hell out of here and stay here myself as decoy. That's my job."

The boy hesitated. "All right," he said. He started to withdraw into the brush. "Hope you get there first, ah, Mr. Peterson. Before this Deerlover."

Robinson strode north through the pine woods because they offered no obstruction, but when he came opposite the northern reach of the field he cut again into the brush so as to conceal his approach to the stepfather hunter. The stepson hated him. Still, Robinson had not shot a man whose relationship with another human being was so apparent, so present as this. But what was the difference? Cooper had a wife and children. What difference did it make that in this instance the child, a stepchild anyway, was on the scene? No difference. Pure sentiment. From the field the ewes and the lambs also were watching him.

He never saw any deer. Probably they were does and fawns. But they must have been there because suddenly before his eyes leapt up the spectre of the human hunter in all his fashionable regalia yelling and waving his arms, yelling, "Yahoo, yahoo," and chasing the unseen deer southward to be shot by his stepson. The sheep milled around stupidly and then stampeded down the field toward safer ground. Robinson took the prone positon in the brush, steadied his left arm under the rifle, the canvas sling twisted around it, and with his right hand turned the ring to 2X. He concentrated everything on a clean shot just under the shoulder to the heart. But from his right somewhere there was the plunk of a rifleshot and the hunter fell backward out of sight. Robinson waited where he was. After a while the boy appeared, examined his kill, and then went off, presumably to reach the car and drive to a telephone. Deerlover would be credited with the kill. That was all that mattered.

Four hours later, Robinson checked into the lodge just off the Interstate in the Upper Peninsula where he had reserved a room. It was a fancy place with an all-night desk. In writing here he had used the Fenimore alias. Now he paid for two nights in cash. He'd stay the extra night partly in hope of getting some rest, but mainly to avoid any correlation between the killing he might accomplish and checking out of this lodge, even the checkout of Fenimore. So far as the records went, Robinson Jay remained at Lutz's motel two hundred miles south. He had rumpled his bedding there before leaving for the pine stand. The maid would notice that he had not slept there tomorrow night, but he did not think there was danger in that. Though very tired, he left a call for 5:00 A.M. A good breakfast in the restaurant here with the other hunters and out on the road before dawn. If a good opportunity did not present itself then he'd have another try in the evening.

All the way up he'd thought about the murderous stepson, the hatred that must have lain behind the intelligent, unhappy face, the ruthless immediacy of the decision and the act. How much of Robinson's fabrication had the boy believed? Had he grasped who Robinson was? No danger in that either, for he would never aid the police. Robinson had found himself shaken by the incident for reasons he could not fathom. He was glad he had no stepson or son of his own to hate him.

NOVEMBER

19

i

He cruised thoughtfully eastward along a state highway that clung to the north shore of Lake Huron. There was something pleasant, even nostalgic about the drive, and he wished that he might simply enjoy it. Last year he had unwisely driven straight north from this area into the deserted, rugged country below Lake Superior and clambered for hours over exposed rock though he'd known the hunter density and kill-density was very low there. He'd found his man, finally, but got lost on the way out and spent the night shivering. This was much more congenial country, though crowded for his taste; empty cars and trucks were pulled over on the shoulder, one every half mile or so. Small islands were scattered to his right, some with an expensive house on them and a path to the dock and a bridge to the mainland. A stiff north wind came off the lake, flattening the cypress that endured here and there along the coast, soughing across the roadway and up the steep slope to his left. At a village on the western tip of the peninsula the highway ended, and according to his map there was only dirt and gravel to the north. A dock on pilings jutted out into a strait. The ferry was coming in from Drummond Island, which lay maybe a mile and a half away. He did not know whether deer lived on the island, and in any case did not wish to risk getting marooned on so small an area. He drove back until he came to the car that he remembered as being farthest from any other.

There was vegetation within sight sufficient to conceal the Vega. So Robinson drove past the hunter's car, a late-model Japanese, parked a hundred yards away, and cut back and up the slope with the .308

slung on his back. At the top he had to lean into the wind, but as soon as he started down the lee side of the ridge the air was calm and suddenly quiet. Here the cypress gave way to scrub on sandy ground. Beyond the gully beneath him was another rise to about the same height. He nearly fell over his hunter, who was crouched half-way down in a clump of brush, his camo suit blending absolutely with the surroundings. The man in fact heard Robinson and turned and glared up at him.

"Quiet, for God's sake," he whispered. "And go away. This is a perfect opportunity here."

Truly, the shadowed man would be quite invisible from the opposite side. Deer coming over the slope and down or along it would be lit in the light from the low sun just reaching it out of the southwest. The range was easy, and the wind, from the backdraft effect off the opposing slope was gently in Robinson's face.

"Yes," he said softly.

When he regained the crest of the ridge, Robinson looked for other hunters, saw none, and strode parallel to the highway in the brisk wind till he was well past the Vega. He did not wish to associate himself with the car until he was certain no one was watching, no vehicle coming either direction. There were two hunters, far ahead of him and half-way down the lee side to his right. He'd appear to them silhouetted against the morning light, unidentifiable. When they waved a friendly greeting, he raised the .308 clutched midstock in his right hand and shook his arm vigorously in response. Maybe after the media had gone to work hunters would be less casual in the presence of an armed stranger. No way to tell whether they were partners with the dead man or from another car. They had seen nothing, obviously. They would have paid no heed to the shot, of course, if it had carried to them. And the body lay sprawled as completely camouflaged as it had ever been.

No one else in sight, no cars, either direction. The hunters down the slope would lose sight of him. He dashed down to the Vega and spun the rear tires getting it out of there and onto the westbound lane. Then he slowed. No pursuit. Once again, he was out clear.

He realized now why this stretch of coastal road with its windblown cypress was so nostalgic. It reminded him of his childhood, the backseat of some big 1930s car, behind his father, driving, and his mother, even the rank smells of the car came back to him, the rough texture of the upholstery at his fingertips, on some wonderful trip along the northern California coast.

He wanted a drink when he got back to the lodge, but the bar didn't open until eleven. He'd not thought to lay in a supply of Scotch of his own, and he was so tired it wasn't worth the effort of going out again for any. Exhaustion had its way with him and he slept long and soundly. Mid-afternoon he went down and read the papers. Nothing about him, not even a repeat in the back pages of Tuesday's front-page report in the *News*. He had a couple of drinks and went back to his room to watch the local five o'clock news on TV. Again nothing. He was not having the necessary impact. Letters were simply too slow. He could hardly dictate or write out telegram messages. He'd have to risk telephoning Cindi Mayer. He might reach her right now, get her home number through Information. He stared at the black telephone in its black cradle. No, he was too drunk and foggy. He'd make some mistake. To-morrow morning.

The day's task done and no further action contemplated until tomorrow evening, he allowed himself another drink before dinner. It was still faintly light outside, good time for hunting, but not for him, not this evening. He'd worn casual clothes. There were groups of men in hunting outfits about the round tables drinking, mostly beer. Like himself, they were evidently satisfied with the day. Or else they were too drunk to care, letting this evening go by. A few couples, middle-aged and older, mostly ranged away from the hunters along the windows. No unattached women. Robinson had not noticed before the mounted heads of moose and elk (though neither moose nor elk survived here) and trophy deer along the walls at each end of the room. In the mouth of one of the deer a cigar had been inserted at a cocky angle.

Three seats away from him at the bar sat a man in uniform bent forward over his coffee cup, elbows on the counter. Not police. DNR? No, State Department of Conservation. Young man, clean-cut with short brown hair. Probably a college graduate from Natural Resources out at the beginning of his career. Robinson had never talked with anyone in conservation (as they called it), only read the publications. Try to draw him out, carefully? He felt communicative. This was no enemy. It was rather a matter of philosophical differences. But careful. No playing with fire. The dead man on that north slope in Mackinaw County had been found now, most likely, and this officer might know of him—if no more, yet, of Deerlover.

"Drinking on duty?" Robinson said. The officer looked

over at him, sat up, and pushed his coffee cup away with a smile.

"I'm not even on duty. Duty starts in ten or fifteen minutes, around sunset."

Robinson nodded, finished his whisky. "Buy you another round?"

"Why not?" The officer sidled over next to Robinson and held out his hand. "Dave," he said. Robinson shook his hand.

"Jay."

"Good to meet you, Jay."

The barkeep brought a second Scotch and poured Dave some more coffee.

"Poachers?"

"That's what we hear. With lanterns. My partner and I'll go out pretty soon and take a look around."

"Hm. What's the difference?"

"Difference?"

"If they hunt with lanterns."

"The deer don't stand a chance, is all. They come and look into the light, can't help it. Same as fishing with lights. You see their yellow eyes glowing like neon, then you aim between or underneath where the chest is. Duck soup." He shook his head.

"Do they stand a chance otherwise? The deer, I mean."

"Huh? Oh, sure. A sporting chance."

"Still, most of the deer will starve *this* winter anyhow . . ."

Dave nodded. "Yeah. That's what we figure. Especially this winter. The acorn count is way down. There'll be deep snow."

"So why stop the poaching? The herd has to be cropped, doesn't it, for its own good? Or Nature's good, something like that?" He was getting a little too drunk. He should break off.

Dave laughed. "You got me. Like they say, I don't make the laws. Too bad there's no more wolves."

"I don't like Nature," said Robinson.

"What you say your name was? Jay? Well, Jay, now you're talking crazy, you know that? What is there except Nature? It's the way things are. It's rough, sure, but it has to be so things keep going. By natural selection. And it's beautiful." He gestured about the room, the seated hunters in their baggy clothing, the two walls of mounted heads. But of course he meant to include all that was cruel and beautiful in the world outside.

Robinson took a sip of Scotch, savored it. "It was men that killed off the wolves. And cleared the land, which meant deer could thrive and multiply. Was that Nature?"

"I guess so. We're sure part of it."

"And those guys at the tables, they're part of it?"

"Everything's part of it."

"Yeah? Well, I don't like it." He stopped, tried to think. "Do you hunt yourself, Dave?"

"I have. I don't care for it much."

"Well, we're not so far apart then." Dave sat staring thoughtfully ahead. So Robinson went on. "Have you thought of the experience, the lives of the deer, between now and when they may starve in winter?"

"Lives? You make it sound like Bambi or something. They're animals, Jay." After a moment: "What do you do, anyhow?"

A possibly incriminating question. "I'm retired. I was a teacher."

"What'd you teach? English, I bet."

"No. High school Latin. And Social Studies. My wife taught English though."

"She up here with you?"

In a sense, yes, he wanted to say. "No. She's dead. Leukemia. Nature selected her out."

After the lad had gone on duty, Robinson gazed across at his own reflection in the dirty mirror behind a row of variegated bottles. *In vino veritas.* In whisky there was yet more truth. Hell, for once he'd drink his dinner, sleep it off. Nothing before dusk tomorrow except a mid-morning call to Cindi Mayer. He'd be OK for that. The morality came down to two issues, didn't it? Animals expressed all the best values in life—love, innocence, dignity, sacrifice, courage, seriousness, humor, intelligence. All individual depravity and evil was human. All. Also there was no God. So the whole idea of men as favored lords of creation over the creatures was a crock. He thought he was the first man in history to put together these two ideas: the benevolence and dignity of animals, the godlessness of the cosmos. He could not quite think it through. It was beyond thought, a new absolute like the former belief in Man. He himself could not behave like an animal, no. As such he'd be no more effectual than deer or dolphin—or Laura. He himself was human and lost. He'd do what he could for animals before the end. By the best instincts in him he simply felt all through himself that that was right.

NOVEMBER

20

i

He woke up groggy from the night before, but not really hung over. He never had hangovers. He showered to clear his head, dressed again in his casual outfit, and glanced over at the phone. No. Telephone companies kept records. He had breakfast downstairs, checked out and drove south over the straits. At Mackinaw City just across the bridge he pulled off the Interstate and found a corner phone booth on the premises of a gas station. He slid in a quarter and dialed Detroit information for the number of the *Detroit News*. Three more quarters got him the *News* operator. He asked for Cindi Mayer. It was Saturday. She might not be in. If not he'd try her home number. There'd be no wiretap now, no set-up for tracing or taping. Later there might be.

A boy's voice. Cindi wasn't there right now. Take a message?

"Is she home then?"

"No, she's here somewhere. Having coffee maybe."

"Can you find her quickly, please? It's important."

Silence while his three minutes ran out. The robotic voice-tape complained and he fed it coins.

"This is Cindi Mayer. What can I do for you?" A low voice that he liked despite the annoyance in it.

"I am the man whose picture appeared on the front page of your paper last Tuesday. Deerlover. Naturally, I'm calling from a pay phone. I wish to speak with you. Will you ask your operator to accept a collect call to you if I call back?"

Hesitation. "Yes. All right. Give me a couple of minutes." He had a sense of competence, capableness. She might do what he needed.

When he was back with her, he asked at once, "Have you received my letter?"

"No."

"It should come this morning. It will be self-explanatory. I said I would continue to correspond, but I realize now that won't work. I'll call you from time to time. I only wish to say now that I am indeed real; that I'll continue to shoot hunters; that I don't look much like your composite drawing. Do you know of the shootings in Alpena Wednedsay, Au Gres Thursday, Mackinaw County yesterday?"

"Wait, wait. This is too fast for me. No. I haven't been following. Look, why are you calling me specifically?"

"The letter will help you understand. Because of your column in Tuesday's paper about drunks in the woods."

"I'm a columnist, not a reporter. What makes you . . ."

"I've chosen you as my contact. It will be a big story. I want you to handle it."

"I don't know . . . You really killed those people?"

"Get your notepad in front of you. What I wish to say finally is that I'm going into Missaukee County the twenty-second or twenty-third. Got that? Monday or Tuesday, or both. Maybe your readers will see that in time to save themselves. I think I'll find one or two who didn't. After that . . . are you with me?"

"Yes, I think so."

"I'll stalk some privately owned land on the Huron coast. I kill at least one hunter a day. Goodbye."

"Wait. I'm not sure I believe you. Missaukee County, Monday or Tuesday. What about today, then?"

"A surprise. You'll believe me because the facts will corroborate what I say. I'll call you again after Missaukee."

"Wait. Why . . . ?" He hung up.

"You're hunting illegally, Mister!"

The light, though only from a small flashlight, blinded him. He held his arm across his eyes. He had been staggering through brush in complete darkness.

"I'm not hunting at all, officer, just lost! Help me find the road."

This was not entirely true. He knew pretty well the direction of the road and his Vega. He came up to the officer. Conservation uniform in reflected light as the man lowered his flash. It might have been Dave out on night patrol for poachers, but it wasn't.

Robinson had no lantern, only the rifle, was dragging no kill. He was obviously a lost hunter in the dark who needed help. It was necessary to preserve that fiction, for of the four men he'd overheard planning some nighttime hunting in a nearby hamburger joint on the Interstate and followed here, one was bleeding to death not fifty yards behind him.

"OK," said the Conservation Officer. "Let's see your license."

This was problematic. His true name was on the license. The dead man would be found here. Yet he showed it. The officer walked round him and also checked the number on his back tag.

"OK. Road's this way."

Robinson followed, and soon they reached the road and the patrol car; the Vega in sight partly around a far curve.

"That's my car," he said, pointing. "Thank you very much."

"Quite all right, Mr. James. Glad to be of help."

Your bad memory just saved your life, thought Robinson.

Afterwards, two or three miles south of Grayling, the scene of the original crime this season, he turned left off the expressway up a winding drive to a motel with an attractive name, The Hideaway. He'd checked in here early in the afternoon. A big family-sized room was available, and he'd taken it for the night. It was the whole top floor of a rustic cabin. He'd napped and then gone out and found the hamburger joint.

Now he put on his pajamas and sprawled on the double bed under peaked rafters and heard the rain start, lightly pelting the rooftop over him, like some boy in a novel by Dickens he'd read in school, sheltered from that rainfall overhead, yet completely aware of it, no two drops exactly simultaneous, each individuated raindrop sounding distinctly, lulling into oblivion.

NOVEMBER

21

i

Sunday. He'd take the day off according to the Lord's example. After all, media impact, not action in itself, was what really mattered, and he'd been working on that. After an omelette at Lutz's Restaurant, he took a nap in his room across the highway. He was nervous about being in Au Gres at all. Police might still be snooping round after the pine stand incident. If the stepson had seen the Vega parked out there amidst the cornfield, he'd presumably not report a description of it, not if he was smart. Still, it was a loose end. Robinson wondered whether the bullet had gone through the stepfather or lodged in him. Not Robinson's problem, except that if the bullet were found and linked to the boy's gun, he'd lose the credit. None of this was likely. He'd lay low during the day, skip bow practice.

When he came out for the paper, he saw the old composite version of the Deerlover's face through the grillwork front of the newspaper dispensing machine. He was back on the front page. The article, a long one, continued inside, was by-lined Cindi Mayer. It was factual reporter's work, not editorialized. She reproduced the letter, quoted the phone call, described the Au Gres and Mackinaw incidents. (The Grayling poacher evidently had not been discovered by press time, or was not attributed to the Deerlover.) A reward of $10,000 had been set up by the Cooper family for information leading to his capture and conviction. She included the Deerlover's threat to Missaukee County and, after that, to privately owned hunting land through Thanksgiving. Robinson was satisfied.

He walked down to Harbor Lights on the river for

a few drinks and dinner. Really, he should start east tonight but he didn't have the heart. The food at T. and C. was better than here. He just didn't want to see Rod, or Phyllis if she was around but unavailable. He let himself get pretty drunk, then had a fish sandwich. No coffee. He'd sleep it off. Missaukee tomorrow. At a big table in sight of his booth sat a group of young men, pitchers of beer before them. One round face stood out, instantly familiar. Who? The stepson? No. Damn. It was the Kid. From Tuesday. In the same baggy outfit as before. The others were in more conventional hunting clothes. Damn it, he was still hunting. After all the crap about his father and his girlfriend and his mother's grave. Robinson nearly got up and walked over. When the young men finally got up to leave, he rose and stopped the Kid with a hand to the shoulder. He had a drunken sense of the others looking at him in amazement. "Damn," he said. "I told you not to hunt. You swore you wouldn't. And here the fuck you are. I ought to kill you."

The Kid's eyes widened in surprise. Then he stepped back with a look Robinson couldn't fathom. It wasn't hostile exactly. Oh hell. The Kid of course had never seen his face. He'd been wearing the mask. Now he'd blown it.

At the motel he had another couple of drinks from his own stock, waiting for the 11:00 news on TV. When it came on, they seemed a substitute crew, a black lady and a callow youth, amateurish somehow. First the usual irrelevancies about the Middle East and Central America. A commercial. A tap at his door. He started. No one visited him. He rose unsteadily, hesitated. Cooper? The Kid to finish him off? The law after all? He simply opened the door. It was Phyllis in the shoddy gold dress.

"Robinson. I'm sorry. I hope you don't mind. I'll go away if you do." He drew her inside, shut the door. "I saw your car outside a couple of hours ago when we went by. I lied to Rod and said I thought you wanted me if I was free. Is it all right? It will cost you the usual. I know you'll have me in a couple of days. But I just couldn't resist the chance."

"Sure Phyllis. If you'll handle everything. I'm blind drunk. Take the money." He patted his right pants pocket. "Call Rod to pick you up. Or a cab?" Was there a cab in Au Gres? "I'm watching television," he added stupidly. They sat together on the bed.

The fleshy-faced youth was speaking. "And finally, Sandra, a man dubbed 'Deerlover' by the media is reported to have been shooting hunters in the northern Lower Peninsula and the U.P. All hunters are advised to use extreme caution in the presence of any stranger. We have a drawing of his face created with the aid of an eye-witness." Camera switched to an enlargement of the composite sketch. He glanced over toward Phyllis. She was watching with interest. This very broadcast, the confirmation of the reality of Deerlover that had led to it, was in a way due to her, was it not? She had shown him the column by Cindi Mayer. He wanted to tell her that. Madness. Sandra herself seemed to have no information to contribute. The fleshy youth continued: "Killings have been verified near Grayling, in Alpena, in Au Gres, in Mackinaw County, and again last night near Grayling. We repeat: all hunters are advised to use exteme caution in the presence of any armed stranger." Switch to commercial.

He punched off the tube. It had been a wretched report. No mention of the Cooper family reward, nor of the danger imminent in Missaukee County and privately owned lands. No quote from his talk with Cindi, though that must have been available. Still, the very vagueness and generality of the report could serve his purpose: frighten hunters everywhere.

"News isn't your kind of thing, is it?" she said. "Especially not that news."

"Well, no. But us guys hunting got to know about him. What do you think of him? You approve of him?"

"I don't know. The idea makes me all mixed up. He's scary."

Robinson put his arm around her where they sat on the bed and gave her a hug. "He won't hurt *you!*"

He looked at her face. She smiled, a little teary-eyed. "He might hire me though."

"He might. But he's just a man."

"I'm not so sure," she said.

NOVEMBER

22

i

He sweated a little, leaving behind the resort town of Houghton Lake, driving along the lower edge of the lake to the boundary of Missaukee County. He'd wanted a drink in town but it was too early, 10:00 in the morning, and he lit a cigarette instead. He'd thought of pulling into a garage that had a side-line renting trucks and four-wheel drive jeeps. "Get into the back country," read their hand-painted sign. He'd actually stopped across the highway and studied a battered jeep. It looked useful, and he was getting more and more nervous about the Vega, which had been in the vicinity of too many actions. But he did not wish to register his presence in this region by renting the jeep, not today, especially not with reference to penetrating into back country, and, besides, the canoe, tied with new white nylon cord to the baggage rack above him would not transfer conveniently to the jeep.

He must be nearly to the county line. He slowed to increase his distance from the camper cruising ahead of him. He'd see whether it was going to be stopped at the line. For an instant he panicked, almost swerved around and drove back. Wasn't it madness to drive in full view on a major road into Missaukee? To have confirmed the reality of Deerlover was one thing, a dangerous thing. But he'd announced the very time and place in advance, today or tomorrow or both, in the county just ahead, twenty-four miles square, and the information had been in yesterday's papers. The law, of course, had been notified Saturday, just after his call. Cindi Mayer had to and presumably wanted to avoid the slightest complicity with him. Yet a sudden U-turn now would be suspicious, while as things stood there was nothing suspicious about him. The canoe up top, the contemporary camping outfit in his trunk, the rifle in its case across the back seat, were these things the equipage of the psychopath? The topo map in his glove compartment was nothing either. He had not yet marked the X where this evening's or the morning's killing would occur.

To the right of the camper, far ahead, the marker sailed into view: MISSAUKEE COUNTY. No roadblock or stakeout. The camper went right through and he followed. Police could be waiting at some intersection. They could be watching from a distance. He still expected to be stopped, if not for interrogation, at least to be warned not to hunt in the county today or tomorrow. Why, after the revelation and the publicity, considering the impressiveness of his record, was there no warning at the county line?

The police might figure, as Robinson himself did, that new hunters would stay away. Their abstinence, if real, was his gift to the deer of the county. Hunters who had already back-packed into the deep woods and remote swamps wouldn't know. Transistors spoiled the purity of the outdoor experience. From such a man he would exact specific retribution on the animals' behalf today or tomorrow.

Then a calming thought crossed his mind. He himself was headed into deep hiding, was he not? In the back country where only the hardy and dedicated could reach. He would shelter and bed down there too (in the expandable man-sized tent and weightless sleeping bag that barely left breathing space within it) led by some sympathetic instinct. He himself was a trophy animal, if you thought of the reward and the magnitude of the law-enforcement apparatus that must be getting organized to hunt him. In the deep country ahead he could most nearly identify with the wild creatures he sought to protect.

Six miles into the county he turned north, pulling the large-scale county road map from the glove compartmet out onto the seat beside him. Four more miles and northern access would terminate in a dirt and gravel crossroad beyond which lay fifteen square miles of wilderness, rocky scrub surrounding the swamplands. From the swamp, or springs associated with it, arose a creek that wandered all the way east back to the lake.

At the crossroad, nothing but brush and a few stunted pines. Amongst these was parked a large pick-up truck, orange-yellow. As he turned left, he read, printed awkwardly in black on the side of it, *The Great Pumpkin.* Family man.

A mile, then right, north again, to where the dirt road perished in scrub brush and hard clay. This was possible, but the creek source lay three miles or more from here, and no place to hide the Vega. Back to the crossroad and three miles east, then north on the county road along the east boundary of his target area. He passed a sort of proto-road, a swath of hard, warped clay in the direction of that area and decided he would try it. But first, while he had the mobility afforded by the car, he wanted to check out the culvert where the creek passed under the road on its eight- or nine-mile way into Houghton Lake. He did so. The creek was four to five feet wide there, maybe eighteen inches deep. It would carry the canoe. He might even park here and paddle back in against the mild current, but that would be a long paddle and, again, the Vega would be exposed on a roadside. A white car of the Sheriff's Patrol drove by without stopping. He turned back toward the rugged belt of clay that seemed to wander in his preferred direction. The Vega jounced and twisted on these hard contours, scraping bottom here and there. He drove more and more slowly, watching the tenths of miles grudgingly accumulate on the speedometer. He was inching toward the putative X on his topo map. But this was not a degenerate road, returning to Nature. It had been an idea, a preliminary scraping decades ago. For what purpose he could not imagine. Mere access into *terra incognita*? Lumber removal whence there was no lumber? He could not tell where baked clay left off and eroded-to-stone began. It occurred to him that on this surface the Vega left no tracks.

Then, in a water-filled dip in this non-road, the promised swamp began. He left the car and walked ahead a hundred, two hundred yards. Here was mush and sinking in of tires and danger of getting stuck inextricably, wild swampy marshland to left and right, blighted trees sticking out of it, and spaces of sheer deep-looking water. He might launch the canoe here. At the last, the psuedo-road lifted to a dead end, and the ground to each side of it fell away into this water. He looked back at the old Vega. Suddenly, by instinct, he knew he must get rid of it now.

He walked back and started it, eased it to the drier, less mushy side of the passageway, worked it nervously to that last high point, got it crosswise, backing and filling, killed the engine.

He untied the canoe and set it down parallel to the Vega, coiling the nylon cord and dropping it in. He took the .308 in its case from the back seat and laid it in ahead of the canoe seat. From the trunk he took the cocoon-tent, sleeping bag, his canvas boots, and the brown double-knit gloves. Once last season he had looked at his right hand in the right glove, clenched the hand, the unidentifiable fabric slightly worn and metallic-looking like the mail worn by knights. For a moment he had been frightened at the sight of his hand, his own gloved right hand.

He sat sideways in the open door of the Vega, removed his tennis shoes and pulled on the boots. The shoes and other things he placed beside the rifle case in the canoe. The .38 automatic, a slim, half-filled box of ammunition for it and some papers—registration, proof of insurance, an Ohio roadmap, the Missaukee County roadmap—he spread on the passenger seat. He had the topographic map in his breast pocket. He put the gun and ammo in the pocket of his wool jacket and replaced the papers in the glove compartment. He considered the elephant-embossed knob of the gearshift. He must leave it. He'd bought this, he could buy another. He'd nearly forgotten to transfer the bag of two cheese sandwiches he'd bought at Lutz's that morning. Hunger reminded him. Already he wished he'd brought more food, something to cook with, a pint of Scotch. He'd known that he would want these thing and denied himself in advance. He'd function best with the irreducible minimum of *impedimenta*. He rolled down the front windows, released the hand brake, and shut the doors. He slid down the slope ahead of the car to the water, steadying himself with one hand on the hard, dusty clay. No fronds or lily pads grew here, and the brownish water had the brackish smell of rotting vegetation. He looked out over the forlorn prospect of the swamp. In a mile or so it held islands of forest and meadowland and the creek began. So claimed his map. The swampland must soon become more healthy then and life-supporting. A few feet down the bank he broke off a dead sapling about five feet long. He prodded it into the water, feeling for the bottom. Here there was mud at about three feet, but his stick went easily into the mud even after his hand was immersed up to the wrist. He climbed back up to the car.

It was not too late to reconsider. There would be difficulties in getting out of here. He had ridden home to Laura in this car. But something inexplicable, some sheer instinct, told him to shed it now. He put his back against the trunk, dug his boot heels into the serrated clay, and pushed with his legs. The Vega inched, then caught the slope and splashed out into the water, nose well into it, rear high and not so far from the bank as he had hoped. But the car angled forward as well as sank, and soon, the surface bubbling with air escaping from all its cushions and spaces, went under and kept going down into the brackish water and hidden mud beneath until from the crest he could not see it at all.

ii

"The land between the lakes," Laura had once read to him, "is swamp and unfit for human habitation." This was from a report by Lewis and Clark to President Jefferson. They meant lakes Huron and Michigan. They must have travelled through Missaukee before first frost, and the mosquitoes must have been frightful.

The hour or hour and a half of watery quietude (he had no watch) had relaxed him, the virtual effortlessness of forward motion even here where there was no current, an occasional stroke of the paddle on left or right. He understood why the Indians had once hunted with canoes of birchbark. The canoe made no sound on the water, left no track of scent. He could watch for trails coming in to watering holes. He could shore the canoe if he wished and step out to check for beer cans or other human junk or for rubs and scrapes indicating the territory of a buck. And, had he reason to take his kill back to camp, he could do so easily without laborious carrying or dragging.

Now, indeed, the marshlands began to look healthier, the timber seemingly more recently flooded, even with small stands of evergreens on patches of dry land. He heard birdcalls. He studied his map and turned a little to his right, northwest, he thought. Twice he had to haul the canoe over flats of mud and dried brush. He was not absolutely sure of his bearings and position. He wished for a compass. The sun was well past its zenith. The time might be 2:00 or 2:30. He had known that he would come to want a watch and a compass and yet had not brought them.

The water where he found himself after the second portage began gradually to narrow into a channel five or six feet wide with firming banks. He thought from his map that this might be the southeast quirk defining the beginning of his stream, and indeed the channel began to round to the east to his right, as it should, and began to develop a current as well as continuing to narrow and deepen.

Then he saw the hunters' camp, pitched a few yards up the right bank in a welter of frost-killed fallen grass. Three A-frames of stripped four-inch poles, the outer frames leaned inward for stability, supporting two twelve-foot overlapped ridge poles. The first of these, an external spine, held up the main tent. The second reached out high over flattened grass to the outer A-frame. He knew what that ridge pole was intended for: to hang up the draining carcasses of bucks. Could he control things, it would remain unweighted.

He studied the camp. A pup tent set up at an angle to the main tent, a rack of firewood. Nobody home, apparently, though it was not the best time to be out hunting. He paddled in, beached his canoe, walked about the camp. Two sleeping bags in the main tent, one in the pup tent. Ten yards behind the settlement the men had dug a latrine. The tents faced a cleared area where they had made a ring of stone and built their fire. Beside this was a green three-burner Coleman stove with a coffeepot. He hefted this and felt it. Cold, but with maybe a cup of coffee left. He worked the red pump on the back of the stove, lit the middle burner, turned its valve down to medium. While the coffee was heating, he searched for the larder, found it in a styrofoam box in the main tent. Some bread and bacon, canned food, canned milk. On the tent floor beside the box were three tin cups and a package of paper plates. Not much. Maybe they were planning to cook venison. Not if he could help it. He took a cup and put a tin of sardines in his pocket for later. He ate a cheese sandwich with the coffee. He used the latrine. At the canoe he noticed a six-pack of beer left in shallow water to cool. He pulled two cans from their plastic membrane and set them beside his sleeping outfit and the rifle case.

He paddled for a long time through flatlands increasingly drier, more continuous, more grassy amidst the brown brush and frequent stands of beech and pine. Here straw grass stayed stiffly upright, interlaced with greenery. His vague channel had become a definite stream, whose current let him rest and proceed in absolute silence. The sun through a thin cloud-veil was much lower now, behind his right shoulder. He was going east and slightly north. He no longer worried that he might commit the classic blunder of the disoriented and make a circle, ending where he had drowned the Vega. He wondered, smiling to himself, whether it was legal in Michigan to shoot from a canoe.

In that moment, he saw two of the hunters and to the right of them and farther away in a circle of meadow under a shaft of soft sunlight, the tawny glow of the bodies of deer. He let himself drift, considering the situation. He lit a cigarette. The hunters were in a stand, squatting behind a screen of aspen that they had supplemented with boughs cut and laid in horizontally. It was a good, natural-looking blind and as he noted from the slow drift of cigarette smoke back over his shoulder toward the falling sun, downwind from the deer. The men were completely exposed to him. If one of them chanced to turn from his intense scrutiny of the meadow and glance upstream, he would see Robinson drifting toward them. Robinson would wave a friendly greeting, hunter to hunter. Out of his impulse to reduce *impedimenta* to the absolute minimum, he had not brought the binoculars. So he uncased the rifle. He set the scope to 4X. He also shoved a shell from the box in the case into the chamber and closed the bolt on it, thus cocking the rifle, not particularly intending to fire it here, not intending not to. He shut his left eye and squinted through the eye-piece at the hunters. They were typical. Heavy-set men in dark, maybe black outfits covering, you knew, webbed underwear, one of them with a red and white check shirt over his suit, beer drinkers, men with rancid breath, athletic once maybe, gone overweight in middle age, heart-attack probabilities. It was a temptation to take them out here and now. Both wore greasy-looking homburgs, like two-thirds of a seedy vaudeville act.

He shifted the rifle towards the field of deer, taking his gloved finger off the trigger. He squinted again into the scope, ranging slightly to take in the whole picture. Does, six or seven in the sunlight, and three, possibly four yearlings with them. In the foreground of his circle of vision stood two large does, the one, its head in profile, kissing or licking the neck of the other, whose raised head was turned towards him, just under the jawbone. They stood in sparse dry grass intermixed with evergreen shoulder-high to them. He marveled at the size of the horn-shaped ears and especially of the Egyptian eye of the doe in profile, so improbably large in proportion to the slim head.

Scoping about the clearing, he tried to assess the situation. The two hunters had a clear shot. They were not much over a hundred yards from the pair of deer in the foreground. They were not interested in this group of deer *per se*. They had not come so far into back country and set up that camp to bag antlerless deer. Maybe they expected their trophy buck to blunder out onto this scene, driven by rut, oblivious to danger, crazy with hormones, and to mount one of these females and present himself to a bullet in the heart even as he was satisfying his lust. But Robinson did not think this scenario would occur. He knew nothing of the rut schedule in this part of Michigan. But these does were not in heat, nor about to be. They were placidly feeding, not mincing about nor restless, looking here and there. They were not itchy. Their tails were serenely clamped against their hindquarters, not half-raised nor twitching invitingly. They were cold, and an experienced buck even in rut was not likely to break cover to approach them. Nothing then, would happen here this afternoon or evening. He could concentrate on the third member of the party. Their canoe was not beached here, and he was certain he had not passed it. The third hunter, therefore, had dropped these two off at their blind and gone on ahead by himself. Robinson was drifting past them now; he would leave them to waste their time. The third member of the team was surely the one whose bed lay separate in the small tent back at the camp. If he did not return, the whole enterprise would be abandoned, and no deer would hang from the ridge pole in front of the main tent where the two bulky men expected to sleep tonight.

The patch of sunlight left the meadow, and Robinson laid the .308 across the gunwales of the canoe and took a couple of strokes with the paddle to speed him downstream. For a few brilliant moments the sunlight was on him, irradiating him as it had the animals, and then it was gone to the east and the whole scene of hunters and does and fawns was behind him.

He alternately paddled and drifted, looking to left and right for the big canoe that would be beached and would indicate the presence of the third hunter. The man could not be very far away. He had to return and pick up his colleagues and take them back to base by sunset.

The stream slowed and widened into a pool under bent and leaning beech trees. It was a beaver pond and there, just to the right of their dam at the far end, tall and gangling, stood a man peering down at it. He carried a huge backpack that seemed as if it would tip him over. Robinson's first impression was of a naturalist or a scholar, but no. As he drifted silently closer and his eyes grew accustomed to the shade he distinguished the jungle-style camouflage and the deer rifle gripped at the balance point in the right hand. The .308 lay before him still cocked. He didn't like to be any closer than this. The proximity had been uncomfortable in Mackinaw County. Yet he hesitated. Where was the big canoe? And the backpack was wrong. The point of paddling in was not to have to lug seventy-five pounds of gear the way this man was doing. He was not connected with the three-man camp back there and its waiting ridge pole. Still he was a hunter. The man could not have heard him slipping closer but chanced to look in his direction, straightened up from his examination of the dam, set the rifle down on its stock, squinted at Robinson coming at him out of the light, and waved his free hand.

"Hello," Robinson called.

"Heigh ho."

"Looking for beaver?"

"They're in there, scared of me."

An idea occurred to Robinson. He drove the canoe up onto the mushy bank, opened the case and placed the cocked .308 into it, stepped over it onto land, hauled the canoe well up behind him. The man laid his rifle on the ground, sat down heavily and struggled out of the straps of the backpack, rose and came over to Robinson, extending his hand.

"Russ," he said. He was hatless, balding, fortyish, a little pink and sweaty in the face whether by constitution or the effort of carrying all that stuff (for the air was cool), frank and somehow innocent-looking. He wore thick glasses. Why did such a man hunt?

"Jay," said Robinson. They shook hands. Russ, whose hand was big and warm, had seen his face now, in here where who knew what might happen before dusk. Robinson weighed this fact. The light was shadowed. Russ did not seem to have very good vision. At worst, this could mean another composite in the papers and on TV. "You, ah, you haven't seen anybody else around, have you?"

"No. Why'd you ask?"

"You got a transistor? See last night's TV, the papers?" Robinson uncoiled the nylon cord and tied it through the brass grommet at the bow of the canoe.

"Man, that's what I came in here to get away from."

Russ looped the cord and the two men portaged the canoe up onto slushy leaves and past the beaver dam. The rifle lying there was an old 30/06 lever action. On the down slope to where the stream dribbled through and over parts of the dam and resumed itself, narrower, deeper and more swift than above, Robinson thought he saw the track of a previous canoe dragged here, and surely the mud at the very edge of the bank barely preserved a human footprint.

"What were you talking about?" asked Russ. The canoe was two-thirds in the water. Robinson clambered in and sat facing him over the .308 in its open case. He had a sudden hunch.

"You connected with that truck? The Grand Pumpkin, or whatever?"

Russ relaxed, smiled. "Yes. You see it?"

"Coming in. I figure you've got a wife and kids."

"Two kids. A boy, Chris, and a girl, Jan."

"Get the hell out of this county."

"Whoa, fella! I live here."

"Then get the hell home."

"What are you talking about?"

"There's a guy walking around here who comes in and shoots hunters. It's all over the news. You'll see when you get out. He's some kind of bleeding heart. Some nut. But he's not fooling. He's shot a lot of guys already. FBI's after him. The news calls him the Deer-lover, for Chrissake. He says he's going to kill some guy in this county today or tomorrow. Maybe both. Some guys told me back upstream. I'm getting the hell out. I wish I had an outboard."

"What? In here? No kidding?" Robinson began to shove off with his paddle. Russ, looking around as though he expected to be shot at any moment, bent and helped at the prow.

The canoe was afloat now, backing slowly away. He took a backstroke, felt the current drawing him into itself. He raised his voice on account of the distance. "Come to think of it, you don't look too much like a regular hunter yourself, Russ. Makes me kind of nervous. My gun's right in front of me, loaded and cocked. If you'll just stay where you are until I'm out of range, I'll feel a whole lot better."

Russ stood transfixed. Robinson, drifting backwards, could no longer make out the scholarly face, whether it had turned pale or not. "Sorry," he yelled. "Nothing personal." Then he spun the canoe about and made a great show of paddling away as though with an energy born of terror.

Ten minutes later, drifting silently with the current, he heard a rifle shot up the bank, steeper now, to his right, just the "plop" of it. He hit the inside of the canoe with his fist in exasperation. He was too late. Immediately, rounding a slight eastward bending of the stream, he saw the big fiber-glass canoe, well beached. He drove into shore, jumped out and hauled up in one motion, left everything and rushed up the slope, tearing through brambles and scrub brush toward where he could see atop the rise a string of trees. What greeted him suddenly, bursting into the open on still rising ground, was classic. He'd seen the image a dozen times in his hunting magazines, the camera held low, ground level, the felled buck in the foreground, its head raised and twisted by the trophy rack, the hunter looming in the background, rifle at port arms before him, coming in to inspect his kill. This hunter was a young man, no jacket despite the cold, but another of the red and white check shirts, tan pants, no boots, a ridiculous pork-pie hat with its brim curled in on both sides, wide grin of idiot joy on his face. He worked the slide action of his rifle. Preoccupied with this, he never saw Robinson, who pulled out the .38 from his pocket, shoved back its casing with the heel of his hand to cock it, held it straight-arm ahead eye-level with both hands and shot him through the chest.

The hunter's arms flung out, the rifle sailed off to the side, and though he lurched back at the instant of impact he fell forward, sprawling over the deer, skidding on his face until his thighs rested on the animal so that his spread legs stuck out absurdly in the air behind him. Robinson walked around, gripped one ankle with his free hand, dragged the body off the flank and haunch of the deer. A bloodstain bloomed around the puncture in the back of the shirt, and blood pooled broadly in the dry leaves under his breast. The mouth was working silently.

Robinson stood for a few moments with his back to the felled deer. The automatic was ready, self-cocked and reloaded by having been fired. This would be very hard. He turned and knelt inside the front legs of the deer. The limpid, tear-shaped eye fixed him. He delayed. He thought how small a full-grown buck was, after all. They said big game. A buck like this, ten-point, had survived by its wits five to eight seasons. Yet it could not be much more than thirty inches high at the shoulder. It weighed two hundred, at the very most two hundred ten pounds, no more than the hunter bleeding quietly to death beside it. He must stop thinking. He must himself, here, deliver the *coup de grace*. He could not bear to point behind that eye into the brain. Instead, at the joint of neck and spinal cord where all the nerves connected. He laid the muzzle of the .38 there, pressed it in, turned away so as not to have to see. A wounded animal could linger in agony for days.

Wounded.

Where was the wound? He'd assumed the buck had been hit by a badly placed shot. He saw no evident wound. He tossed aside the .38, examined the animal more closely. The neck was swollen. That was just a sign of hormones. It had been in the rut, therefore maybe the carelessness that led to this misfortune. A deep scar high on the neck, but rectangular and healed. No sign of bleeding anywhere. He had to be sure. A wild animal could be traumatized by human handling, but he had to be sure. He grouped the four hooves together as best he could, held the pasterns with both hands, raised up and rolled the animal over, feeling the trembling in its legs as he stepped around the rump and set them down. Again, no sign of recent injury. What had happened? Then he saw a trickle of blood along the base of the animal's right ear, dripping onto the neck against which the ear now lay. This scratch could not explain the buck's condition. It led his eyes, however, to where a chunk was broken out of the base of the right antler. The ear raised, alerted, would have paralled, even pressed against the antler. The bullet, striking in there, far higher than intended, had blasted away this part of the base and grazed the adjacent ear. It might have knocked the antler, which would be shed in winter anyway, clear off its base. Instead, it had sent shock waves down into the skull and brain. The buck might not be in shock in the medical sense but only badly stunned. He rubbed the back of its neck, pressing his fingers into the warm pelt. The animal shuddered its whole length, and rolled an eye. He was only terrorizing it. He stepped away, sat down against a tree, and lit a cigarette, watching in the gathering dusk. Once it raised its head, then let it fall. After a while it began to try to pull its legs under itself, fell back, tried again and rose shakily like a new-born fawn, stood testing its balance, staggered away. It would be all right. He didn't care anything about his own fate at that moment as against the miracle of the resurrection of the buck.

The water of his creek glimmered in the last after-
glow of sunset. It was imprudent to have stayed so long
here, but he didn't care. He felt suddenly drained,
exhausted, unable to think or plan. He wanted just to
push off in the canoe and sleep in the bottom of it and
let the current carry him where it would and awake
under whatever cover of branches upon whatever shore.
He shook his head to clear it. He couldn't afford the
luxury, and it was getting cold. Yet he must sleep soon.
He shoved off with his paddle, drifted down past the
big canoe shored by the man now dead. He might pull
it out, let it drift. Better to leave it. He wanted the spot
marked, the man found soon. He drifted blindly, doz-
ing, until he thudded up against something, a fallen
tree or roots, against the side of the canoe. He'd been
drifting crosswise to the current. He had to stay here
and sleep. He took the silvery .38 from his pocket and
dropped it into the water. He took out the package of
shells for it, dropped them in, tore the box into small
pieces and tossed them into the invisible water. The
night was utterly black now, moonless and starless. He
clutched at the log he couldn't see and pulled himself
along until the canoe touched shore. He stepped off
the prow, one hand still on the log to steady him, pulled
the canoe after him wholly onto the bank. He felt blindly
for the sleeping outfit and bag of food and lurched with
them into the invisible brush, scratching his hands and
face, until he felt himself in some kind of clearing. He
fumbled for a match and lit it. All right. A leafy area
maybe six by six, twigs and pine cones lying about.
The match went out. He had no paper but the brown
bag itself. He dumped out his provisions, crumpled the
bag, and lit it with another match. It was succeed now
or sleep hungry, unsheltered, and cold. He laid twigs
across the burning bag, then, as they caught, added a
couple of the sappy pine cones. As the circle of firelight

widened, he could find and break up large twigs and dead branches to add. Soon the fire gave him warmth as well as light. He set up the cocoon tent, the foot open toward the fire, and unrolled the sleeping bag into it, unzipping it. He squatted, supplemented the fire, tried to think. It might be folly to camp this close, but he had no choice. Still, nothing could happen tonight. Those heavy-set hunters back at the blind, when their young friend had not returned for them, they'd stumble back to camp, if they could make it in the dark through marsh and swamp and across the hip-deep stream. They wouldn't blunder downstream in total darkness to seek their friend, nor try the five miles to the nearest road with the virtual certainty of getting disoriented and lost. Not those two. It would be hours into daylight before they could communicate with the outside world, hours more before any search would penetrate to here.

In the flickering firelight he pulled the key off the can of sardines, opened it, and placed several inside his last cheese sandwich. He snapped the tab on one of the beer cans. After his meal, he crawled into bed and slept the sleep of the just.

NOVEMBER

23

i

As he drove east on the cross-state M-55 toward private
property, the snow began to flurry and then to fall
thickly, streaming at him with the velocity of the car
from some illusory point of issuance always just ahead.
The radio said it would end by nightfall at one or two
inches. That meant a wholly different world for hunters
and hunted. The new snow remembered what had
tracked in it, but told what it knew only to men, not
to other predators or to prey, until it was no longer
new and became confused, overloaded with information, and at last erased its memory either through
its own renewal or by melting away. It vitiated the arts
of concealment and camouflage for those animals who
had no lairs to retreat to and must be continually hiding.
It favored hunters, but not the hunter of hunters. Behind him in Missaukee it was laying an indifferent blan-
ket over the prone body of the young hunter, his rifle
and his hat.

Robinson had risen at dawn, packed his gear in the
canoe, and driven hard downstream, stepping out and
crouching to drag it through a culvert, hauling it around
fallen logs, all the way to the upper lake and then south,
another eight or nine miles, to complete his circle at
the public-access park in Houghton Lake. He ate
breakfast at a restaurant on the highway, where he
could watch the unprotected canoe and plan his course.
By folding the county map and slicing with his table
knife he cut off the northeast corner, the general area
of last night's action. He'd throw away the rest. He
bent and studied the ten-inch square and drew a black
X to mark the spot. This was an indulgence in melo-
drama but had a practical purpose too. He'd mail this

map to Cindi Mayer. It might appear in the paper and on TV. It held something frightening. People could imagine he'd marked the X in advance, as, indeed, he'd planned to. Knew somehow where he and each victim inevitably made their rendezvous, had other maps so marked. He re-checked the coordinates of the site, folded the map into letter-size and wrote the coordinates on the back.

The paper. He'd got a copy of yesterday's *News* from the coin-operated box outside the restaurant and brought it in to read with his second cup of coffee and a cigarette. The morning *Free Press* was sold out or had not arrived. The *News* front page offered only a reference to an inner section, B-1: "Killer still a threat. Man calling himself Deerlover threatens death to hunters." Considering that, so far as they knew, nothing had actually happened since the front-page article of the twenty-first, the editors had presumably declined to grant front-page priority to a repeat of the story. Maybe Robinson could revoke that decision. He turned back to B-1. Under "Deerlover" he read:

> The FBI, local and State authorities are now involved in the search for the killer known as the Deerlover. He is believed to be from out of state and to have murdered hunters in other states. A red, two-door Chevy Vega, 1974 or 1975, has been associated with at least one of the crimes. Anyone seeing such a car in a hunting area, or abandoned, should report it.

There followed a reminder of his warnings for the next couple of days and of the reward. Contributions might be mailed to the *News*, addressed "Cooper Fund." No by-line. The style did not seem like Cindi Mayer's, but he could not tell. He leafed through the back feature pages for her column, couldn't find it. Among the

classifieds, his eye chanced to catch the heading ANI-
MALS. The usual birds, dogs, cats for sale, or lost or
found. Monkeys, horses, tropical fish, pet memorials
to honor the dead. An ad for the Humane Society. In
the box beneath this, with no heading, were some lines
arranged as verse. He read them, could not quite take
them in, read them again:

> I never knew how their lives at last were spilt,
> But I have hoped for years all that is wild,
> Airy, and beautiful will forgive my guilt.

He might have written these words himself, or at
least chosen them and paid for their insertion. He felt
a kind of envy for whoever had thought of doing this.
But then, more fully, a kind of kinship. He had an
unseen ally.

So there were new developments after all. The FBI
was involved. Possibly the reports of related killings in
other states had been fabricated to make that legal.
Someone, somewhere had seen and reported the Vega.
Cooper? Was it within the range of technology now-
adays to run down the registrations of all such cars in
Ohio? In the forty-eight contiguous states? He didn't
think so. Anyway, if they did a computer check of two-
door red Vegas for 1974-75, Robinson would not be
hearing from them because the Vega was, or had been,
of 1976 vintage. All the same, he thanked the impulse
that led him to dispose of it.

He'd inquired the name of the outfit down the highway that rented trucks and four-wheel drive vehicles and telephoned them from the restaurant. He said his car had had an oil leak in the main seal; he'd let it run dry and it had seized up and he'd sold it to a junk dealer that Triple A towed him to. He needed transport for his canoe and his gear. The man said they had a car for rent too and maybe that would be better than a truck, and he'd drive it down to the restaurant and pick him up.

The car had proved to be a huge "full-size" wagon out of the past, two-tone, brown on the top half, white below, like a fish. He liked it on sight. He walked out to meet the garage man. "Vista-Cruiser" read the logo on the rear fender. The wagon had a baggage rack but was so large that the canoe could be put inside it, diagonally, prow over the lowered passenger seat against the windshield. That was where the canoe lay now, beside him, as the snow whirled over the hood of the Oldsmobile.

At the garage, negotiating the rental, he'd learned that the car was also for sale. He'd listened to the engine on the short drive. It sounded all right. The two slab-faced owners, evidently father and son, excused themselves and conferred in their office on the question of price. A thousand, said the son, who'd picked him up from beside the public park. Robinson frowned. Actually, the car was worth that if it had no hidden defects. If it had been a rental, they probably serviced it now and then.

"What if I pay cash on the spot?" he'd asked. The garage did not look prosperous. It was a long time till the tourists started to come back next Memorial Day to Houghton Lake.

"Cash, check?" asked the father.

"Cash—money." Robinson pulled out his thick wad

of bills. Often, cash transactions had let him handle a situation without leaving written records. The car would be OK. If necessary, he could sleep in the rear. He'd trade it in back home.

"Eight-fifty," the father said.

First he'd driven the Vista-Cruiser the few miles west back across the county line. He wanted to mail the segment of topo map from Missaukee County and, if possible, call from there too. Just as the county marker whisked by and he was remembering all that had happened since he'd last passed it, there appeared the roadblock he'd anticipated yesterday. Or at least two white County Sheriff's cars, one on the shoulder and one along the midstripe, an officer between them waving him to stop. He tensed and sweated, though he knew rationally that there was no threat here. Had the young hunter been found, which was nearly impossible this early, the police would be stopping cars leaving the area, not entering it. The body still lay face-down undiscovered up that slope from the stream and his empty canoe. This was only a warning to men coming in, or a vaguely generalized and harmless dragnet to catch Deerlover. It was the first positive evidence of Robinson's effect. He was the cause of this stop-and-check-operation.

"See your registration?"

"Car's rented." This was true. Robinson produced the rental papers. Tweedle-dum and Tweedle-dee back at the garage had signed over the title to him but had also rented him the car for today and tomorrow so that he could use it more or less legally until he could call his man in Aurora for an insurance binder and also get the registration into his name. "My own car's little. Rented this monster so I can take a bunch of guys in hunting next couple days. We'll tie the boat up top to make room." In the midst of this fabrication it occurred to Robinson that a bunch of guys wouldn't fit in a twelve-foot canoe. "Yep. Picking them up in Lake City. Camp out. Have a helluva time. Get some trophies and some venison."

The officer returned the papers. A car had pulled up behind to take its turn at interrogation.

"We're instructed to tell guys not to hunt around here."

"Not hunt?"

"Have you read the papers? Heard any news?"

"Hell no. That's what I come up here to get away from."

"Well there's a man dresses up like a hunter that shoots real hunters. He says he's going to do it around here. Some kind of maniac, but he's dangerous. If I was you I'd stay the hell out of the woods. Some nut."

"OK. I'll tell the guys."

He wasted ten minutes driving over and down to the town of Merritt, which had neither post office nor a safe public telephone. The other nearest town, probably four or five buildings at an intersection, was Star City. It was on the county road toward where he'd seen the Great Pumpkin and beyond which lay the wilderness where he'd slain the hunter. Easiest just to cruise across the county to Lake City, as he'd told the officer, the largest town on his map, even though he did not wish to remain long in Missaukee County.

The town was grouped along the highway, which

became its main street. He picked out the post office from the flag and blue roadside box in front of it. It was closed for lunch. The bar across the street proved deserted except for the proprietor, and it had a solitary phone booth. The man was capable of reluctantly producing food but nothing Robinson could eat, only hamburgers and hot dogs. It was 1:00. The post office was opening. He took a double Scotch with ice into the booth, fumbled with the coins, dialed the *News* and asked for her desk. The proprietor had returned to his station behind the bar. He'd scarcely glanced at Robinson while serving him.

"Hello. Cindi Mayer." He liked her husky voice.

"Hello. I'm calling you from Missaukee County in the north. If I give you the number, will you call back *immediately?*"

"The *number?*" Incredulously, but then, "Yes. Yes. I understand. Immediately." Background sounds of a busy office.

He read her the number from the dial in front of him and hung up. He took a long sip of the whisky. This bravado would magnify the media coverage. And the risk made him feel better somehow, less tired, more alive. Maybe also the little fear distracted him from the other fear. The digital clock over the bar said 1:08. If she did not call right now . . . The phone jangled.

"Thank you for your promptness," he said. "Have you scribbled the number and 'Deerlover' on your scratch-pad? Are you handing it to a colleague?"

"Just scribbled. No colleague."

"You will have to give it to the authorities."

"Yes."

"Give me ten minutes after we are finished?"

She hesitated. "I can't guarantee anything." She was straightforward with him. He hoped that while she must stay within the law and the confines of her morality they might still work together in some sense in this enterprise.

"That's all right. Now I want to report to you the location where they will find the hunter."

"You have already...?"

"Yes. It's five miles north of someplace called Star City. I have the precise readings. Will you write them down?"

"Yes."

He read from the back of his folded map: "Forty-four degrees twenty minutes, fifty-five seconds west, thirty-four degrees, twenty minutes, thirty seconds north. Got that?"

She read back the coordinates.

"It's by a stream," he added. "They'll find his canoe. He's up the bank just a few yards. Maybe he's found already."

"I haven't heard—"

"He had two friends who will start a search for him. I merely wish to take the credit. It—happened yesterday just before sunset. Also: you will have confirmed by now my report of the episode in Mackinaw County. And Saturday night there was a hunter near Grayling. He was hunting after dark with a light." He did not add that on the seventh day he had rested.

"So that was you also. What—what about today?"

"No place in this state is safe for hunters. Make that clear to your readers. I particuarly urge, again that owners of private hunting lands stay at home and watch TV if they wish to enjoy Thanksgiving dinner with their families. I shall probably not take the holiday. After that, I may concentrate on the West Coast, along Lake Michigan. But no place is safe. It is not true what your paper printed this morning that I have hunted in other states. Not yet. I'd better be leaving here now."

"Could— Look, is there any way I could interview

you? Tape a real conversation over the phone maybe? If you had a chance to make yourself clear, and not just, just shoot people, it might help your cause and you wouldn't have to keep—"

"I don't see see how. I'll think about it. Goodbye."

He replaced the receiver and wiped it with the back of one of his gloves, also the door handle of the booth. The keeper of this establishment would wash the glass. Maybe the rest of his day behind the bar would be less routine than might have been anticipated.

At the post office, Robinson bought a stamped envelope and slipped the folded map into it, wiping it too just in case. He dropped it into the box outside and walked down to the Oldsmobile, parked where it could not be seen from inside the post office or the bar. He drove east at the speed limit, back the way he had came, hoping the same officer might be on duty at Check Point Charlie. It had been less than an hour and a half since Robinson re-entered the county. As he drove, he tried to puzzle out a way he might indeed be interviewed by Cindi Mayer. That *would* further his cause. A long conversation from a pay phone or motel phone seemed too dangerous. To meet her in person seemed out of the question. He wondered whether the talk they had just completed had itself been taped. The feds would think of that, set up the equipment, insist that she do it. Or would that violate freedom of the press? Well, if there was a tape and it was released to radio and television, so much the more drama and effect. He wished he'd tried to sound more ominous. Maybe, come to think of it, he'd sounded ominous enough.

If they'd had a tap on her line, they'd have started to locate him even while he was still talking to her. Startled authorities rushing to contact the phone company for the address, others to telephones, police radio.

The two patrol cars were positioned the same as before at the check point. Just possibly, news of his call had already been radioed out here, or news of the discovery of the body. He'd thought it safest to go out where he came in, though westward departure from the county would be much quicker. He'd entered this area less than two hours ago. He could hardly have penetrated deep country, shot somebody, and returned, much less made a phone call about it to the *News*. No, he was potential victim, not assassin. They'd let him through.

The pick-up ahead of him slowed as it approached the patrol car parked over the center lane, but sailed through. An officer was speaking to the driver of a westbound car, but no one was stopping eastbound traffic. It was the same officer. Robinson pulled to a stop. No car behind him. When the officer was free, Robinson called out through his open window, affecting the chagrined sportsman.

"We decided to take your advice, officer. Keep the hell out this region."

"Hope everybody does!"

The radio buzzed in the patrol car parked on the shoulder, and the officer waiting in it picked up his receiver.

"So do I," Robinson said with sincerity, and drove away and out of Missaukee County for good.

iv

Now he was boring eastward into snow, a little worried by practical problems, preoccupied so he did not brood upon the more general problem he could never define or understand. He had to get rid of the canoe. He'd rented it on impulse in Omer, a few miles out of Au Gres, on the Rifle River. The rental agency had been officially closed. It was for summer tourists. Robinson told the recalcitrant proprietor, quite truthfully, that he wanted to try hunting with a canoe. He thought the agency should re-open for the hunting season, was missing a good market. As for himself, he and his wife would take the canoe up north on top of the Vega, and after he'd had his two-days' hunting drifting down the Rifle, she'd pick him up here. His cash rental money and hundred-dollar deposit for the twelve-foot battered canoe had prevailed. Now he must return it. So on M-23 he took what he thought was the last county road before Omer and angled till he came to a bridge crossing the Rifle maybe a half mile above town. He put the rolled-up sleeping outfit into the canoe, leaving everything else in the locked Vista Cruiser. He paddled and drifted down toward Omer, watching snow crystals dissolving all around him in dark water.

It was a temptation simply to drive on the few miles to his reserved room in the old-fashioned motel beyond Au Gres. He was tired as well as sore in his arms and back from the six hours of canoeing this morning. But the season was more than half over, and he did not want to waste the evening. Besides, Phyllis was unavailable until tomorrow. So he turned north on State 65 two miles out of Omer. It ran north some twenty miles according to the flip-map on the seat beside him, then veered west and crossed the Au Sable River. His hunting magazines said that Arenac County, behind him, Iosco where he was now, and Alcona just ahead were especially difficult of access for the casual hunter because the best areas were closed, posted and reserved for private use.

He liked the sound of that name, Au Sable, though it had undoubtedly been bestowed by French trappers. The river was wide, pooling, where the highway crossed it, and no human habitation marred its snowy banks. He stopped for a moment. The snowfall had ceased. Deer would water here, though maybe a little farther from the road than he could see and a little later into the gathering dusk.

On his search yet farther north and then east for choice private hunting land, he shot a target of opportunity not twenty yards off the M-72.

V

He was hungry as well as tired and turned into the first decent-looking diner somewhere on the Huron coast. The color TV displayed a professional football game under daylight on the West Coast. There was evident interest in this. The sound was up, audible over the racket in the room. No chance of getting the barkeep to switch to the news. And he had to settle for fish and chips with his Scotch, nothing else on the menu being possible.

Too tired to think clearly, he let a vague idea cross his mind, intermixed with the words of the football sportscaster. He was not getting careless, no, but his sense of style and his compulsion to gain the maximum of notoriety and publicity for the sake of his cause were creating dangers beyond any calculation. That he could only trust to luck and instinct to get through. That after this season he had done what he could here and had better shift to a new field of operations.

After a while, a waitress brought his food from be-hind him, having come from the kitchen through the dining area to the bar. She had whispy blonde hair and an acned face. She looked malnourished, anor-exic. She said there was a table, actually a little nook in a corner, if he preferred. She carried his plate there while he followed with his fresh Scotch. He asked whether there was a good motel around: he was aw-fully tired. She said Logan's, five miles down the high-way on the right. Forget the others. He said it would be booked up then, if it was so choice. She asked his name. He was too far gone to care why. Fenimore. James Fenimore. He ate his food, drinking his whisky, smoked a cigarette. When she returned, she said he had a room reserved at Logan's, if he wanted. She was Logan's niece. Would he like anything else? He looked up at her sickly face. She was in some trouble, and probably he could help. She wanted him to try. He could not alleviate all suffering. Suffering was every-where. He must specialize where he was most effective. He shook his head. He left her a ten-dollar tip.

At the motel office, the entire wall behind the pro-prietor was covered by a coarse-grained blow-up of an aerial photograph of the area, presumably by the state topographical society. He asked the man—Logan?—whether he might have a piece of paper to make some sketches from the photograph. At first Logan looked at him strangely. Then he seemed to understand.

"You're out hunting, Mr. Fenimore."

"Yes."

"That there's posted territory," he said, pointing at the center of the blow-up. "But it's good. Lost Lake Lodge owns it. Nine square miles. There's Lost Lake. A deer drinking spot." He put a thick finger to an oval blob at the upper middle of the territory. "Ain't lost on the photo. But try and find it when you get in there."

Maybe he would. "What road is that running west from the highway? That is the highway?"

"Yep," said Logan conspiratorially, handing him a piece of writing paper with the motel letterhead. "And that there's Delano Road."

"Can I leave a call for eleven?" He was so tired— He started a little sketch of the area. There were clearings in the woods and what looked like an abandoned orchard, small trees in rows, open fields to the north and west across county roads.

"Eleven A.M.?"

"No. Tonight. I need to do something. What's your checkout tomorrow?"

"One P.M."

Robinson paid for the room in cash. "Call me again at noon."

That would leave time.

He started up groggily at the jangle of a telephone. Where was he? He'd snapped out of a bad dream in Missaukee woods, in the dark, hadn't he? *A telephone?* Then he remembered and rolled his legs onto the floor and sat up, fumbling for the table lamp. His arms and shoulders ached. He felt grundgy. It was the second night he'd slept in these clothes. He'd buy new tomorrow. After the telecast he'd take a bath and sleep naked till noon between clean sheets.

The big TV was bracketed high on the wall opposite the foot of the bed. He tuned in the news. It had already started, something again about the Middle East. He was thirsty. Maybe there was a soft drink machine outside. No, a can of beer remained from his raid on the hunters' camp yesterday afternoon. It would be cool from being outside in the car. He went to get it, leaving the door open so that he could hear the pair of announcers bandying the day's events. In the two inches of snow he realized that he still had on his shoes. He'd not even pulled them off before falling into bed.

Inside, he did so, and stripped off his khaki pants and the red wool shirt. He propped himself up with pillows and watched the screen in his underwear. He pulled the tab and drank some beer from the can. The very next item after the international news was about him. He knew even before the serious young anchorman spoke. Over his left shoulder was the stylized background graphic of a hunter, in silhouette, just having fired his rifle, and opposite him another, identical hunter, doubled up and starting to lose balance and fall. The images told the story without words.

"Our next report is a grim one. Evidently, as you have probably heard, there is a middle-aged man loose in the northern woods who has taken it upon himself to defend the deer population by shooting hunters. A term has been coined to describe these murders: *hunterized*. It is believed that the man known as the Deerlover has 'hunterized' at least eight men since the start of the current hunting season, November 15. Every man out hunting in the state is advised to be extremely cautious in the presence of any stranger in the fields and forests. The course of greatest prudence would be to refrain from hunting altogether until the killer is apprehended."

Yes it would, thought Robinson.

The screen switched to the anchorwoman, behind her a large graphic showing ten or twelve identical cutouts of men with rifles held across their chests. "The killer, Bob, is the object of a local, state, and federal manhunt. The problem handicapping law-enforcement officers is that he resembles other hunters and seems to have no personal ties with the men he kills. He seems also to exhibit amazing mobility, prompting some authorities to speculate that there is more than one such killer.''

Robinson sat forward. He wished that this speculation might prove true, might be prophetic.

Bob again, over his shoulder now the menacing portrait Robinson had first seen in the *News*. The camera zoomed in on this until it filled the screen, simian, inaccurate, not Robinson, and yet as he studied it again not without some elliptical reference to his physiognomy after all.

"The so-called Deerlover, shown here in a drawing prepared by an Otsego County artist in collaboration with an eye-witness, has put himself in telephone contact with Cindi Mayer, a columnist with the *Detroit News*. Through Ms. Mayer, he has begun to specify where he will strike next. Yesterday, and possibly today also, it was in Missaukee County. Tomorrow on privately owned land. Thursday, Thanksgiving, anywhere in the state. Friday and Saturday on the western coast along Lake Michigan. Authorities do not know what weight to attach to these threats, but clearly hunters should be advised and cautious.

"Now a special message from Otsego County Sheriff Ralph Pitago, interviewed earlier today by our own Jenny Drake."

The sheriff sat in a swivel chair in his office, ruddy, heavy-set, an obvious hunter, Jenny seated facing him. She introduced him, thanked him for making himself available, asked what hunters should do in this unprecedented situation.

"They should stick together, go out with men they know, avoid strangers."

"What progress can you report in the investigation?"

"We have a number of leads that of course I can't reveal. County and State police are coordinating their efforts with those of the FBI. We have computerized investigations now. There's one thing I'd especially like to stress—"

"Yes sir." The camera approached Pitago, full ruddy face, obvious pleasure in being suddenly important.

"On behalf of Chief Hinchly and everyone else associated with the investigation, I urge every armed man out there to report anything unusual to the police and not try to handle the situation yourselves. If any of you hunters see a suspicious man, don't take the law into your own hands. Don't get jumpy and shoot. There could be a bloodbath out there if people started doing that. The law is fully capable of apprehending this criminal. We need citizen support of course. But don't start shooting each other!"

Back to Bob. "Thank you Jenny and Sheriff Pitago. Finally, we remind you that a reward, now in excess of fifteen thousand dollars, has been posted by the Harold Cooper family for information leading to the capture of this man. Anyone with such information should contact . . ."

On the whole, satisfactory. Would that Pitago's worst fears might be realized. Robinson could retire. He left the set on, ran his bath during the sports news, listened, soaking his sore muscles, to the weather forecast: cold tonight, around freezing. No precipitation. High tomorrow near forty. Not enough, unfortunately, to melt off the snow. But then: "A late report, just in, on the Deerlover killer. The body—" Robinson was leaping from the tub, throwing a bath towel around himself. There was Bob, seated before the composite again, reading from a slip of paper. "—of Hugh Sligo, thirty-two, of Southfield, Michigan, was found today in a wilderness area of northeast Missaukee County. He had been shot through the chest. Mr. Sligo's body was found late this afternoon, but authorities withheld the information pending notification of his family. The pre-

144

cise location was specified in the call from the killer to the *Detroit News* that we mentioned earlier in our newscast." Bob raised his eyes to the camera. "Obviously this maniac is a real and present threat to all sportsmen in Michigan."

True. But now he had to finish his bath and get twelve hours' sleep.

NOVEMBER

24

i

He turned west off the highway onto Delano Road. It was still midday, too early to park and enter the woods that were slipping past on his right unless an irresistible chance offered itself. The woods were well posted: NO HUNTING alternated with PRIVATE PROPERTY every fifty yards.

He'd circle the area, reconnoiter it, and return this afternoon. From what he could tell, this was solid ground. Good. He was tired of swamp and marsh. Up Delano three miles then right along the western edge of the preserve. On Delano there had been a blur of car tracks in the snow, scattered houses to his left explaining these. Here there were no tire marks, and it was hard to keep to the road over the undifferentiating snow. Harvested fields to his left now showed no track of man or other animal. The southwest corner of the woods was cut out by a square field maybe three hundred yards on each side holding at its far corner a failing, once-red barn ready to fall sideways and pitch itself into the trees. This was deer country. In spring and summer you could drive at dusk and probably find several, high of head, does mainly at the divide of woods and field, sometimes closer, feeding on corn gleanings, or even bounding across the road in front of you. Or you might come across them, ghostly and only half distrustful in your car lights, just the glowing pairs of eyes first, then the whitish tawny bodies.

At the corner of the enclave he turned west, back toward the highway. Soon he'd done the whole perimeter. He'd not expected to find the parked cars of hunters because there were abortive access roads cut into the woods. He'd seen them on the aerial map as well as here. They revealed no tire tracks or footprints. No one was in there unless they had packed in before the snow. No one would camp in nine square miles they owned or hired whose western boundary was M-23.

Of course these woods might not be hunted today. Yet it was prime territory with only a few days left in the season, and the fresh snow would attract hunters. Still, on the way down to East Tawas he'd try to locate a back-up area just in case.

He'd learned on the phone after brunch that the nearest town with a Secretary of State's office was East Tawas. He wanted to legalize the Vista-Cruiser in his name. On the way he drove twice into woodsy farmlands off the highway and lined up alternatives to the property of Lost Lake Lodge.

East Tawas was another resort town waiting for Memorial Day, not much going except a couple of ski shops and snowmobile dealerships. But across from the cinder-block office building of the Secretary of State were the packed windows of a sporting goods store. A camo suit in a dark brown, fallen-leaf color, hung there and especially caught his eye. Through the office window, dialing his agent in Aurora, he admired it. It might be wrong for hunting in snow, but he suspected that in any thick woods the brown leaf-fall would still predominate, and the brown would hide him. In any case the suit was new and clean and would serve to get him out of the rank garments he had sweated and slept in. He'd sat in a remote corner of the restaurant this morning for fear of offending people. In due time the agent called back, verifying the insurance, and Robinson presented his title and registration application and paid his fee. It occurred to him to call Cindi Mayer from here, but the phone, though secluded, was not enclosed in a booth. Call her tonight, at home, to elude that tape recorder, when the business around Lost Lake was concluded.

The camouflage suit turned out to be perfect. It was polyester, bulky like the canvas suits that made hunters resemble moon-landers walking town streets or supermarket aisles. It was so warm, claimed the salesman, no other clothing was necessary under it, even in the coldest fall weather. It was soft and very light. Close up, it was not solid brown but brown with a trace of white as if after a light snow. Best of all, though thickish, it was reversible, and the other side was snow white. Just right for the present conditions. The white made him think of films of Russian soldiers white-clad, on skis, silent, terrifying, all but invisible as they swooped down on retreating Germans.

He drove till he found a laundromat. At the nearest station he ordered ten dollars worth of gas. In the men's room he stripped and zipped himself, naked, into the camo suit, brown side out, stuffing his soiled clothes into the plastic shopping bag from the sports store. At the laundromat he sat bulky and conspicuous among gaunt local housewives and their children, reading old hunting magazines, while his clothes sloshed in suds and then flopped and dried in hot air, ten cents for each ten minutes. Even the notorious shooter of hunters had to do his laundry. Afterwards he drove to another station, ordered the other ten dollars worth of gas required to fill the tank, and in the men's room got back into his socks and underwear and then the polyester suit. Deerlover was freshened and ready to return to the precincts of Lost Lake Lodge.

ii

Again he cruised the whole perimeter slowly and thoughtfully. Now the county road along the west border was bleary with car tracks, and one of the access roads off of it into the private park showed two sets of tracks going in. He would not follow, an obvious trespasser to the men in there. He completed the circuit. No other evidence of human presence in these woods. Heading west on Delano, he stopped to think what to do. Suddenly this whole enterprise seemed ill-considered. At least four men were in there, probably more, who knew each other and would immediately recognize him as an interloper. He'd have to stay camouflaged, unseen. Even if he succeeded in that, how could he select and pick off one and get out of there without being caught by the others?

Well, he had to try. His credibility required that. Besides, the men should be widely scattered in the nine square miles. Unless they'd followed the news, he had the benefit of complete surprise, inexplicable violence out of nowhere. A rifle shot in there would cause not alarm but rejoicing. If they had kept up with the news, they'd not be there at all, would they? They'd be cultivating wife and children at home, or drinking at their favorite bar, like many and many a man he hoped he had already influenced.

There remained the problem of the snow. If he simply parked here and trudged in, there was the car to be seen beside the reserve and the obvious tracks. If all went well and he was fast enough getting out, no matter. But it didn't feel right. He started the car and eased forward. If he had a companion, someone who could drop him off here, there'd be the tracks starting from nothing, entering the woods out of miscellaneous car tracks, and the man who made them coming out anywhere, unpredictably, as arranged with his collaborator.

A daydream. At the corner of the county road, the square of farmland behind and to his right, he paused in the car, thinking tactics. He pulled across the county road and over onto the shoulder of Delano, actually a slight gully dipping toward bare snow-covered field. From any distance the Oldsmobile, light brown over white, would be inconspicuous, nearly invisible. He slung the rifle over his shoulder and strode the fifteen paces back to the the county road. All right. A man had parked here for some reason anyone would suppose, probably to hunt, walked back to the road, all trace of him disappearing in the welter of its meltings and markings. This man had not returned to his car.

He walked in the muddled car tracks all the way to the northwest corner of the field with the reddish barn. Then he crossed the field to the barn, leaving a clear set of tracks. He walked around the barn on the side that leaned towards the trees and entered at the south end where the high sliding door was open a couple of feet. The interior was eerily lit by the afternoon sun through slits in the west wall and spaces where boards had fallen off. His segmented shadow on the dusty floor was easily ten feet long. He crossed to the side facing the woods and peered at them through a crack. A board at eye-level was loose, and he found a jack iron and knocked it out. This would be a good place to hunt from, using the barn, which the deer were accustomed to, as a blind and waiting till they came out for scraps of corn husk left by the harvesting machine. Here too the woods were posted every so often, but the farmer had not posted his field. So technically it was public hunting from the barn. For Robinson's purpose the site was unsuitable, however. He could not afford the time to wait on the chance that his prey might appear. And if anything went wrong, if there were others he had not seen close behind, there was no escape from here. He'd come here out of his instinct to create a confusing situation. Someone had walked in, presumably to hunt, presumably not the owner of the Oldsmobile since he came from a different direction, and this hypothetical hunter was still in the barn. Robinson decided to leave him there. He hid the .308 under some boards and waited at the barn door till no cars were in sight either direction. He laid a plank fallen from the loft in the snow outside the door and walked out on it, faced toward the remote corner of the field in the general direction of the Oldsmobile, checked again that no one was likely to be watching him, and taking strides as long as he could without losing his balance walked backwards into the trees.

On this windless day the trees, chiefly densely needled pines, held the snow in their branches so that the ground under them still showed its autumnal brown. He looked at the tracks he had made. The effect was that of a man who had rushed out of the woods and been snatched up to heaven. Placing his bootsoles carefully, he walked out in his own tracks, paused at the starting point to look around a last time, and ran all the way out to that far corner of the field. If seen, queried, he'd say that the hunting looked good and he'd forgotten his shells in the car. Then, getting his breath back, he walked down the road past the field to his original point of entry and casually retraced his steps to the barn. Inside, he slung the rifle, stepped out again onto the board until he could get his feet into two of the footprints coming out of the woods. He backed again,

looking behind to place his feet precisely, into the shade
of the pines. The sun straight ahead of him was low
over the horizon. He must hurry. Yet he took a moment
to appraise the situation as it would appear to any one
coming upon the scene or investigating the area. It was
this: a hunter had entered the field and gone into the
barn. He was still there. Another man had run out of
the woods for some reason and disappeared at the
intersection of the road. A third man had parked his
car near the intersection and had not yet returned to
it. This until another snowfall, or wind, or rain, or ob-
literation under the trample of human feet. Robinson
Jay, who was all three of these men and yet distinct
from them also, all in white like a Russian soldier, unslung his scoped .308 and prowled as so often before
into *terra incognita*.

The apple orchard surprised him, though of course
it had been on the map. He tried to recall the relationship of this clearing to Lost Lake itself and the
boundaries of the preserve. He'd mislaid the crude
map drawn from the photo, taken it from his shirt or
trousers when he had laundered them and left it useless
in the car. He'd seen deer droppings in paths through
the surrounding brush, fresh too, but mushy and un-
formed, and then suddenly, as he moved ahead, the
shapes of deer in the orchard, bright-tawny and shadowed in the sloping sunlight, does with their speckled
fawns, heads down mostly, eating apples from the snow.
The wind was so slight—it seemed to have no direction—that even if it was vaguely from behind him his
scent would not reach them for a while. He wanted to
watch them feed and nuzzle each other. He'd reconnoiter around the grove slowly, cautiously. The club
must know of this place, hunt it regularly. Members or
guests might be on either side or across from him,

hidden as he was by foliage and windlessness. If so, very probably they were waiting for a buck to appear and by pulling back and making a circuit of the orchard he could come up behind one of them. This course seemed right and prudent, but finally he rejected it. The chance was too great that they would settle for an antlerless deer and he would hear the crack of a rifle and one of the very animals before him would crumple or stagger and fall. He could not risk that. He'd never witnessed the actual moment of the killing of a deer. He would not add that experience to the gallery of images that haunted him and troubled his dreams. So he rose deliberately into the clearing with its remnant of an orchard. The does startled at once of course, noses raised and sniffing, ears raised and turned toward him as they walked quickly to his right into cover on the east. He loved the way they moved, head and neck and shoulders working ahead of the step in the way of all hooved animals and then body catching up, over and over. The mothers didn't wait for their fawns or nudge them along. It was a matter of instinct that the fawns should follow and cling to them. Sometimes this instinct failed, and a man might find a fawn alone beside the trail. It would reach its mother if he let it. Now two fawns lingered, curious and naturally friendly. In some other world, Robinson could pluck crab apples from these enduring trees and offer them. Not in this world. He waved his arms and shooed them out of sight.

He looked about him. How many decades, generations, ago had some staunch couple, family, thought that they could grow apples here and farm a living? They must have built a house somewhere, outbuildings. No trace of them. And yet the apple trees, untended, untrimmed, had renewed and renewed themselves in this solitude, the fruit no doubt smaller and more crabbed each fall. He reached up and plucked a wrinkled apple from its stem and nibbled it. Sour, but not inedible. He ate around the core and tossed it away. He was studying the pattern of hoofprints in the snow when for no reason he raised his eyes, and there was a hunter, ten yards away just out of the woods, stocky, middle-aged, ugly in his hunter's hat and dirty orange jacket and black shiny pants, rifle at an angle across his chest, fleshy face accusing.

"What the hell you doin' here? This is private property."

"I know," said Robinson. He unslung his rifle and worked the bolt.

"Well clear the hell out. You just scared off all the damn deer."

"It's the private property of the deer."

"You some kind of maniac?" But the man's voice broke in the middle of the words and he stepped back, doubtful, thinking maybe about his friends in the woods somewhere, whether to call out to them—

"Yes," said Robinson.

Something like realization affected the dull face. "Wait. For Crissake," he wailed. "You're what's his face, ain't you?"

"Yes, I am."

What a scramble, ducking low as he ran through brambles and grass, trying to keep in snow or behind any screen of trees against a background of snow. He was winded. Too many cigarettes. He had added to his lead on the hunters, maybe with luck shaken them altogether, but could still hear them yelling behind him and must risk only a moment's rest. He crouched, gasping, in a circlet of alder saplings. The sun was very low now, out of his sight but not yet set, the shadows long. They ran a few degrees north of east. So he was fairly sure of his direction. If he ran with the shadows, he would come out somewhere along the edge of the field where the barn was.

He'd not dreamed there would be so many of them. Another carfull or two must have driven in after his check of the perimeter. Enough so that some could stay with the wounded man, others go for help, and a group of several come after him. He had not anticipated pursuit, either. Maybe, after all, he was getting too old for this kind of thing. He had miscalculated the whole situation. He should not have fired and drawn them in as he had, but slipped away and told the terrified fat man to stand there and be quiet. By the time they gathered and learned what happened, Robinson, keeping to heavy timber where there was little snow on the ground to show his tracks, would have been safe. As it was he'd had to run a straight chase away from them, and if they were any good at all they'd track him down. Indeed, the voices sounded closer. He rose, peered into the woods the way he had come, leaning to left and right to see more deeply into them. No glimpse of human movement. But they were coming. He felt it. They would track him and he had to get out. He turned, ready for the dash, stepped out and caught himself at the last second, sagging forward on saplings he had thrown his arms around to keep from falling. Under his eyes was water, greenish against a mossy bank. He raised them: an acre, acres of it stretching ahead to the far extreme of a circular shoreline, water lying placid and lustrous in the reddish sunlight it reflected. He had found Lost Lake.

He could not go forward. If they were smart, and thinking, and knew the terrain, they would split up so as to head him off no matter which way he went round. Maybe he could ambush them or simply shoot it out.

He doubted that. If they were not smart and came straight after him to this spot, he still had his lead. He moved left, scrambling again, not taking much care to hide his trail when doing so would slow him. He kept the lake, or the clearing that held it, in sight so as not to get disoriented, until he had run half the distance past it. Here, if they were going to intercept him, would be the place. They'd agreed to keep quiet. Or given up. He heard only the normal sounds of a forest in the fall, rustling of an occasional squirrel, bird calls, one distant woodpecker. He did not think any one was close. He had to sweat it through. He cut away from the lake in what he thought was the direction of the barn. For the sake of speed, he ran down a winding corridor, probably a snowmobile path in winter, the ground rising a little, dark green ahead, pines, maybe those that lined the field. He thought: I stand out against this green. Instantly a voice— "There he is! There goes the white bastard." But it was distant, carried it seemed across the water. He looked back. By a chance alignment of spaces and openings the lake was visible from just this point, though it would not have been in spring or summer, and across, about where he had stumbled on it, stood some men in hunting dress, a couple already starting around to him, maybe others already ahead of them whom he could not see. He plunged into the trees, slashing with his arms at the low branches of pine saplings that obstructed him, hauling himself through if they swung back and tried to cling to the rifle on his back. He broke into the cathedral formed by tallest pines where, long ago, pioneers to the area had ceased clearing the land and lumbermen had never come. Ahead was blank snow, the field. He despaired, staring left and right to get his bearings, nothing familiar. Time was essential. He couldn't just wait here.

Then, at the edge of the field, when he looked again to the right, much farther than he'd calculated, leaned the barn. He retreated a little under the trees and raced along the carpet of pine needles and cones and loam that blessedly, would keep no record of his passage. At the place where the hypothetical fugitive, now embodied in himself, had already crossed the whole field, he glanced back. If they broke into the arbor now he was in plain sight. Not yet. He forced himself to step with care—camouflaged now against snow—in his own footsteps till he was opposite the slit at the barn doorway. He crouched, estimated the distance, and, twisting as he went, leapt sideways onto the end of the old board from the fallen loft. Inside, he slid the board in after him. You could see the depression where it had been but they'd not, he hoped, figure that out. He heard voices, very close, as if at the precise point where the fake tracks began. He unslung the .308, fumbled with the zipper of the suit. How could they have gotten here so soon? He struggled out of it. He yanked each leg through itself all right and the right arm, but the left stuck half-way. Here he was in his long underwear in an old barn with six or eight armed men closing in, and he couldn't reverse the left arm of the camouflage suit. He pushed it back, started over, got it through and jammed himself in, zipping it even as he staggered for the barn door. The main thing was to choke down his need for air, hide the fact that he was out of breath from running. And then act surprised by it all. Brave it out. He'd been in this barn hoping for a shot when deer came out to feed at dusk. He was not the man they were chasing. Who were they chasing? The figure in white who had just hurtled past the barn door. He stepped out into a gorgeous midwestern sunset, the red orb perched on the horizon irradiating a streak of sullen western clouds. Men silhouetted against this beauty were faceless. The path of his own tracks was darkened by the late shadows, more visible than before. Fake them out.

"What the hell's happening?" he gasped. "Trying to bag something here. Some bunnyrabbit runs past like a lunatic . . . All you guys coming in for the kill, for Chrissake."

They were looking at him, assessing him. One of them separated and went round the back of the barn. He was looking for the tracks of Robinson's entry. He would find them. The rest regarded the indisputable evidence of the tracks leading away across the whole field.

"I never saw nobody go so fast," Robinson said.

"Don't seem human," said one of them, gazing at the tracks.

"No, don't."

The man who had surveyed the barn came back. "Maybe we can still get him, " he said, satisfied. "It's that bastard calls himself the Deerlover. We'll split the reward."

"I heard about him!" Robinson said. "I'll help. Let me get my gun." Robinson re-entered the barn, choked in air. He wouldn't have to talk much more. Re-emerged with the .308. "Let's track that bastard."

He spent a wet hour chasing himself.

Westward, past the T. and C. and through the town of Au Gres, looking for a phone booth or a place that might have a secluded public phone. Over two hours till he could meet Phyllis. Just as well to put a little distance between his new motel and the place of origin of his call to Cindi Mayer. In his pocket he had a scrap of legal paper with her home number and a list of names of bars and restaurants, also a dozen quarters for the phone. But as he drove, a way came to him of testing her and not having to pump quarters into a public phone.

Back at the motel, he'd showered and dressed in casual clothes. He'd been too tired to think of eating anything. Maybe after his call. He'd taken a look at the day's *News*. His killing of Sligo, reported by Cindi, began on the front page, no photos or composite, but the article was OK. She mentioned his forecast of the "murder" and his "audacious phone call to this re-porter" boasting of it, the usual uninteresting details of the man's life. No preaching about staying out of the woods, but the message was fairly implicit. No quote from his call. His map with the X marking the spot had not of course reached her by press time. Nothing about the killing up that road off M-72, presumably not yet discovered. He'd wished he had access to the Detroit TV news broadcasts. He hadn't the time to drive the seventy-five miles or so south to see them. He'd missed even the local evening news, being preoccupied then with saving his skin. The schedule said that national ABC news was aired here at 6:00. He'd try to catch that when he could. It came at dusk, prime hunting time, but he would manage once or twice before the close of the season.

He'd remembered to glance back at the classifieds. In the listings under Animals was a new verse, only a line and a half of type, no numbers with which to respond through the *News* office, just the words: "How careful of the type she seems, how careless of the single life." Quite different from the previous sentimental lines, and yet he was sure the same person had paid for the insertion. He could not place the allusion, yet the words were familiar. Laura had once quoted them to him. He knew who "she" was. Again, the uncanny identification with his own thinking, as if he had arranged the entry himself.

He'd got her home number through area information on the motel phone, "in Detroit, Cindi Mayer." Luck was with him, for she might have dwelt in any of the numberless suburbs and he'd have had to try them one by one.

In Standish, twenty miles from Au Gres, was an Amoco station, closed, dark, but with a lighted phone booth at the corner of the intersection with the highway. Someone had left the door closed activating the light. He disliked the idea of standing in that center of light, but the anxiety was irrational. In the booth he dialed her number, inserting seventy-five cents for the long distance call. Her phone began to ring. Again, the question that had come to haunt him this season: risk vs. impact. The greater the risk, the greater the impact, and impact was of the essence. No answer. And now, since he'd come so close to death or capture this evening, since death or capture seemed suddenly imminent, he must speak out through the best channel he had—Cindi Mayer. She professedly disliked drunks in the woods so maybe, despite the rhetoric of today's news article, also the more dangerous sober killers in the woods. No answer. He was just about to hang up when the periodic buzzing stopped and her voice came across, husky, sleepy maybe. "Yes? Hello."

"Are you alone there?"

"Yes. Is it you?"

"Yes. No bug or tracer?"

"No. I don't think so."

"I am going to give you the number of this phone. This time I am asking that you not report it to the authorities, or not until later. If what you say is true, that should be possible. I want to try to arrange an interview. It may not work out. Even so, it should make a good story. Shall I give you the number?"

"Yes."

"You must dial back immediately. The slightest delay and I will be gone."

"I understand." He gave her the number on the dial before him, hung up and began to count. He pushed the folding door aside to extinguish the light. She had eleven numbers to dial or to touch. A touchphone was much the faster. He would give her until fifteen, no, twenty seconds. If she took longer she had called the police first. The phone jangled on the count of twelve. She had passed the first part of his test.

"You realize," she said without waiting, "that my telephone might be tapped without my knowledge. I don't think it is. That would get them into a problem."

"I'll risk it."

"But how can we arrange to meet? You said—"

"I'll tell you. But first I want to report the killing of a hunter off Michigan 72 one mile past M-65. The twenty-third, Tuesday. It wasn't in your report. They'll see his car, blue Pinto wagon. He was hunterized. That's the phrase, I think."

"All right. I'll remember. I won't be able to mention that in the paper, you know, not on your say-so or this talk we haven't had."

Stupid of him not to realize that. The official report would reach her paper soon. He said only: "You hadn't heard about it?"

"No. We heard about Rogers City, of course, this

evening, after I was home. My editor called me. And also something that happened a little later north of Tawas. That's very confused. I'm driving up tomorrow to talk to the witnesses. The paper is sending me up. On Thanksgiving. But a story is a story, isn't it? There'll be local TV and I think the networks too. You're getting famous."

"Rogers City?"

Anyway, she was coming up here on assignment. It seemed like providence helping arrange the interview.

"Yes. Wasn't it you? It's a town north of Alpena. Presque Isle County. You said you were going to 'strike'—that's what you said—on private property, and a farmer there was shot down at four o'clock practically in his own backyard, going out to hunt deer from his pasture. It doesn't look very much like an accident."

Robinson hesitated. Rogers City. Best claim the credit, think about it later. He said only: "He should have stayed inside."

"No doubt. But we have a problem with the north-of-Tawas business. It was in your style. The people up there seem to be saying that you admitted (if that's the word) to the victim who you were. Boasted? Anyway, I can talk to him at East Tawas Hospital tomorrow. He'll live, though he seems to have been scared out of his mind. Are you losing your touch, going soft, Deerlover? Our problem is that we don't see how—it doesn't seem humanly possible—you got from Rogers City to above Tawas in a couple of hours to shoot two men on private land."

"I see the difficulty," he said. "It was me though. I had a close call at Tawas. Ran like hell but they nearly caught me. Which is why I want to talk directly with you. Next time they might finish me. I want to be on record."

"There are problems in communicating with a—

excuse me—criminal. I don't know. I can't condone the shooting of people, human beings. I would like to help convey your message, whatever it is, if there's some way I can. Then you might be able to stop, retire." She laughed. "Turn yourself in." When he said nothing to that, she added: "How might I meet and talk with you?"

"Perhaps it will be impossible. If your line is being tapped, if you're lying to me, I'll know tomorrow. Otherwise, I want you to consider a list of bars and restaurants for our rendezvous. Copy down the list, please, when I read it to you. After Tawas, I want you to drive back to Standish and be prepared to head north a second time. There's a restaurant cum gas station there called Forwards. If I wish and things look OK, I'll join you there." (The place was diagonally across the street from him, gas pumps brightly lighted before the restaurant entrance. It was non-alcoholic, family. She'd have an easy time there, though she would not meet Deerlover.) "If I'm suspicious or get nervous, somewhere later along the line. Stop next at the Omer Bar in Omer. It's the only place in town. Then, in Au Gres, Harbor Lights, and after that a half-mile farther, Town and Country. Then the fifth place, Beartrack Inn, six miles farther. Then Wabens, nice restaurant overlooking the Lake, few miles out of Tawas. Keep going till I make contact. I'll know you." The other four places he named were chosen at random—

He had already decided to meet her at Beartrack. He repeated the list of ten names to be sure she had Beartrack right. If she turned the list over to State police or Feds, let them try to arrange stakeouts at each establishment. Still, there was great danger in his plan. But an actual interview, reported well, might have sensational effect, beyond many a shooting in the relative safety of the outdoors.

"All right," she said. "I'll go to those places. If you don't mind my saying so, it sounds like a hell of a Thanksgiving."

iv

On the way back he pulled into the gravel lot at Harbor Lights. Still an hour till his reservation of Phyllis, and he didn't want to spend it out at the T. and C. watching Rod transact other business, Phyllis coming back from whatever previous assignment. Above all, he needed a little time to process, assimilate the events of today and the past few days, time to sleep and to dream them away. Was it only this afternoon he'd escaped by the skin of his teeth from capture or death at Lost Lake? Yesterday he'd left Missaukee and returned the canoe and hunterized the man off M-72? Only the night before the impromptu killing of the idiot young man in the check shirt, Sligo, Hugh Sligo, and the resurrection of the buck? Was this chronology right at all or muddled, compressed, imaginary? He was so weary—

As for Phyllis, he didn't regret the reservation. But he'd just get her out of circulation for the night, take her to his '40s motel, apologize and fall asleep.

The lot was crowded: mostly old broken-down cars, some pick-ups in good shape; mainly locals, few tourists or hunters. But at the far corner nearest the highway a new white Mustang stood out. The Kid, maybe. Robinson paused. He wasn't up to another unpleasant encounter. Well, what the hell. The Kid was about as harmless as a hunter could be. He'd taken Robinson for a deer, hadn't he? Or had he? Robinson was too exhausted to think or care. Maybe in effect the Kid out there with his blunderbuss was an asset to the cause.

He threaded his way past the pool table through the crowded room to a small table against the far wall under a window fringed with plastic curtains. He stood for a moment gazing out. Below, light glittered on the surface of the river where it flowed past the deserted stalls of the marina. He sat heavily, put his head in his hands. He'd just sit like this, maybe begin to unwind. Place was busy. Waitress would be a while. No matter.

But someone was approaching. Unwillingly, he raised his eyes. It was the gaunt blonde from behind the bar, Mary, who he thought was the wife of the proprietor. She held a drink, smiled, placed it before him, ice clinking. It appeared to be a double Scotch. He looked up inquiringly. Did she remember his drink from earlier visits? Was this gesture his recognition as an habitué?

"Courtesy of the gentleman at the bar," she said and left with a vague wave of her hand in that direction. Far down the bar near the entrance a man had turned toward Robinson, a glass of beer in his hand which he raised in salute. It was the moon-face of the damn Kid.

Robinson didn't raise the glass in reply, but nodded and then stared down at the drink. What in hell was going on? When he looked again, the Kid was saying something to the young companion on each side of him, slid off his bar stool and started down the bar and across toward Robinson. Same baggy outfit, an expression on his face that Robinson could not read, not hostility—

The Kid thrust out his hand. Robinson hesitated, took it from where he sat, staring up at the bright fleshy face, a little sweaty. The boy's grip had surprising strength and warmth.

"May I join you?" The voice was slightly choked.

Robinson shrugged in bafflement. The Kid sat across from him. There was a pause. "I'm sorry to intrude this way on your privacy. But you didn't look too good. I just want to tell you not to be discouraged."

"Not discouraged?" What the hell was he driving at? Robinson shook his head, couldn't help smiling at such earnestness. He raised the glass toward the boy, caught the moist eyes, then drank deeply.

"I'm only tired," he said cautiously.

The Kid nodded. "I couldn't resist the chance to meet you, either," he blurted. Robinson tightened his eyes, tried to think. They had met before— "And to say just this once," the boy choked, "in case we don't have a better chance to talk—" He looked across the dance floor at the hustling room, no other table near theirs. "—How much I admire you." Robinson nearly asked *for what*? but held back. "Privilege to meet you. Also, to tell you not to be afraid." The Kid turned an open gaze upon Robinson.

"Afraid?"

"I mean of me." He leaned forward, dropping his voice to a level just above the chatter and laughter and the garbled music from some juke box outlet on the bar. "You could be," he whispered. "I want to tell you that you absolutely needn't be, far from it. I'm *with you*. Realization began to stir— Robinson felt sweat beading on his brow. "I think you are a hero." The Kid seemed near tears. A cracking and clattering sound came from across the room, someone breaking the racked-up balls to start a game of pool. Softly, reverently, half heard, half read from the Kid's lips: "Deer-lover."

V

Phyllis squinted at him with possible affection. "You look awful."

He certainly must. On top of everything else he was trying to handle, the damn Kid had somehow deduced who he was. He just couldn't take that in. If there was something to be done about it, he couldn't think of it now. Maybe nothing. The Kid pretty obviously approved, would not intentionally sell him out. Yet it was a dangerous loose end. Robinson did not think he could bring himself to kill a man who was with him in spirit, though conceivably all the sympathy had been pretense. Anyway, the boy was probably out of reach now. Nothing to do but sweat it. After his disclosure, he'd returned immediately to his friends, not looked toward Robinson again nor acknowledged Robinson's departure from Harbor Lights.

Robinson had picked up Phyllis after ten according to the reservation, driven her north to his backwater motel. She'd said nothing about the direction or the different car but added now, looking about as they stepped into the room, "Hm. And you've come down a little, haven't you?"

"Didn't want Rod to know where we were, so he could come spying on us like he did before."

"You changed motels just on account of me? Being with me?"

"Mostly." He didn't want to lie to her. "I had another reason as well."

She didn't ask what. He fell into the one armchair.

She stood before him a moment in the short-skirted whore's dress, then pulled out the straight-backed chair from the vanity and sat down. The skirt pulled back on her thighs. Robinson was unaroused despite himself. Too tired. "God," she said. "What happened?"

"I've had a rough couple of days."

"Bag anything?" There was an edge to her voice, of sarcasm over the deeper sympathy.

"No." He had to go into his act. "Had some good shots. Didn't take them. I'd only shoot for a trophy."

"Trophy?"

"Trophy head. A male, a buck, eight to ten points on his antlers. Phyllis—" She looked across at him, sloe-eyed, doubtful, trying to understand. He wanted to beg off and fall into bed. He would. Something in her face held him. "Has it been OK for you this last couple of days?"

"It's been OK, yes. But like I said you look terrible. Like you were going to fall onto the floor—"

"Phyllis, I've been pretty busy." She nodded, uncomprehending. How his arms and shoulders ached from the canoeing, his legs from the sloshing in marshland and running in the snow. His nerves— Maybe after all he should not have contracted with Rod for her tonight. He hadn't foreseen—

"Come over to the bed and let me undress you. You need a good rub, a massage. The first thing Rod trained me for was work in a massage parlor." She drew him over to the bed and pulled off his shoes and socks, unbuttoned his shirt, unbuckled his canvas belt and tugged off his slacks and his underpants, rolled him over on his stomach and began to massage his neck and back under the loose shirt. Her fingers were strong. Then his buttocks, his thighs and calves. All the tension had moved down to this feet, so that when she first touched them he jumped, could hardly bear the electric sensation. But as she kept on the tension drained away and he was all right.

Then she tugged at the side of his hip to tell him she wished him to roll over, and he did so and she made love to him subtly and gradually until though he was half into sleep and supposedly he could not respond he burst into a soft reverberating climax. If only life could have ended then, in the heart attack perfectly timed. But no . . . It would end otherwise.

His face was toward the mechanical digital clock supplied by the management: 11:05.

"Phyllis, thank you. I–" She eased herself off of him, sat on the side of the bed and tucked her legs together.

"What, Robinson?"

"I know it's going to sound stupid, but I want to watch the TV news again, about this hunter-killer. I'm afraid–"

She rose and went to the set. "I can understand *that*," she said.

The picture flickered on. The same young couple as last night, behind them the two symbols black on white of the hunter seen through crosshairs, the one hunter rifle-to-shoulder shooting the other. Phyllis turned up the sound.

". . . slain on Monday," the man was saying. Switch to the camera close to him. "Has been identified as Hugh Sligo of Farmington." There was film of an area not familiar to Robinson, probably back of where he had slept, the body being carried out under canvas to a waiting helicopter. "A late killing has been reported. The body of Thomas Parkinson, slain Tuesday, was found today near Highway 72." Again film from a hand-held mini-cam, this time of a walk Robinson dimly remembered having taken along an overgrown logging road to where he had found and shot this Parkinson. "Today, for the first time, there have been two incidents. As reported in our six o'clock newscast, Henry Jackson of Rogers City was killed while hunting on his farm about four P.M. And only two hours later on private land five miles north of Tawas City another hunter, Tony Massini of Tawas City, was gunned down while hunting with friends. He is expected to survive. Mr. Massini has told authorities that the man who shot him claimed to be the so-called Deerlover. Members of the viewing public will recall that this killer had vowed to slay hunters on private property today, and it appears that in fact he has sought to do so. All hunters are again advised by State Police and federal authorities to use extreme caution in the presence of any stranger in the outdoors or, preferably, to refrain from hunting altogether unless or until the killer is apprehended. Gloria—"

Switch to the girl, the composite drawing of Robinson behind her, over her shoulder, rather frighteningly. "This Bob, is the only drawing of the killer." Another switch to a close-up of the drawing while the girl's voice continued. Phyllis sat on the bed and watched without any sign of recognition. "However, in a new wrinkle in the bizarre case, he has been in touch with a reporter, Cindi Mayer, for our affiliate paper the *Detroit News*, so that we are able to play a tape of his voice—"

He looked again toward Phyllis. Would the voice be more recognizable than the face? Might she put that together with the switching of motels? Should he—? No. He'd had to miss the 6:00 P.M. airing and wanted to hear himself, what he sounded like to the public. And it might seem suspicious to her if he got up and switched off the set, having expressed such interest in the news about Deerlover.

"This segment," Gloria's voice continued while the simian version of Robinson filled the screen, "has been released to the media by the F.B.I.: "No place in this state is safe for hunters. Make that clear to your readers. I particularly urge, again, that owners of private hunting lands stay at home and watch TV if they wish to enjoy Thanksgiving dinner with their families. I shall probably not take the holiday. After that, I may concentrate on the West Coast, along Lake Michigan. But no place is safe. It is not true what your paper printed this morning that I have hunted in other states. Not yet."

The voice sounded to him distant, distorted, alien. But of course a man could never know, except through reproduction like this, what he sounded like to others. He glanced at Phyllis. She was merely intent upon the screen, quite without suspicion or realization.

Certainly the segment was sufficiently intimidating for his purpose. Why, though, no mention of his audacious reporting of the Missaukee incident itself, in the very conversation from which they had excerpted those words? He'd hoped for film of police converging on the bar from whence he'd called Cindi. Why no further mention of the growing reward for his capture sponsored by the family of the late Harold Cooper?

Again the face of Bob on the screen: "We repeat, all hunters are advised to stay indoors until the case is solved, or, if you do hunt, to observe extreme caution upon sight of any stranger." There was fear in official quarters of accidental killings, he added, jumpy hunters shooting one another. No re-run, however, of the exclusive interview with Otsego County Sheriff Ralph Pitago.

Then a detergent commercial.

"May I switch it off?" he asked, pulling himself up in the bed.

"Robinson." He looked across at her, kneeling now on the corner of the bed in the tinsel, half-transparent dress, tears starting in her eyes. What had he said to touch her so? "May you? Nobody but you has been polite to me like that for years, maybe never."

"Phyllis, I just act like I feel. Please don't cry. Look, I'm completely played out. I've got to sleep. But if I take you back to Rod, he might give you another trick."

She smiled, maybe at his grasp of the vocabulary. "Probably. There's a lot of horny guys up here."

"Stay with me two, three hours, whatever. We'll sleep. Just sleep. I'll put in a call to the desk of this establishment, if there's anyone there, to wake us. I'll take you back—"

"Don't do that. I don't sleep good. I'll wake you. Bless you, Robinson."

"OK. If we oversleep it's on—" He was almost dreaming already.

"The meter," she said softly, waking him.

"Tomorrow night? You can't do anything?"

"I asked him. He's got something special set up. I couldn't push too hard. He'd get suspicious."

"Suspicious of you and me? It's all been commercial."

"Suspicious you like me. He couldn't stand that."

"It's Thanksgiving, Phyllis."

"Thanksgiving? Yes. I'd almost forgotten there are days like that. Thanksgiving for what?"

She'd pulled the dress over her head, still kneeling on the bed, and slipped in beside him now, between the fresh sheets, pulling open his shirt and pressing herself against him.

For this, he thought, slipping into oblivion. Something held him back. "Are you still all mixed up about that Deerlover?" he murmured.

"Yes. He thinks he's doing something good. Maybe he even is. He scares the hell out of me, Robinson."

"Me too."

She was saying something more, but he could not stay awake.

NOVEMBER

25

i

He slept in, with a vague memory of taking Phyllis back. He must have—she was no longer beside him. He dozed, and glanced now and then at the digital clock, its number flipping noisily: 6:00, 6:20, 7:00. He could not force himself to get up. He hadn't the heart for any dawn expedition despite what he'd said about not taking the holiday. He was exhausted. It was too much to ask. He *was* getting too old for this sort of thing.

Some accident might be attributed to him, some woodsy murder of a rich uncle, something like the stepfather above Au Gres, some mystery like Rogers City, and it would be the same as if he himself had acted. Maybe he was even being relieved of the sole responsibility. Replaced, immortalized? Not quite yet. He thought of the green appointment book in his breast pocket, the remaining obligations.

Today, though, it was important to rest for the possible interview with Cindi Mayer. Could he really talk with her? Unlikely. Yet he'd give her the chance for direct communication. Further his purpose greatly, her career too, though maybe not so much as if she set up his capture. He must be rested tonight, alert, and infinitely careful.

He slept till 11:00. A shower refreshed him and he decided upon brunch at Lutz's and some bow practice to pass the afternoon. The practice involved no danger and would not tire him. He'd had no opportunity for a whole week, since the Thursday afternoon before the episode at the stand of pine.

By habit he glanced along the single row of cars

facing the cottages of the motel. At the far end, nearest the lake, stood the white Mustang. He thought there was someone slouched behind the wheel. Rather than investigate, he slid into the Olds and pulled onto the highway, turning south. Sure enough, when the motel was just going out of sight, the Mustang swung onto the road behind him. The damn Kid, the only person alive who knew who Deerlover was.

He parked at Lutz's, went inside, not looking back. Now between breakfast and lunch, off-season, the restaurant was nearly empty. He took a small booth beside the windows, ordered a mushroom omelette, eyed the highway east over the bridge. The Kid had pulled off somewhere and was keeping him under surveillance. What exactly did he want, having expressed his adulation? An opportunity to talk in private? Best to take no chances, shake him . . .

Yet Robinson lingered, drinking extra coffee, smoking, thinking. No sign of Kid or Mustang. It was helpful, in a way, this specific problem, something concrete to worry *about* that took his mind off the recurrent fear for which there was no focus. When he finally left he drove slowly toward the bay and right on the Shore Road. Past the slim line of scrub brush and trees was a soggy beach and reeded shallows favorable to waterfowl. He'd seen a heron there, last season, standing on one extended leg resting or sleeping, and he'd shut off the motor of the Vega and stayed for an hour till it chose to ungather its wings and flap away.

He parked on the gravel shoulder to the right of the road and took the bow, the packet of arrows and his makeshift target down to the beach. He set up the target, paced off the twenty yards. He took the sitting position sideways to his target, ready to sight over past his left shoulder. He set and drew an arrow. The fifty pounds was easier this time. But he anticipated the old difficulty: how to release quickly enough with the first two fingers of his right hand so as not to diminish the thrust given to the arrow and cleanly enough not to send the arrow however slightly to one side or the other. He squinted down the shaft of the Heartslicer, blade on target, then raised to two inches above center to compensate for the curve of the trajectory. A car motor sounded on the road. He relaxed the bow and let it down, pivoted toward the road. Past the strip of brush and scraggly trees the Mustang stopped behind the Olds. The Kid stepped out and came toward him. Robinson rose to his feet, center of the bow still gripped in his left hand, arrow against the first section of the forefinger, set in the string, aimed into the sand.

The Kid stumbled into view, baggy pants tight at the knee, blue corduroy, knickers. Heavy shoes. A brown ill-fitting tweedy jacket over a blue shirt. Round pudgy face without the fake glasses. Apparently unarmed. This Kid, alone on the planet, knew who he was. Yet he knew that Robinson knew that, and here he stood, helpless before him on this desolate beach. He stopped short. His expression, what was it? It could be read as veneration. Robinson would not have been surprised had the Kid dropped to his knees. But that was crazy—

"Who are you, son? Why are you following me?"

"*I shot two plovers once,*" said the Kid incomprehensibly."

> *They swam out to sea*
> *With jagged ivory bones where wings should be.*
> *I never knew how their lives at last were spilt*
> *But I have hoped for years all that is wild,*
> *Airy, and beautiful will forgive my guilt.*

"How the hell could it?" cried Robinson without thinking. "Why should it?"

"Exactly. That's why I'm here now—Deerlover."
The last word was a prayer, almost. Something choked.

"It's you in the back pages of the paper."

"Yes. I—I'm doing a major at the U. of M. in American Culture. I just want to pay my respects to you and explain what happened." The Kid stayed where he was, five yards away, abashed or fearful. "I guessed, last year, that you probably existed. I came up this season to help you. Christ. I damn near killed you. That's a danger we face."

Robinson bent and laid his gear on the sand, the arrow still crosswise to the wicked bow. "We?" he asked.

"You and your followers, like me. That we might shoot each *other*." So the Kid was the plump incarnation of a dream—

"Are there others you know of?"

"Not for sure. But it figures there are, or will be. I shouldn't have followed you, should have been satisfied with meeting you at the bar. But . . . , well—" The Kid stepped forward and held out his hand. Robinson pulled off his double-knit glove and gripped again the hand of his first disciple.

"We should wear a badge."

"That wouldn't be too practical. But it's why I wear stupid outfits like this." He glanced down at himself. "So I won't get shot by one of us. You aren't so careful," he said, taking in Robinson's regulation wool jacket and khaki pants.

"What were you doing in there, playing decoy?"

"I was practicing. I couldn't hit a barn then. Or I didn't think I could."

"You came pretty close to me, Kid."

"Oh God. If I hadn't lost my nerve at the last minute. I thought you were a regular hunter. How could you have come into those woods where I was target practicing? I figured you were an offering or something. Now I stick to farmers, people like that, so I won't make any mistakes."

"What about your father?"

The Kid's face darkened. "He died couple of years ago. He taught philosophy at Michigan. Wouldn't have hurt a fly. I'm a chip off that block you could say. The gun was grandfather's, mother's father."

"Glasses fake?"

"I don't really wear glasses."

"Your mother's grave—you swore on that."

"Yes. She hasn't got one, yet, thank God. I swore on it not to hunt deer and I won't," he said, smiling at the understatement.

"Nope. Your girlfriend?"

"Haven't got one, never had, really. The mirror tells me why, most mornings. When I do have, if I do— I won't impress her with my exploits up here. By the way, don't worry about today. It's taken care of. Outside Prudenville around dawn. I botched it but it's OK. You claim credit. I think it's scarier if hunters think there's one guy who's everywhere and he never gets tired. You must be exhausted."

Robinson nodded. What had he created? Well, nothing out of line with his own views, nothing wrong given the planet as it was. "How did you know me?"

"Well, there was that gaffe at the bar, when you forgot you'd had the mask on out there. You were *so* mad that I was still around. It wasn't because you were scared I'd kill some guy by accident. You didn't want me to *hunt*. I still didn't put it together. There'd been the drawing in the papers and on TV. It doesn't look like you exactly but like somebody might half remem-

ber you, like I did. Yesterday I heard your voice on
TV, chewing out the hunters the same way you did
me, same tone, and it hit me. I hung around the bar
where I'd seen you a few times hoping you'd show
up. You came in looking dejected and I had to, you
know, encourage you, give you my moral support. For
what it's worth. And then I didn't want to lose track of
you. I wanted this talk, too. So I followed you to the
other bar and your motel. Then I left to get some sleep.
You had the girl. I drove out for Prudenville before
dawn. On the chance, I checked your motel afterwards
and your car was in the lot. I napped until you came
out and went for lunch and came here."

"This is all a little difficult to take in," said Robinson.
"But I'm glad that you exist. Don't tell me your name,
and I shall not tell mine. We really can't meet again.
It could sabotage the whole enterprise. We can't communicate, as you said. It's a privilege to me also to
have met you again under these circumstances." He
looked into the intelligent, fleshy face at a loss for what
else to say. Then a thought came to him: "Was it you,
yesterday, at Rogers City?"

"Rogers City? No, Deerlover. I assumed it was you!"

8:00 P.M. Beartrack Inn. He'd driven by it before, to
and from Alpena and Lost Lake, but had not realized
how capacious it was. The lot in front was full. Across
the highway cars were pulling into an auxiliary lot. He
drove over and parked there, crossed toward the restaurant entrance, trudging on light snow. There was

another full lot to the south of the restaurant facing the
rock-packed Huron shoreline. Too many cars. It was
impossible to do his usual check.

Inside he had to wait at a little counter to be seated.
He looked around. Indeed the place was huge. A bar
area with some tables to his left. Soundless TV flickering behind the bar. Ahead of him a large dining area
fronting through glass on the wind-troubled lake. A
dance band he could not see except for the back of a
twisting youth with an electric guitar, was setting the
beat for dancing around a corner out of his sight. Past
the corridor to his right he inferred by the echoing
chatter a yet more vast roomful of diners. Then he saw
a painted placard by the cloakroom with an arrow
pointing that way: The Elks' Thanksgiving. He smiled.
The Elks.

But the place was wrong for his purpose. Safety lay
in these numbers of people, true, yet they would make
it difficult or impossible to make the contact he hoped
for here. If she came at all. Even if she did, he would
not approach her unless the circumstances were absolutely perfect, unless his instinct told him it was safe
to do so.

He decided not to seek a table. From the dining
room he would be unable to see the entrance and
might miss her, and it was better not to be conspicuous
as a man, alone Thanksgiving night, of approximately
the Deerlover's description. For all he knew the whole
place might be taken over in the search for him, might
be infested already by plainclothesmen.

He had to stand at the bar but was served his Scotch
and ice quickly, and he took a deep draw to steady
his nerves. It would not do to panic and flee conspic-
uously either. He had to remember that he was invisible
here for what he was, indistinguishable from a hundred
men his age and build in these rooms, and from five

hundred on Cindi's itinerary, could not be identified even if searched and interrogated. The mask in his pocket was not incriminating in itself. Only if his motel room were searched . . .

Again he looked around. Though not elegant, the place was a cut above the other taverns in the region— the clientele mainly well dressed—attracting the better class of tourists and the lake shore society. No one in bulging space-suit hunting outfit, though he was sure the men at the bar were hunters, as were those drinking in small groups at tables in the bar area around him. He was glad he'd worn his sports clothes. When someone left the bar he would sit with his back to these tables and to the entrance and watch for her in the mirror behind the rows of bottles.

But when a man at one of the tables caught his eye and motioned toward an empty seat there he accepted the invitation. It would seem odd not to, and now he was apparently part of a foursome of men and could hardly be Deerlover. The man who had beckoned him over gave his name as Rick, and the names of the three others, which Robinson let himself forget at once.

"Thank you," he said and raised his glass.

"Filled your license yet, Jay?" It was the younger man across from Robinson. He was atypical—harder, healthier than most hunters, trimly bearded, some sort of outdoorsman. He reminded Robinson of someone. It was Corbett, the white tail guide, pictured in that hunting magazine, whom he had been thinking about more and more.

"Not yet," he said.

There followed a desultory conversation, Robinson half listening, pretending interest, saying little. The three were well ahead of him in intoxication though they drank only beer. "A bunch of drunks in the woods," he thought, raising his eyes to the entranceway. The Corbett-figure ordered another round. It seemed the men had hunted together for several seasons, establishing a base camp far up the Rifle River. But last year was just too wet and cold in and around their tent, and now they had rented motel rooms. They could bring girls there, too, from among the prostitutes imported up from Florida for the season.

"Good thinking," said Robinson. Such a group as this had rented Phyllis for tonight.

He recognized Cindi Mayer immediately. She was tallish, tailored suit with a knee-length skirt, the gauntness of face in her photograph softened almost to beauty in the flesh. She looked nervous and tired. This was the fifth place she had entered, a pretty woman alone, and for all she knew five more lay ahead. She looked the reporter, mannish cut to her suit, leather purse on shoulder strap, businesslike expression. She did seem to be alone, though it was impossible to be certain.

She stood uncertainly at the reception counter, glanced into the dining room, then about the group of tables where he sat. He sipped his second Scotch, waiting for her to resolve the same dilemma he'd faced half an hour earlier: where to go in this vast place so as best to further the encounter? The heavy-set hostess appeared and they talked. Robinson could not hear. If seated in the dining room, she must be reasoning just as he had, she could be lost in the crowd. And also, if by chance she was first to arrive, she could not see Deerlover, or a probable Deerlover, enter. She could hardly take an empty seat at a table of strange men. She shrugged at the hostess, said something and walked toward and past him to the bar. He could have touched her.

"Nice pair," murmured the Corbett-figure. And when a man at the bar perceived in the mirror Jane Fonda,

more or less, standing behind him and offered his seat
and she accepted, 'Corbett' added, "Nice ass." He did
not seem inclined to act upon these observations, nor
did the man who had relinquished his seat pursue his
advantage but only stood uncertainly behind her, drink
in hand. Robinson himself feared to act, make contact.
Could he approach in this context, tap her on the
shoulder, and say, "I believe it's me you wish to interview?" It was impossibly risky. Why had he set up
this arrangement at all? Then a rather bland-looking
man from around the corner of the bar, who must
have seen her take the seat there and order her solitary
drink, did it for him, came round and tapped her on
the shoulder. They spoke. Robinson could not quite
hear. Her face, partly toward him now, brightened
doubtfully. The man could pass as well as Robinson
for the subject of the composite sketch in the *News*.
But she must have been approached by other irrelevant men in the bars this evening. How could she
know? He appreciated the perplexity she must be going
through, the need to encourage Deerlover, at the same
time to shake off some lush trying to pick her up. She
smiled and slid down from her seat and let the man
take her hand and lead her across the room. For a
moment Robinson supposed they would get their coats
and leave. He could hardly rise and try to prevent that.
What would happen to her then? But instead the man
led her past the partial screening behind the band and
out of sight onto the dance floor. He'd only asked her
to dance. The invisible band was playing something
slow and sentimental and Robinson wished that it was
he and not the irrelevant stranger who was dancing
with Cindi Mayer.

The music changed to country and then to hard
rock. Soon after the beginning of this, Cindi emerged
from the dance floor and went down the corridor away

from him into the ladies' room. When she came out she got her coat from the cloakroom and, tugging it on, headed for the exit. She had realized that Mr. Bland was not Deerlover. She was on her way to number six.

If he was to act it must be now. She had gone. He looked at Rick, 'Corbett,' and the nonentity with them at the table. Corbett at any rate had watched the whole process.

"No score," he said.

"Hell," said Robinson instinctively. "I'll try my own luck."

To his surprise the Corbett-figure rose when he did. The thought flashed into his mind: this is the police plant, it's all over. The man thrust out his hand.

"Good hunting," he said.

Robinson shook the strong hand, caught the knowing glances of the others, uttered thanks for the drink, and hurried out, his pursuit of Cindi Mayer covered by the erotic motive.

She had vanished. But down the walkway beside the building to his left he made out footprints just disappearing in the lightly-blowing film of snow. Nearer him they were already obliterated. Her car must be in the south parking lot.

From the corner of the building, across the diagonal of the lot, he saw her beside her car clearing her windshield of snow. She had backed into a space among the row of cars ranged just a few feet from the rocky lakeshore. He walked towards her. She was getting in, hadn't noticed him. He glanced about. He half expected a cordon of sheriff's deputies to spring from nowhere and apprehend him. There was no one. He took the web mask from his pocket and pulled it over his head, adjusting the eye holes, when, just like a woman, she switched on the headlights before starting the motor. He froze there. Through the glare in the soft light from her dashboard he could make out her startled face. She switched down to parking lights. Then slowly she twisted round, fumbling for something behind her. A gun? No. She'd have that in the glove compartment. She had found the handle to the rear door on her side, unlatched it, and cabdriver-style pushed it slightly open. Back behind the wheel, she let him appraise the situation, study her face—serious, expressionless—in the dashlight. He decided to accept her invitation and strode to the car, pulling the door closed behind him as he slid over into the corner opposite the driver's seat. She started the engine.

"Tell me where to drive," she said.

He said left, south, and she followed the instruction, driving slowly for a minute without speaking. No car followed them. He did not think this was a trap.

"I would like to tape our interview," she said, "if that's all right." When he raised no objection, she added, "We'll have to park someplace quiet. I can't think when I'm driving, and I don't want road sounds on the tape. I'll tell the authorities I had you on the telephone. If they knew I was physically with you and didn't, you know, do anything about it, I'd be an accessory after the fact. And before the fact too—if there is anything further on your agenda for this season, Mr.—" She paused. He couldn't see her face in the rearview mirror but thought she might be wryly smiling. "You have the advantage of me."

"Deerlover," he said.

"You choose the place."

He knew that the highway was swinging imperceptibly westward and, soon, that they were a mile or so above Saginaw Bay. He had her turn toward it at the next crossroad. Maybe one of the wooded driveways of the summer people would do near the beach where he practiced archery. "Slowly," he said, looking back, but no car turned after them. "Right here." It was the narrow shore road where this afternoon, many miles farther along, he had chatted with the Kid. "No, wait." She stopped in the intersection, the turn half completed. Their crossroad continued, the pavement sloping, it seemed, right on into the bay. No posts or fence. A drunk losing his bearings here would plunge his car right into the water. The road modulated into a ramp for launching boats in the summer. "Down there," he said, pointing.

"Down where?" She did not look back at him.

He told her, and she drove the car around and down about half a block toward the water, an equal distance now ahead of them. She stopped close to a cleared area beyond which stood a cottage, presumably already winterized and deserted. She shut off the engine. "It will get cold," she said in the near silence, "but we'll take some breaks and I can run the engine and warm us up. I want the tape to have breaks in it, actually. The pretext will be that I spoke with you several times over the telephone. My home phone. In between, we can talk off the record, if you wish."

In the car lights the wavelets of the bay lapped toward them. Then she punched the lights off, and as the light shrank back to them the bay went invisible in the moonless night. The dashboard glowed softly, and there was faint light from a streetlamp back at the crossroads. Even with the windows up, the faintest sound of lapping was audible.

"My tape recorder is in the glove compartment," she said. "There is nothing else there. I'll take it out now." She hesitated. He said nothing. She did so. It was dully black, the size of a cigar box. "I want to test whether the sound of the water will register." He had not thought of that.

"All right."

She placed the machine on the rest between the bucket seats, behind the boot of the stickshift. When she started it a tiny red light came on. She waited a moment, then made the machine whirr in reverse, and touched another button for the playback. She did all this blindly with the fingers of her right hand while staring straight ahead into darkness, and he watched the back of her head, barely visible from the distant streetlight, the rich brown curls. No sound from the machine. The light went off.

She spoke: "I'll adjust this so that it is voice-activated. So you needn't hurry with your answers. You can tell by the light when it's set to record. Touch my shoulder if you want me to turn it off awhile." She paused. "I am going to record a little fake introduction to the series of phone calls this is supposed to be. Then I'll switch off the recorder. Get your OK on the intro. When you're ready I'll start up and ask my first 'official' question. All right?"

"All right."

The red dot of light.

"I have arranged," she said, "over the telephone, to conduct a series of short recorded telephone interviews with the man in Michigan who has come to be called Deerlover. He is the admitted killer—he probably would not say murderer—of nine or ten men out hunting the last ten days. I do not know whether he has killed, or will kill, anyone today. He has admitted, or rather claimed, taking fifteen human lives a year ago in this state, one every day of the firearm season. The situation in the woods and fields in the major hunting counties of our state makes it fairly easy for a good marksman to do this, if he has no compunction against taking human life or if he thinks that animal life is equal to or better than human life. Understandably, the man does not wish to conduct extended conversations, even by phone, with a journalist. I hope that he will contact me again, from various public phones as he chooses, and respond on this tape to my questions. This procedure that he has initiated seems to me in the public good. Of course I cannot condone his killing, and should he contact me, I will make available to state and federal authorities seeking to apprehend him, this tape and any other information that might come into my possession by mail or phone."

The dot of red went out.

"Is that acceptable?" she asked. "I'll erase and do it over—"

"It's acceptable," he said. "Let's have question number one and get started."

She held up to the dashlight a little pad of white notepaper with some sort of list written on it. The hand holding the pad trembled. She, maybe more than he, was afraid. He'd not realized. She was alone in her car with the murderer of twenty-five men, could not know that to such as she he was harmless. The dot came on.

"Thank you for having called me again. I won't waste your time. Why do you shoot deer hunters?"

He took a deep breath. It was going to be hard to find the right voice for this, not a threat but an explanation. "Because I wish to diminish the terrorizing and slaughter of innocent creatures. I believe that I act on behalf of a majority of people who in their hearts applaud me. Even if they are not a majority, they are the best people, the most sensitive and kind, the ones who understand the situation. Some of them belong to societies that share my objective. Contribute money.

192

Lobby, boycott. That is futile." Laura had been such a person. "But even if there were no such people I would do what I am doing."

"You speak of kindness and sensitivity?"

"Yes. Of course."

"I see. What is the situation?"

"That there is no God."

"What has that to do with killing deer, or killing hunters?"

He knew that he would sound preachy, that he was more effective in the ominous than the explanatory voice. Yet he must try. "Everything. The alleged superiority of human beings over other animals with nervous systems, love for their offspring, consciousness, souls all depended on the idea that human beings were special to God. Some God. Now all the animals along with us are on the same level so far as that goes. And the other animals look a lot better to me."

"In what way?"

"With their love, their gentleness, their innocence, their utter lack of cruelty, their simple, beautiful lives. They didn't fall when we fell. Do you understand what I mean?"

"I think so, maybe. But isn't it cruel to shoot men?"

"I've thought about that. I am human and capable of it. It is a tiny cruelty intended to reduce a vast cruelty."

"Lions are not cruel, then, or wolves, and so on?"

"No. They have to live. It's not their fault. Anyway, they don't terrorize whole populations. For sport."

"Whose fault is it?" Still she spoke straight ahead of herself into the darkness.

"Nature's."

"You mean you're not a Nature lover?"

"No. But I don't wish to talk about that. I don't think your readers would understand—the distinction, I mean.

I tried explaining it to a conservation officer a few days ago. He, no—"

This was a mistake. He'd gotten carried away, thinking of this problem at the core of his philosophy. He leaned forward and touched her shoulder. She jumped, gasped.

"Oh! Oh, I'm sorry. It was my own signal, wasn't it?" She turned off the recorder. "It's just that we hadn't, you know, made any contact till then, I guess. You weren't quite real to me."

"The conservation officer will remember my face," he said. "More importantly, where we talked."

"Yes. I understand."

She reversed the machine for an instant, stopped it. "It will be good to check that we are recording OK." She put it on play. ". . . have to live. It's not their fault. Anyway, they don't terrorize whole populations. For sport."

She cut it there, wound it back again and replayed. After "sport" the machine ran silent.

"I'll put it back on voice-activated. Is that all right? And we'll continue?"

Again, his own voice sounded menacing to him, more so than he felt when he spoke. A danger half-formed in his mind. That conservation officer! *She* could initiate a search for him, Dave. That might lead to the lodge in the U.P. He brushed this away. Too late.

"I gather," she was asking, "it is not only deer you love." When he did not respond, she added: "You—you love all creatures great and small—with, of course, the possible exception of men. So, then, why—"

He considered trying to explain about the whales, the dolphins and baby seals, the elephants, the gorillas. Hopeless. He thought instead of a mordant reply: "I cannot be everywhere at once."

A long pause. Was it his imagination or was her voice different, huskier, somehow, as she went on: "You know that the societies you mention, national organizations for the protection of wildlife, have all repudiated your way of sparing wild animals."

"I didn't know. But they have to say that. They don't mean it."

"I see. What about laboratory animals? Vivisection? At the Highway Research Center in Ann Arbor they plan to strap a baboon into the driver's seat of a car to see what happens when—"

"*Please* don't make me think about that. I can only repeat what I said before. Maybe I'll get around to them." Delegate the job in Ann Arbor to the Kid, he thought grimly.

"I'm sorry. What about farm animals? Slaughter houses? Are you a vegetarian?"

"Yes. I don't eat any flesh. How could I? And I don't wear anything that came from the body of an animal. For me to wear a leather belt or leather boots or shoes would be like eating venison, like being a Nazi with a lampshade made of human skin."

"Your *shoes* are not leather?" She spoke as if she might twist round in the car and look down at his feet.

"They're canvas, like my web belt, like the boots I hunt in."

"Then you do value human life, from what you say about the Nazis."

"Of course I do. I venerate all animal life."

"Except hunters."

"Hunters, Nazis, highway scientists . . ." Other depraved and perverted specimens of it who torment and mutilate and destroy it.

"What of the survivors? The wives and children of men you have killed?"

This took him off balance. He hadn't thought much

about it. He said so. "I've always shrugged that off," he added. "It doesn't weigh on me. I guess I've thought more of the does and fawns. I guess I've thought the kin of those men better off with the insurance money. I don't know. If the men stay home during the season, Ms. Mayer, their wives and children will still have them around."

"Are you married?"

"My wife is dead. We had no children. Now," he added, "I'm getting nervous. I'll hang up. Somebody might be tracing this call."

"I thought that went all right," she said. "Are you ready for another bout?"

"In a few minutes. Do you mind if I smoke a ciga-rette?"

"No."

"You?" He reached forward to offer her his pack.

"No. I'm trying to quit. I'll run the engine some to generate a little warmth. OK?"

"OK." He suppressed the impulse to ask her how the interviewing and taping had gone in the morning in East Tawas. He'd see the results of it. He didn't want to get into mere conversation, waste time, lose his tenseness and alertness.

She started the motor and let it idle. Indeed, the cold had begun to reach his feet and legs. The heater had a blower to the back seat, and almost immediately he felt warmed. She started to say something. Were there specific questions he would like her to— but a car was coming down the road behind them, stopped at the intersection, its lights like a pair of eyes fixed in what seemed an interminable stare. They both watched in the rearview mirror. The interior of her car was lit hardly at all and yet light glittered on the tips of the wavelets in the bay ahead of them.

"Don't worry," she murmured. "It's nothing. No

one knows I'm with you. Trust me, Deerlover. I only want the story."

And the car swerved onto the crossroad and disappeared.

"Your questions are all right. They help me say what I want to communicate to the public. Don't you worry either. I only wish to reach the public—" He smoked, tapped the ash of his cigarette into the armrest ashtray beside him. "You aren't a hunter."

"You're fascinating," she said, "and scary too, even to a non-hunter. I can't approve of what you are doing, and yet somehow I respect it too. Is that possible?"

"Absolutely. Because it is a small and godless planet."

"Hm. I wish that we could talk more—openly, face to face. Share a dinner. Have you taken off that terrible mask? It must be uncomfortable. I won't look back. I couldn't make out your face in here anyway. Did you have dinner back at the restaurant? It's Thanksgiving."

"No. I'm not sure whether turkeys have souls. I couldn't take any chances." Despite himself he was yielding to the temptation to relax and get humorous, off guard. Careful.

"You could have, oh—shrimp. Shrimp don't have souls, do they?"

"I don't think so. Maybe."

"Tell me about Nature, what you don't think my readership would comprehend."

"I'm not sure I can. What's the point?" Still, he was glad to get away from chit-chat.

"To make me a more sympathetic vehicle for telling the world about you."

So he tried to explain. It had been all right, the principle of the weak perishing, the strong surviving, when there were amoeba, sea plants, and lichen, things like that, trees. The essential heartlessness of the scheme didn't emerge until there were elaborate nervous systems, true consciousness. There'd been no love, feeling, sentience when it invented itself. Yet they were implicit. In time it produced them. "Yet they are alien to it because it is unfeeling. Nature is only the great big DNR, cropping and managing feeling creatures as if they were roses or bean sprouts. There's nothing in the soul of an animal that is akin to Nature."

"I'll have to let that sink in," she said. "It's certainly a novel way of looking at things. I'll remember it. I have a question, on my list, about the DNR. Shall we switch on the recorder?"

"All right."

A second pair of lights came down the road behind them. This time she remained silent, waiting. The car stopped, stayed, its light probing mindlessly into the dark, then turned and vanished out of sight and hearing. She cut the motor and they resumed.

"Thank you for calling. You knew, sir, that by your contacting the press—me—your existence would become known positively to the authorities. You are now—" she paused, as if realizing anew whom, helpless, she was with—"the object of a huge state and federal, ah, manhunt, if you'll permit the term. Why did you contact me and pose this great risk to your mission, and even your life?"

This was a question she herself already knew the answer to, of course. He explained about the magnification of his impact that the press could bring about. He added, "I contacted you specifically because I happened to see your column on drunks in the woods. I thought you might be sympathetic, not to me but to the problem, interested in the problem, that's all. I killed a man this morning in the woods. Hm. Near Prudenville. Yet by speaking with you now I can do more good than I did then. Not that you are in any way responsible for or encouraging what I do."

"And it was 'good' that you killed that man?"

"Yes."

"The media you speak of have dubbed you a psychopath, a psychopathic killer. Are you?"

"Not the way they mean it. They mean sick. The word used to mean 'feeling,' you know, 'having feeling.' In that sense I'm a psychopath. A monomaniac too, I suppose."

"Excuse me. Are you a scholar?"

"Yes. Yes, I am. Or I was."

"You have sensitive feelings?"

"That is why I am here."

She asked her prepared question about the DNR: their argument that the deer would die anyway and should be managed. He answered well, having thought much about this. He was skeptical, with so much money involved. In any case animals had a right to live the cycle of their lives in such peace and dignity as Nature allowed.

"What of the loss of sport and the waste of venison?"

"I won't answer a question on that level."

"Sorry. Those points are made in various publications. Assuming you are right, how can you justify taking the solution to the problem—the abuse of harmless animals—into your own hands at the cost of human life?"

"I wouldn't mind if others joined me."

"That isn't what I meant."

"I know. I justify it in the name of life and in the cause against terror and pain."

He was suddenly tired, and signaled for her to break off the interview. As the car warmed itself she was quiet, thoughtful it seemed. She asked whether, when he was a schoolboy perhaps, he had read a story called *Bambi*. He'd heard about it, he said. Someone had mentioned it to him recently. But he'd missed reading it somehow. "Should I?"

She gave a little laugh. "I guess not."

She had a few more questions, and he agreed to a last round on the tape. Then she would drive him back. "Thank God I don't have to go into the rest of those bars!" she added. "Oh, I forgot. There isn't any God."

They resumed the formal interview, faking an exchange on the phone as before.

"How did you start, Deerlover? How and when did you receive your—your mandate for this mission?"

He explained about his life with Laura, why not? The forty societies she joined that had no effect, his brooding at the time of her death, his reading about the suffering of animals, his decision that he could be most effective in Michigan. But all that did not quite explain it. He thought silently while the machine waited for his voice. The conversation he'd overheard in a Toledo bar before ever meeting Laura, how it was a good idea, but of course they'd never do it because of the penalty. The animals he'd always had around him as pets. Frank Buck—the book his parents gave him for Christmas which, when he was ten or twelve, he'd read with a fascination that turned, to his amazement, to revulsion, placing in his mind an image, the image of a tiger in India with its lips sewn shut, that he could never extirpate, changing him. No use speaking of that. Many factors, but not *Bambi*, he concluded.

"Would your late wife condone what you are doing?"

"I don't think so. She was gentle, like an animal. I mean that as the highest praise. But I don't know. She is dead." And then he added, because it came to him, in answer to no question, "Animals cannot help themselves, being what they are. And yet they must be helped. That is where I enter the picture. That is what, for me, sums up everything."

"Thank you. Do you plan, may I ask, assuming you are not arrested in the meantime, to resume your mission in Michigan next year, next season?"

"I'll decline to answer that. I shall be somewhere. I shall not be idle, not then, nor ever while I am alive. But any specific answer might reduce my effectiveness. I could be many places at many times. I am retired, I can afford to travel. I will say that I have been thinking quite a lot about deer hunting in Texas."

"Texas will be sorry to hear that."

"I hope it may profit from my words."

"But aren't you afraid of being captured and punished by the law?"

Actually, he was not, or he seldom thought of that. He was in fear almost all the time except when he forgot to be, now and then, when active, preoccupied, drunk. The fear was worst when it had no immediate cause. The machine was waiting with its tiny red light. "I would have a platform, then," he said, "for a while, to broadcast my message to this state, the nation, the world. The notoriety, the trial reporters and so on would give it to me. And then I'd be a martyr for animals. A man could do worse. But I can achieve more with my freedom. I do not think I can be caught."

"One last question, if you will. This is the twenty-fifth of November. You don't mind if I record the date of this third conversation?"

"No."

"There are five days left in the firearm season. Do you plan to—"

"Yes."

"Is there anything I could say that would dissuade you?"

"No."

"Then may I also ask— there is, I understand, a bow-and- arrow season after that, through—"

"December thirty-first."

"Do you intend—"

"I'd better not comment. I will say that I own a bow with what's called compound action. I have been practicing with it. I have a plan for it. I am not so accurate as with my rifle."

"Thank you. If I may say so, I find you terrifying." She spoke, still, into the wavy darkness of the bay ahead of her.

"That's my whole intention."

"Is there, finally, anything further you would like to communicate to (as you say) the state, the nation, and the world?"

"Not at this time."

A third pair of lights appeared on the road behind them and stopped at the intersection. He watched in her rearview mirror. The car was white in the streetlight. It came on, not veering away but drawing up behind them. A red quadrated light twirled on its roof, making of the roadside trees and the bay and the summer house beside them a sudden crazy merry-go-round.

"Oh Christ," she said, in the midst of this. "It's the sheriff's patrol. I'm coming back—"

"What?"

But already she was clambering between the bucket seats, all knees in front of him, over the recorder, then falling into the seat beside him. He twisted round to look behind them. There were two officers, the driver just getting out with his flashlight, the other remaining in the car for back-up, the light still spinning insanely.

"Put your hand up my skirt," she said. He couldn't react. "And for Jesus' sake pull off that damn mask! Look, my eyes are shut, in passion and in esctasy. Trust me, Deerlover!"

Her eyes were indeed squeezed shut. He yanked off the mask, stuffed it under him. The officer was at the window, playing his light on the front seat. She clutched for Robinson's right hand, put it on her knee. The fabric of her hose was unexpectedly coarse to his finger tips. "Not like that," she muttered through clenched teeth. "For Chrissake, like you mean it. Grope me." He thrust his hand up her leg. "Kiss me, dammit." With her free hand she hauled him over almost on top of her. The flashlight was on them now, steady, voyeuristic. He kissed her and kept kissing her. Her delicate perfume touched his nostrils. She responded to encourage him and wriggled underneath him convincingly. He worked the hand on her thigh. Then she pushed him away and they both looked sheepishly into the glare of light with the smirking face behind it. Would he make them get out? Ask to see their licenses? He'd remember the name Cindi Mayer, the bastard. Robinson rolled down his window.

"Well. Everyboy cozy in there?"

Cindi spoke: "Just fine, officer." She made a feint at adjusting her skirt.

"Just wanted to make sure." He kept the light on them. "You're not local people, are you?"

"No, officer," Robinson said quietly.

The light stayed on them, and stayed, and then flicked away.

"It's all right, Charlie," the officer called back to his partner. Two consenting adults, after all.

They watched out the rear window as he returned and the patrol car backed, swung round, blinked its brake lights at the intersection, vanished up the road. They were in darkness, in the backseat of her car. The tiny red light of her recorder...

"Thank you," he said breathlessly, "for—uh, this, and for interviewing me. I think you had better erase the last segment of the tape."

NOVEMBER

26

i

I MET "DEERLOVER." The headline on the front page of Friday's *News* cut into him with a sense of betrayal. Somehow, despite her apparent loyalty last night, she had sold him out. But as he read, hastily, the lead-in to the transcript of the interview, he began to understand what must have gone through her mind. She had realized that the fiction of the series of three telephone interviews would not wash with the authorities, even if they were supposedly over her phone at the apartment. Too risky. Also: publication of a talk person-to-person with the killer had far the greater news value, so long as she could avoid implicating herself as an accessory.

This she had managed very cleverly in the lead-in. She'd been returning from assignment in East Tawas (the related story was on page two) when she'd glimpsed a red Chevy that she thought might be following her, but it disappeared. She'd stopped for coffee at a place called Forward's in Standish. (This was presumably true.) Coming out after dark, in the parking lot, she had been accosted by a man wearing a web mask and holding a gun on her. He'd forced her to drive to a remote place and tape an interview. He'd had his own tape-recorder, but since she had hers with her they'd used that. He supplied a short list of questions but invited her to ask her own, and she had done so. He had made her return his list to him. For his own protection (he said) he'd insisted on the pretense that the questions and answers were over the telephone. She couldn't maintain that fiction. They had been together, though through force and against her will. Except for his holding the gun on her, this multi-murderer had acted like a gentleman, and was obviously educated, even scholarly. It seemed his purpose was to try to explain his actions to the public at large. The result was the following transcript. The tape itself, the very voice of the killer "Deerlover," was of course already in the hands of the police. With their permission, it would be excerpted on local and national radio and TV.

The transcript, running into the back pages of the first section of the paper, was so far as he could recall verbatim. She omitted the introduction that he had approved, erased it presumably along with the coda involving the county patrolman, before turning over the tape. Good. Surely her story and the transcript would be picked up by the national news services, and the voice excerpts would be on national TV.

His responses, in print, seemed satisfactoy. He hoped that prospective hunters the next few days might hear the voice itself, laconic and terrible. He did not know from whence within himself came that sound and tone.

Cindi's report from East Tawas was also satisfactory. The fat man Massini had babbled to her of the deadly man all-white who had shot him down in cold blood in the orchard. Adequate testimony from some of the men who had chased and lost him in the snow. No mention (just as well) of the hunter from the old barn who had joined the chase. He would not have been available for an interview. Maybe there'd be film on tonight's TV, the Lost Lake area, killer's tracks in the snow. He'd like to see that from the safety of this room.

After dropping him at Beartrack she must have driven back to Standish and called the State Police or the FBI with her story. Or maybe just found the nearest Sheriff's Patrol headquarters in that direction. He was a little worried about fingerprints in her car, but the only thing he could remember touching (that would bear prints) was the inside door handle on the driver's side to pull shut the door, and those prints would be blurred, surely. His mission was greatly advanced by the interview. Everything was all right still, unless in the haste and complexity of the last few days he had forgotten something crucial to his impunity.

And maybe after that she had driven on to her parents' to tell them the official version of her adventure and have some delayed turkey and dressing.

He'd tried, again, to sleep in, to doze and unwind, but again his mind wouldn't let him, and he had repeated the pattern of the day before, going out for breakfast and the morning *Free Press* and then archery practice on the same beach where he'd talked with the Kid until time for a late lunch, after which the *News* was delivered to the rack outside Lutz's. He wished, not for the first time, that chance had established his contact with the morning paper instead of the afternoon. The *Free Press* merely reiterated the Rogers City and Lost Lake episodes and did a review of the whole history since Cooper on the fifteenth. The third slaying near Prudenville (if the Kid was telling the truth about it) had evidently not been discovered at press time. Then in the *News* was Cindi's great scoop, the enforced and terrifying interview with Deerlover directly, her very life endangered while yet her tape recorder captured everything. He had to hand it to her. She had come through to the maximum for them both. Unless through some implication he could not decipher she had sold him out, through his naiveté. Time would tell, the assault on his car in some tavern lot, a knock at his motel door.

He sat with the paper on his lap, staring at the inactive screen of the TV which night before last had carried his portrait and his voice. He remembered the Kid's poetry in the classifieds. He'd check whether there was anything new. As he leafed back through the paper, his eye chanced to fall on the tag CLUBS in the middle of a page. This was the continuation of an article from page three. It started in mid-sentence, something about safety in numbers and in familiarity for men who still wished to go out hunting. He turned back to the beginning of the article, HUNTING CLUBS. It reported the setting up of a number of impromptu hunting groups, mostly among business associates in the Detroit area, to foster safe hunting during the remainder of the firearm season or until the capture of the "so-called hunterizer." The movement had begun sporadically, here and there in Detroit, a week or so ago. Evidently it had only now come to the attention of the *News*. The idea was that men who knew each other might more safely venture into the wild where an intrusive stranger would be immediately conspicuous. Each club also had distinctive dress or insignia. Membership was usually by invitation, either by word of mouth or by letter.

Well, there was something to this scheme. It was amidst the private club at Lost Lake that he had nearly perished, and they had no uniform or insignia. But these clubs were different. They did not, so far as the article revealed, hunt on private territory. He wished he'd learned of this movement earlier. Now there was not much he could do about it.

Still, he glanced down the list. Most of the clubs hunted out of lodges that were not on his possible itinerary the remaining few days, even supposing he could devise a way to infiltrate. But the last caught his eye because its name was a direct insult to him: "Deerslayer, Inc." He read the details. Eighteen men recruited from the moving business in Detroit. They'd had bright blue blazers made up with the image of a stricken deer on the back, leaping into the air before dying. So you could always tell an authentic Deerslayer on sight, isolate a stranger. They'd rented the Leland Hotel in Leland for the last week of the season. That was two or three miles from the Homestead in Glen Arbor where he had a reservation. It seemed like the hand of fate. He'd look into the matter. There might be nothing he could do, but it was intolerable. Deer-slayers, Inc. As bad as Corbett, the whitetail guide.

Somewhere recently he'd read about someone in the moving business in Detroit. He sat back, trying to recall.

The telephone jangled. He quite jumped in his chair, looked with fascination at the black instrument within reach of his left hand on a side table. Never, in all the lodges and motels he'd used, had there been a phone call. The phone rang again. The law? They wouldn't telephone. Cindi? She could not know where he was, could she? Would not telephone and endanger him if she did. He rested two fingers on the back of the receiver and felt the vibration of the third ring. Mrs. Hibbard, maybe, his house sitter in Aurora? But he'd forgotten to call and give her his new number. Old lady at the motel office? But why she, he'd paid cash in advance? He lifted the receiver and put it to his ear.

"Robinson?" A woman's voice, troubled. What the hell?

"Yes."

"You don't know me. I'm—with Rod, you know?"

"Yes."

"I'm calling for Phyllis. Some guys beat up on her and she's on ice in the hospital. East Tawas Hospital."

"How bad?"

"She'll live—at least until Rod finds out."

The connection clicked off before he could think how to respond.

He put on his sweater, went out to the Oldsmobile

and drove north. On earlier trips he'd noticed the Hospital sign marking the turn-off in East Tawas at a place where the highway ran along Tawas Bay.

In the near-empty lot of the hospital, he paused for a moment in the car, considering. The fat man Massini was here, unless already moved to some larger facility. The press people would be gone now, but there might be a police guard. Would they interrogate every man of his age and build who came, on the theory that the psychopath might want to finish the job and eliminate a key witness? Or figure what would be quite correct except for Phyllis, that this would be the last place Deerlover would barge into? Have to chance it . . .

In the emergency room, no sign of the law. The situation felt all right. The receptionist, middle-aged, hatchet-faced, was arguing about visiting hours with a black man who wanted to see his wife. Robinson had never before seen a black in northern Michigan. They were mysteriously excluded. Blacks of course never went hunting. He feared trouble with this receptionist. Disgruntled, the man took a seat, grabbed a magazine.

"Sir?" This was promising. He decided to fake being her distraught husband, a gamble because he did not even know her last name, Rod's last name. Maybe it wouldn't come up, would be taken for granted. If he lost the gamble he'd simply look in every room of this little hospital and find her. But no. Easy. Then he'd look like the maniac.

"My wife Phyllis," he said. "Ah, we had an argument last night. She ran out. I've been desperate trying to find her. I just found out she's here. Some people beat her up, they said. They are coming to talk to her about it, I think—the police. But I've got to see her—"

The woman looked at her register. "All right, Mr. Robinson," she said. "The state police *are* coming to talk to her. I'll see whether you can see her before that.

She very much wants to see you. Unlike some wives I could name." She glared at the black, who ignored her. "Take a seat. I'll be right back."

Robinson. Phyllis had signed in under his name, the name she knew him by, hoping her colleague would reach him, hoping he would come for her, hoping maybe to disguise her identity in case Rod came first.

The receptionist was checking with her superiors or maybe by phone with the state police, taking forever. Phyllis had had the wit to make sure Robinson would not be suspected of beating her. So it might be all right.

He stood at the desk, resting his hands on it and tapping it nervously with two fingers, trying to consider contingencies. If Rod burst in now, or the police came to interview the beaten girl—here in the same building where Massini was recovering from his gunshot wound . . .

At last the woman returned. He could tell from her smug expression that it was all right. Maybe she made a special effort just to spite the black guy, who still had to wait. Anyway, Mrs. Robinson was in 103.

Phyllis shared the room with an elderly woman in leg traction either drugged, asleep, or lapsed into senility; out of it in any case. Phyllis' face was bruised, a welt raised on the right of her forehead over the old scar. She was alert, and her face brightened at the sight of him.

"Robinson," she said, "I knew you'd come and get me out of here."

"Can you leave?"

"Yes. Oh yes. There's supposed to be stuff today about tests for internal injuries, but I think I'm OK. One of them hit me here (she touched the welt) and knocked me down."

Impulsively, he bent and kissed her forehead.

"Robinson. You came." She sat up and began to

push back the sheet and swing her legs around. "I've got this stupid hospital gown with the slit down the back. My dress is in the closet. I don't know where my underwear is. It doesn't matter. They kicked me, with their boots on, mostly my legs." He couldn't see, beneath the gown. "I guess I fainted and they got scared. I don't know what's happening."

He handed her the skimpy dress from the hanger in the closet, turned away while she slipped off the hospital gown and wriggled into it. There were ugly bruises on her knees. The high-heeled tinsel shoes were on the closet floor, and she took them from him and carried them while she walked with him barefoot along the corridor to an exit at the back, then, doubling back, across the whole exterior of the building to his car. Down another corridor he thought he had glimpsed from the side of his eye two state troopers talking, just an impression of tan uniforms, Texas-style hats, bulging holsters. He'd forced himself not to turn his head and look for sure.

"Rod," she said, now, in the car.

"Yes, I know."

He drove out of the lot, turned south on State 23. Just then a blue wagon roared past them toward the hospital.

"I can't stand it any more," she said as they drove. "I'm more afraid of the men he sets me up with than of him. Oh God, I'm afraid of everything. I wish I was dead."

"It's all right now," he said. "I can help you."

"He gives me to all the creeps now, creeps and groups. It was never like that before."

"It's all right. I'll take care of you. You don't have to worry any more. You won't have to do it again."

After a few moments' silence she responded: "You did say you'd lend me money. Drive me someplace safe, to a bus stop maybe? If you give me your address I'll pay you back. I promise. I could get a job . . ."

"Don't worry about that, Phyllis. Money is not important to me." It was true. He had no heirs, no needs, no responsibilities beyond, for the moment, her, his mission, and the animals at home. "I'll get you out of this."

"Why?" she asked frankly. He looked across into her brown eyes in the battered face.

"I don't know. It makes me feel good. I just will."

A little later she pointed to the right and said, "That's where the suite is. Where Rod keeps us." It was a modern cinder block motel with a curved driveway, sprawled on the bluff rising away from lake level. "I should get my things. I can't travel in this rag. But I'm too scared."

"Right. Rod is probably just behind us." He could handle Rod easily enough, but here was not the place, with people around, the police to be called if anything untoward happened. "Let's buy clothes for you to-morrow."

"Robinson, if I could trust you, it—"

"Trust me."

On the door to his room when they arrived was Scotch-taped a hand-printed note on the motel paper: "Suitcase with manager." No signature.

"Kathy," she said. He let her into the room and fetched the suitcase from the office, the wizened lady there asking no questions. It was packed with Phyllis' clothes.

"It was thoughtful of her, but I'm not sure it was smart," he said as they looked at the jumbled clothes. "How did she get them here? Is there another car?"

"No. Just the blue wagon."

"What will Rod think when he finds out your stuff is gone?"

"Robinson, I don't know. I'm scared out of my mind. Maybe he'll think we stopped and picked it up after you took me from the hospital."

"Maybe. Or maybe he'll figure it out and put the pressure on Kathy. She knows where we are. I think we should get out of here tonight, in case he breaks her down. It would be an ugly business if he came here. I can't get into that. Put on some slacks, why don't you, and we'll get something to eat along the way and stay somewhere and tomorrow I'll drive you clear across the state. I have a reservation at a top-flight place on Lake Michigan. I want you to come there with me. Rod won't have the slightest idea where we are."

"You said you'd lend me money, drive me to a bus stop. OK. But for me to go with you—I don't know. So many people have said they'd help." She broke down in tears.

"I'm different from them," he said. "I won't let you down."

"How can I believe you?" she cried.

"Because I'll put myself in your hands, too, the same as you are in mine. Because I am capable. Because we're both fugitives, equally. No, I more than you. Not just one man but the whole law-enforcement apparatus in the country is trying to track me down."

"What are you talking about, Robinson? I don't understand. Are you a criminal?"

"I'm Deerlover," he said.

For once he was shaken, and it was by his own incredible rashness, the uncharacteristic and impetuous act. He had not weighed consequences at all. Now, as he looked at her standing wide-eyed and utterly nonplussed across the bed from him, they flooded over him. He bent and dropped the sweater he had been holding on the bed but kept his eyes on her, gauging her reaction. He had put everything in jeopardy, not only the last few days of this season but anything here or elsewhere he might do later, his whole mission. And for what? To preclude a little human suffering, insignificant in the total balance of things. To gain for himself a few moments' companionship, a little gratitude, a little love? He couldn't believe it.

She backed away, into a padded chair before the closed drapes of the front window, reached behind her for the arm of the chair and sat down. The drapes reminded him of the night in the other motel when Rod had come. They must not stay here. Her skirt hitched up above her knees showing round and purplish bruises. Except for the one inconsistent welt from the blow to her face, they had confined themselves to areas that hardly showed when she was dressed, even in the whore's dress.

"You?" She motioned toward the TV.

"Yes."

"All this time you have been going out and doing that? And last year you did?"

"Yes."

"My God. And, and it's just because you like deer?"

"That's right."

"Robinson! You shouldn't have told me. Now I'm dangerous to you, and you, you–"

"Phyllis." He crossed over to her and she shrank back in the chair, but he gently touched the welt on her face and knelt before her and laid his head against hers. "I made a mistake in telling you," he whispered. "But it's impossible to undo it. Something came over me. You are a great danger to me now, it's true. But I can't hurt anything innocent. It's not in my make-up. Not even—Not for anything. So don't be scared of me. Please don't." She was still teary-eyed, trying to rub her eyes with the back of her hand, trying, he thought even to manage a smile. He had no handkerchief. He rose and went into the bathroom for the box of Kleenex there and brought it to her and sat opposite her on the bed. She dabbed her face. Everything, he thought, would be OK for the next few days, the rest of the season, and maybe he could do something about the so-called bow-and-arrow season to follow. As for the long-term future, even next year, Texas . . . That was unreal. One season at a time.

"Innocent?" she said, almost managing a smile.

She was thoughtful. "If I come with you, if we go together to that spiffy place across the state, would you still do it—"

He could see that she wanted to come . . . Of course she did.

"I think so. At least once or twice. At least once."

"I–" She hesitated. "I wouldn't have to be with you?"

"No, of course not."

"Then you'd leave me alone sometimes, once or twice?"

This was one of the consequences he had not weighed.

"Yes, I would. For an hour or two one or two days and one morning till the afternoon. I can buy you a handgun just in case," he added. He could use his Ohio permit to get one.

"No. No, don't do that. I couldn't possibly use it. Not even on Rod."

"All right. But there's no conceivable way he could know where you are. You could lock yourself in your room if you wanted. He'll never find you, though."

"We couldn't just drive completely away, out of the state, to wherever it is you come from?"

"Not now. I'll take you there, if you want—as soon as I can. It's a beautiful place. In Ohio. Who knows, you might even decide to stay?"

"How do you know I won't report you to the police while you're away? You'll come back and you won't know but what the law will swarm in and I'll be counting greenbacks."

"Partly I know because I'm your safety and escape from Rod. More because you wouldn't do that." He smiled. "It's not in your nature. Maybe you'll refuse to come with me and take your chances. But if you do come, you won't turn me in."

"Oh Robinson." Hysteria was beginning to overwhelm her, she'd had too much, tears came down her face and she twisted her lips in an effort at self-control— "you'll come back. And I'll ask you how, how the *day* went!" She broke down utterly.

He pulled her up from the chair and hugged her. "We won't talk about it then. It need only be twice more. Then it will be over. But now we must pack my things and get away from here."

He doubted that she heard, in her fear and misery. But she was coming.

She sat in the chair with her back to the window drapes and sipped a weak Scotch he had fixed while he loaded his *impedimenta* into the big Oldsmobile, the one suitcase with his clothes in it, maps, magazines, and the folder of clippings and notes on top of them, the .308 in its discreet leather case, the hideous bow of black steel with its thick black cords. And her little case. She had changed into slacks, a tan blouse and white sweater. He left her for a few minutes to consult with the proprietress, to tell her he and his wife were leaving a day early. Of course he expected no refund. He just wanted her to know. She held a sign-in card on which he had printed a false license number and description of the car. He wanted to win this woman's dubious good will in case Rod came and started asking questions. Bribe her implicitly with the day's rent. He'd brought the whore's dress from the room (crumpled, it squeezed into his right hand) and released it into the rubbish can on the way to the office.

Phyllis, quiescent now, joined him in the front seat, and he drove out of the motel. He'd thought of going over to I-75 and striking north, stopping at some motel around Grayling, then cutting West to the Homestead next morning. He'd still do that. But if it was OK with Phyllis, he'd stop across the highway for awhile in the lot of the grocery store there just to see whether Rod arrived and judge what to do thereafter. He preferred to get behind his pursuer, not to be chased. Phyllis understood. They waited. After a while she said, "All those men?"

"They were men like the ones who beat you."

"How do you know? You didn't know them."

He shrugged. "They were hunters."

Then the blue wagon streaked into view, screeched left into the motel lot. Rod jumped out in his sleazy sports outfit and strode without hesitation to number seven. He had pounded the truth out of poor Kathy. He twisted the doorknob, tried to peer through the drawn drapes, went directly down to the manager's office. He was there only a minute, then returned to his station wagon and burned rubber out the lot, hurtling out of sight down the highway, following no one. The proprietress had given him some description of his quarry, accurate or not.

"He'll never give up," whispered Phyllis.

"Maybe not. It doesn't matter. He's looking out there into the whole world, and we're behind him."

This was the truth, and Robinson was glad of it. There were threats enough to the remaining phases of this season, against Corbett and the Deerslayers, without having to worry about Rod.

He drove well under the limit, turning north off State 23 as soon as he could, cutting north and west on two-lane roads. He figured that when Rod reached the north-south Interstate and had failed to run them down he'd turn back on 23. He'd have no clue which way to go, and he had his girls to keep active, business to attend to. No use running into him, even in this dusk. Conceivably, he might continue the chase and, even, turn north, though south toward the population centers was more likely. Still, the odds were overwhelmingly in their favor. Only a freak coincidence could bring them face to face with Rod. Robinson would try to come out on the Interstate just south of Grayling. He'd take Phyllis to the lodge up the hill away from the highway where he had stayed six nights ago, drive them over to Glen Arbor in the morning. He had no reservation at the lodge, but that would present no difficulty. Half the tourist rooms in the state were vacant, thanks to him. He felt again the sense of his power. He'd made an impact, he'd changed things. He'd made the right decision in assuming this mission. That had not been certain after last season, but it was now.

Phyllis was quiet, thoughtful. As they drove he tried to explain his philosophy, his atheism and concomitant love of animals. The influence of Laura. He spoke in simple terms as best he could. She seemed to understand. Maybe he was underestimating her.

She asked: "What did you do, Robinson, before you became Deerlover?"

"I loved Laura. And, if you'll believe it, I taught Latin in high school. For twenty years. I retired early. We both did. She had money from her family."

"Tell me some Latin."

"Oh, I'm full of it. *Arma virumque cano . . .*" He could do the next twenty lines, but what was the point? She'd say, 'Well, it's all Greek to me.' "*Et ego in Arcadia.* Hmm. *Caveat Venator.*"

"What was that last?" she asked. "You said it with more feeling."

"It's my motto. Let the Hunter Beware. Don't be scared by it."

"*Venator,*" she said. "Like in venison."

"That's right." He looked across at her, centered in her half of the seat, looking straight ahead, hands clenched in her lap. He felt a wave of affection for her, or maybe it was only protectiveness. She was so small and helpless and after all, despite her own mockery of the term, so innocent. They were pulling up behind a big Buick wagon, a family in it, four or five children with their dog in the back behind their parents.

"Oh, Robinson!" she cried. "Look at the bumper sticker."

Actually there were three. "Jesus Saves" on the left,

in the middle "I Brake for Small Animals," and on the right he could hardly take it in—red against white, DEERLOVER. This was himself. There was something underneath in small letters. He drew a little closer. "We Love You!"

"Robinson, there might be hundreds of those, all over Michigan. And it's you they mean. You know? I still can't really cope with what you told me."

He'd thought much the same. Ordinary people like these, and there must be very many if not hundreds, in support of him. Someone was printing and selling stickers to the public. This expression of sympathy with his cause was the antithesis of the organization of Deer-slayers. Surely it would be larger and more powerful. Phyllis slid over in the seat and snuggled against him, and he put his free right arm around her and held her against him, letting them drop back from the vacationing family with the bumper stickers.

"You're strong," she said, "and even if it's crazy to say so, you're soft-hearted."

"Yes, both," he said. "I think that's true. I'll take care of you. I can and I want to. I have trusted you and put everything in your hands. You must depend on me also. I'll get you through this. I'm steady. I don't drink too much, not usually. I'm well off. I'm not violent." He was at a loss for words.

"The next few days, I'll probably be a mess on account of Rod coming after me and you, you know—I can't think about that. But Robinson, after that's over, if you'll really take me to your place . . ."

"I will. What then?"

"Well, I'm a pretty good cook, or used to be."

NOVEMBER

27

i

He snapped awake, the brown knotted rafters and planks of the peaked roof above him suddenly in focus. He had, again, the Dickensian sense of being a child: comfortable, warm, and dry at the top of a household some drizzly morning. He shoved a pillow behind him and hauled himself to a sitting position against the knotty-pine wall at the head of the big double bed. He looked about. The spacious room held three additional single beds. It was designed for a family like the one in the Buick, or, of course, for a group of hunters. Then he remembered eveything since he'd been here before, looked over at the tousled bedding beside him, panicked for an instant: she'd waited till he fell asleep, taken the keys, the car, driven to the nearest state police to turn him in for the reward, all the evidence in the car, flee Rod with police protection and the money. But no, no. He heard the reassuring splatter of the shower water in the bathroom somewhere behind him. Everything was all right.

They'd checked in at about 8:00. The proprietor remembered him from before, but there could be no danger in that. The slaying that night had been miles away. If he wanted the big attic room again at $40.00 it was available. A group of hunters had cancelled out. To tell the truth, business was suddenly miserable. It was that bloody maniac. God damn his hide. "You heard about him?"

"Yes."

"Ruined the whole season. Cost me a fortune."

"Sorry. Can you recommend a place to eat dinner?"

He'd recommended the Cozy Lady up the road, which sounded like the proverbial greasy spoon but would be OK for breakfast. He'd take her there now, then they'd come back, pack up, and he'd try to call Corbett before starting the drive across to Glen Arbor. She came out of the bathroom wrapped in a blue and white striped towel, in something like happiness, patting it against herself to get dry. "Morning, D.L."

She sat on the far edge of the bed and let the towel fall away as she picked up her underwear from the chair beside the bed and slipped it on, the panties without quite standing up. Then she stood and turned as if she were modeling to show the bruises blooming violet and black on her thighs and buttocks over the bikini underwear. A contusion, smaller, dark, with what looked like dried blood showed over the groin, from a particularly vicious kick. This, she said, was what had alarmed the men, and she'd fainted right after. The doctor was going to do tests, but she felt all right, inside. She shrugged. "Everything works."

Last night they'd just stripped and slid into bed without bringing anything in from the car. He'd not realized the savagery of the attack upon her. He could not risk taking her to another hospital. She agreed. She'd heal. She'd had a lot of practice.

At breakfast, she was nervous, even frightened, constantly gazing about, tensing whenever any man entered the room. She asked Robinson to sit on the same side of the booth with her, between her and the people. It was her first moment at all out into the world since giving Rod the slip. He put his arm around her and she sidled closer to him, turning her bruised face towards him, sloe-eyed and pale. Her black hair was still wet from her shower. "I'm pretty scared," she said. "You'll take care of me?" It was half assertion, half question.

"Don't worry."

"Don't you worry either. I'd be nutty to do anything,

you know, bad for you and lose my bodyguard, even
if I wanted to. I mean even if I could figure out what
I think about what you're doing and decided it was
wrong. I can't though. I'm in no condition to do anything except keep glued together, and not get caught
by Rod. Oh Robinson, he'd kill me."

"Don't worry about him. I'll take care of you." Their
food arrived and he took away his arm, nudged her.
"By the way, don't say anything too definite about me
in public places, will you?"

His humor seemed to help relax her, and she ate
pretty well. While they were eating, he told her his
thoughts about the next few days. There were the two
matters he must attend to, or at least try to attend to.
He considered it best not to be specific about them to
her, though he would if she wanted. She said no, she
would feel easier not knowing. On the other hand, he'd
have to make some calls maybe and do some harmless
reconnaissance, and she could be present then. She
nodded, thinking maybe about the reconnaissance. It
was only in fact to the town of Leland, he said, just a
couple of miles from their inn. And he'd have to be
away from her twice for a few hours in the morning,
possibly on one other occasion, but never overnight.
The few hours he was away, she could stay locked in
their room and use room service. He stressed the safety
features of the inn. It had security guards and a twenty-
four hour reception desk that would not give out one's
room number to strangers or allow any except guests
to explore the premises. The public could use only the
dining room, and that only with advance reservations,
even in the off-season, and so forth. In case anything,
well, went wrong with him (but it wouldn't) he'd leave
her all his spare cash, directions to the house in Aurora
with the key and a note to his housekeeper. The inn
had a limousine that went to the Traverse City airport

or she could call a cab. If arrested, he would not say where he was staying or he'd give the motel address in Au Gres. He would not mention that he had a companion, and they'd never suspect that he had. She must take *everything*—his clippings, maps, clothing—with her in the suitcases. This was important because she was now an accessory to what they called murder, and she must not be connected with him.

But these contingency plans were frightening her again, and he dropped the subject.

They'd kept their room till after breakfast. By instinct, he wanted to check the backtrail, whether any pursuer was behind them. He eased up the curving hill-road till the parking lot of the lodge levelled into view. Just the five cars as before, none familiar, no police. Oh just to stay here, the rest of the season or longer, leave everything to the Kid, *et al*. Eat, rest while Phyllis healed, make love under the peaked roof, walk in the woods.

He wanted to use their phone, now that it wasn't too early, and Phyllis came up with him, afraid to stay in the car alone. He dialed Corbett's number, copied from the summer issue of *Hunting News*. No answer. He tried his own number in Aurora. He'd been remiss in not checking frequently with Mrs. Hibbard. She answered, a bit sleepily, probably awakened by the call. Everybody was fine. Pincushion had had a recurrence of her ear infection, but there were still some of the drops left from the veterinarian last year. A new sack of thistle seed had finally come for the finches. The porch steps were as good as new.

Through this Phyllis sat on the edge of the rumpled bed opposite him. When he hung up she shook her head bemusedly. "I don't know how it's possible," she said, "but I can't help feeling you are a good guy, Robinson, whatever that means."

"I don't know about that," he said. "I do what I feel is right."

ii

He drove them slowly the few miles westward across the state through Kalkaska and Acme and along the south shore of Sutton's Bay into Traverse City. He remembered a big department store on the main street here, and he parked and took her in to buy some clothes. Again, at first, she was frightened to be exposed, in public view even though with him. But inside the store, Milliken's, surrounded by other customers and salespeople and racks and racks of apparel, it was inconceivable that Rod should appear, and she relaxed. "For the first time since I met Rod," she said, " I feel a little bit free."

"Buy anything you want."

She chose a tweed skirt-suit, a little austere for her, he thought, but she must be trying to escape the image she'd been cursed with all those years with Rod. At the counter, as he was paying, she asked about a coat or at least a jacket. She'd always been cold up here, everytime she had to be outside. She owned no coat. She'd pay him back. But it didn't really matter, did it? She'd be afraid to go out anyway. So forget it. He persuaded her to buy a lady's coat by London Fog and a polyester jacket too and wool slacks and some walking shoes in case they took the ferry to one of the Manitoulin islands or climbed the Sleeping Bear.

Driving westward out of town, they passed a car rental agency and he suggested they replace the Oldsmobile. Possibly Rod had a description of it from the woman at the Au Gres Motel. He was thinking also that the Kid knew the car, and he'd had enough of him. These were improbabilities. Nonetheless, on general principles, it was smart to leave a baffling trail. She nodded, a little worried again by this kind of thing, these precautions of the hunted. Probably she realized that it was not only Rod he wished to shake off their trail. He rented a new Dodge, a white four-door Aries, because it looked nothing like a hunter's car and ironically invoked his sign, the Ram, energy, imagination, independence. In the agency lot he transferred everything while Phyllis sat in the new car. Then she waited there, all four doors locked, while he drove the Oldsmobile to a side street a few blocks away. He did not wish to leave it at the agency and potentially link his old car and his new one, if there was any pursuer. They'd retrieve it on the way south Wednesday evening, when the season was over. He'd arranged to drop off the Aries after business hours, putting the key in the mail slot of the office. He paid with his Visa card in his true name.

A few miles and they were in the dunes area along the Lake Michigan coast. Glancing across at Phyllis now and then, he pointed out the variety of landforms and of flora here, sand-dune deserts right against stands of hardwoods or of pine, cedar swamps, this browngreenness set off by occasional stands of white birch, brilliant and shadowless under the noontime sun. In back, though you couldn't see them from the road, were treacherous bogs with moss on them that looked solid enough to step on. He thought this talk of natural things might help relax her, and indeed she seemed less tense, her color almost normal, looking and nodding as he pointed. She said she'd slide over against him again but couldn't on account of the bucket seats.

She put her hand on his knee and he placed his right hand on top of it. It was cold. Adjustment from life with Rod would take a long while.

Then she thought of something: "Robinson, did you, you know, do anything around here last time?"

"No. I was here ten years ago, on vacation, with Laura."

The thought, and the beauty sliding past on each side of them, filled him with nostalgia. That had been a good time. And what if we could see into the future? If he, tenured teacher of high school Latin and Social Studies, his young bride of a year beside him, could have caught even the barest glimpse of now: widower, practiced marksman, number-one fugitive in the state, maybe the nation, driving this same road again with a battered woman he was rescuing from hell.

"We camped out, up ahead, at the tip of the peninsula," he added. "Tomorrow or Sunday, if you like, I'll show you the place."

They reached the Homestead in time for lunch. It was two and a half miles beyond the tiny town of Empire and so, he figured, about the same distance south of Leland, where the Deerslayers were convening. The spread was expansive beyond his expectations, small groups of condominiums and cluster-townhouses ranged widely over several acres of wooded hills. He'd chosen an upper-floor suite at the site called Ridgeline, he wasn't sure why. It was high and central, with a view to the lake from the sitting room and over the woods behind from the bedroom. It had seemed from the brochure secluded yet convenient. Probably he'd thought also: no *cul de sac*, no getting pinned with your back to the water. They registered at the Reception Center just off the highway, drove in and out the curving roads of the place to get oriented, parked and took up their bags. She stood for a moment on their little wrought-iron balcony overlooking the distant lake, ruffled and scintillating in the sunlight. Then she changed for lunch. She'd wanted to wear the new suit but it showed bruises around her knees. Later, in Ohio, she said. He'd have to settle for the new slacks. They walked down a wooded path to the Inn and the dining room and a window table for two, lower and closer over the bright lake. Amidst this well-to-do roomful of vacationers, largely older people who might just have come in from tennis or nature trails, but with children of all ages, not a hunter anywhere, Rod, she said, could not appear. People like Rod didn't exist here. He agreed.

Some people, he thought, noticed her face and exchanged glances or whispered about it. But he held her hand across the little table. They talked affectionately. The bruising had happened in some accident.

After lunch he dialed Corbett again and a man answered. Phyllis was putting away their clothes in the bureau and closet.

"Yes?"

"Is this The Whitetail Hunter?"

"Yes. I'm accepting reservations for the fifteenth and after. Booked up until then, I'm afraid."

Maybe Robinson could cancel those bookings.

"Hm. I was thinking of this month. Tomorrow or Monday."

"Sorry, sir. We start up December first, and we're booked to the fifteenth." A sense of impatience, desire to hang up.

"I know that. But I'm here now. I haven't had any luck with the rifle. I want to go back with a trophy head, you know? I hear you've got the odds. If I got in first, first crack at 'em—"

"Yeah. But they're spooked by the gun hunters. You have a firearm license?"

"Yes."

"That's good for one buck, firearm season with bow and arrow. You have a bow?"

"Browning compound action."

"Good with it?"

"Platter at twenty feet, every time. I just can't find the damn buck to hit with it."

"I gotta see how good you are. I worship those damn animals, you know, almost call 'em by name, watched 'em since April, how they come and go. A wounded one, hit wrong, I don't want that. And I like to meet my people."

"I won't hit wrong," said Robinson.

"OK. But I gotta see your stuff. Now it's three hundred per person for a three-day guide, if you want a trophy, Pope and Young class buck. Kill fee on top of that. Hundred for a spikehorn to six-point. Hundred-fifty for a seven- to ten-point, two hundred anything over. I think, if you're coming in now, I might be able to put you across from a ten-point I know about."

"I haven't got the three days. I'll pay the three hundred for one day, if you'll put me across from that ten-point."

"No guarantees. I think I can. I gotta see your stuff first, though. And there's a hundred-fifty deposit. I usually fix that up by mail."

"Let me come down tomorrow morning, around ten. I'm at The Homestead in Glen Arbor. Name's Jay. I'll pay you the deposit or the whole three-hundred and show you my stuff with the bow."

"Well, OK. That's an extra hundred-fifty for that ten-point. If you get him."

"If I get him. Right."

"You know where I am?"

"I know exactly where you are."

Phyllis had been listening to his side of the dialogue. He could not gauge how much of the substance of it she had gathered. As he hung up she sat with her back to him across the room, one hand on each drawer-pull of the vanity. In the mirror her bruised face looked worried. "You're going to kill that man," she said. She turned and faced him.

"Maybe. I have to try, Phyllis."

"I know. And we agreed not to talk about it, didn't we?"

"I think it's better if we don't, easier on you."

She rose and he took her hand and they sat side by side on the bed.

When she spoke again, her tone was warm, not pleading, her fine almond eyes moist with feeling. "Do you have to do it again, Robinson? You've—" she tried a little laugh with a smile, but there was hysteria in back of it— "You've done so much. Nobody will dare to hunt these last few days anyway. So why?"

"I've thought of that. It's tempting, just to stay with you and take you home." Corbett, however, dared, and so did the convention at Leland. That was problematic. He had bad vibes about it. But if the showdown below Travis with Corbett was flamboyant and well-publicized, he'd cut down or eliminate the whole month of bow-and-arrow season. He'd never forgive himself back at home, for not having made the effort. "I have to try."

She said it wasn't only the hunters, though she couldn't get used to that, but the risk to him, and to her also, because truly she didn't know what would happen to her without him. He could only promise to be careful and remind her of their contingency plan in case he did not return. As she watched from the bed, he fetched the fat billfold from his jacket in the closet (it was of leather, but old and worn, and from Laura) and placed it behind her things in the back of the vanity drawer. There was nearly a thousand dollars left. He'd have to take half of it to Corbett—though with luck that might be refundable. For now he could leave it all. He had a few dollars in his money clip. The thousand would be safe here. She would be with it. He'd decided against the vault downstairs: too tricky her trying to retrieve the money without proper identification as his wife. As he closed the drawer a current of the original panic when he'd told her flashed through him. He was in her hands. She could leave while he was out. She could arrange the police reception, saying he'd kidnapped and beaten her—*ecce signum*. Exonerate herself as an accessory. Well, he'd told her. Betrayal wasn't in her nature. Just keep steady.

"You're going out now?"

It was awkward. "Well, yes, just for an hour. Nothing dangerous." He laughed a little and shrugged: "I have to practice."

She came with him. Though it might be scary to watch him practice, it was far less so than waiting alone imagining Rod in the woods outside. She simply couldn't face that.

They found a place on the lee side of the road, five miles back, just past Glen Lake and within walking distance of Sleeping Bear. There was a fifty-yard patch of level sand behind a scraggly stand of young pines trying to root themselves in soil too sandy even for them. He saw it from the road and parked far over on the left shoudler and got his equipment from the trunk of the Aries. In the sandy clearing she sat on a fallen log while he set his target twenty paces away and checked his bow. Since his first experiments on the beach of Saginaw Bay he'd bought two new pieces of equipment beside a proper target: something called an arrow rest, which supported the outer shaft of the arrow at mid-bow when the arrow was drawn so he didn't have to lay it across his knuckle or thumb with the risk of variation and of damage to his glove from the slice of the plastic fletching; and something called a release. This he held in the crooked first and second fingers of his gloved right hand and drew the string with it. A pin engaged the string, and when he pressed down on the trigger with his thumb the action retracted the pin and released the string, delivering the arrow uniformly and with no pull to either side; none of the awkwardness of having to unbend one's fingers suddenly to launch it. He explained these things to Phyllis, showed her how the devices worked. She just nodded.

Ever and again she looked back toward the highway and their car. He knew she was thinking *Rod*. To occupy her mind and calm her he kept talking. He told her of the catalogue he'd discovered at the sporting goods store in Au Gres, full of other accessories: bow tuners, stabilizers, strings, string servers, chest and arm guards, archery gloves, arrow straighteners, bow sights, dampers or silencers, *ad infinitum*. These last (he did not elaborate for Phyllis) muffled the slap of the strings upon release of the arrow. Just as he'd surmised back there on the beach, since sound travelled faster than an arrow, a buck could conceivably hear the release first, even over twenty yards, spook, leap, and evade the razor broadhead. Robinson could do without this refinement. Let Corbett hear the slap. Test his reflexes.

Let him think in that split instant what the sound meant.

She seemed disturbed by his account of the para-phernalia of death by bow and arrow. Or maybe it was something in his tone of voice as he spoke about them. He'd not realized before, he should have prepared over the summer, that hunting by bow and arrow was more cruel than firearm hunting, though it seemed at first more primitive and simple, the hunting of the Indians. But the impact of an arrow, drawn at fifty pounds, was nothing as compared to that of a lead bullet in the thirty-calibre range blasted out of a rifle barrel on the explosion of thirty or fifty milligrams of powder. The shock of that impact could knock an animal off its feet directly. It was the end of consciousness. But an arrow, even straight to the heart, might leave energy for a hundred yards of running from the site of the baffling blow and sudden pain. Usually, the hit was not so conclusive. The wise hunter, still in his tree stand or his blind, shot a second arrow into the earth where the deer had been, to confirm the spot. Then he left the scene for a couple of hours, even if it was getting dark. Had a few beers at the local tavern while the animal was dying. No point in rushing the search. Then re-turned to the site and proceeded in the direction of the largest part of the blood spot. Important to watch not only the ground but up in brush along the trail. If an artery had been hit, the lungs would blow the blood out. There might be pieces of lung matter also. The buck, though with the arrow lodged forever in his side, knew that cold water helped stop his bleeding and would head for a stream if there was one, or a slough or swale. After the cooling he'd come out straight across and you could pick up the trail. If he didn't emerge, but died in the water, and if it was shallow and you had wading boots, you'd find your quarry soon enough, submerged and dead. If there was no water, you'd find a pool or pools of blood, meaning a steady flow and the animal had stopped to rest. Then the blood trail would stop. You could follow it up till then even better after dark. Blood would virtually glow. If the blood trail played out, that probably meant the wound had clotted and the animal was bleeding internally. Some hunters lost their venison at this stage. You should search the area, first the thickest cover near where the blood trail stopped—blown-down tree tops, honeysuckle thickets, blackberry patches. That was where the animal had most likely gone to die. Had it not, then explore an expanding circle up to a radius of a hundred yards around the last sign of blood. The strongest buck could stagger no farther.

She sat on her log, thinking—what? He couldn't guess—as he practiced. With the aid of the arrow rest and the string release, his accuracy was much improved, and he held the bow vertically, not tilted or crossbow-style as at first, shooting from standing and kneeling positions, without any support. He invested only two of his arrows in the practicing and so had to walk out to the the target after every two shots. The other two arrows he'd save in mint conditon. The arrows sailed with an audible whirr in the air and zinged into the styrofoam behind the target. He never missed the target altogether, though once he hit in the outermost circle of it. With anything to rest his bow hand on or against, he'd be steadier yet. At first the effort of the fifty pounds separation between his left and right hands seemed, as when he first hefted the bow, too much. Indeed, he was a little out of shape, too much smoking and drinking, but the ability came back and he was all right, he'd be all right tomorrow morning when he qualified for Corbett.

When he was satisfied, he packed his equipment in the trunk of the car. Phyllis carried back the target. He said he needed to check out Leland. He'd drop her off on the way. She said no, she'd come. Of course she knew in a general way why he wanted to scout the town. But she did not yet dare to be left alone. And it would be safer for him, entirely safe, to approach the village in this family sedan with the woman obviously his wife (though bruised about the face), in sport clothes, a man who could not possibly be Deerlover.

At the one intersection in Leland he turned right in the direction of the hotel. It was a sprawling frame building, obviously built for the summer season, not fitted for cold weather. The whole right half at ground level was a glassed-in restaurant, closed down, all the chairs up-ended on top of the tables. Something was wrong. He felt as he and Phyllis approached the entrance, just to the left of the shut-down restaurant, a sense of entrapment. He almost took her back to the car. The cream-painted door was unlocked. Inside, in the small foyer of the same color, stairs led up to the hotel rooms and there was a doorway into the restaurant. On the newel post of the stairs was pinned a note: "Mr. and Mrs. Orlevsky. Your room is number 30 upstairs. Please leave the rent there as per agreement. Welcome Leland." Maybe this couple had arranged to stay in the hotel after the season, the staff gone, restaurant closed, maybe as a base for the ferry to the islands or down to Sleeping Bear. A late vacation, just the two of them. Very probably. But what then of the convention of hunters that was supposed to be here now? The whole situation was spooky. He wanted to get away. He took Phyllis by the arm and tugged her back toward the entrance. Outside was a man in a camo suit, black leaves in their pattern against a soft brown background, like the fall of Nature personified and lifted up and before them.

"Looking for somebody."

"No. Place to stay. Place to eat. Wife and I were up here last year a little earlier."

The hunter studied them, seemed to make up his mind about something. "You're too late. Hotel's closed except for us with special reservations. Hunting party."

"There're a lot of you?"

"Yeah. So what?"

"Where do you eat?" Robinson indicated the closed-up dining room.

"Bluebird, cross the road on the channel. It's open special for us." He regarded Phyllis, her bruised face. "Public can come too, if they want."

Robinson was not convinced that the hotel was in fact booked full of hunters, nor the Bluebird specially opened for them. Maybe. But something was false. It was dusk, hunting time. The others were supposedly out in the woods and fields, with their cars. Why was this one man here in his hunting outfit? Where was his club blazer with the deer insignia on it? He might have just filled his license or come back for something. But where was his car? The Aries was alone on the parking strip. The place really seemed deserted. And why was his manner so peremptory, as if he owned the place? Well, maybe he did.

Phyllis was staring at the man. Robinson couldn't read her feelings. She had been abused and humiliated by many such. Yet she knew why Robinson had come here: to investigate with a view to killing him or such another. How could a frightened and beaten girl reconcile all that? She was intelligent and brave, grateful to him surely. Only a couple of days more and he'd take her home.

"Phyllis," he said. "What about some dinner at the Bluebird?" They looked frankly at each other, into each other's eyes. He had a sense that something was at stake, he couldn't tell what. He couldn't think she shared his sense of danger or figure how that bore upon his suggestion to her, yet somehow it did.

She hesitated, glanced at the hunter. "No," she said. "I'd rather find a place for us to stay first if we can't stay here. It's getting late. Let's find a nice motel and eat around there. Please?"

"OK," he said, nodding at the expressionless hunter, taking Phyllis' arm and leading her back to the car. She had intuited his nervousness and fallen into the act perfectly. Again, he had underestimated her.

He'd wanted to cruise the Bluebird across the highway and down the road beside the channel to see whether it was really open. He remembered it. He had taken Laura there. But the hunter in black and olive drab—in the rearview mirror—was watching them steadily from before the hotel and could see which way he turned. It would seem suspicious if he drove across toward the restaurant, having agreed with Phyllis in the man's presence not to. Why he cared whether it seemed suspicious to that stolid specimen of insensate humanity he asked himself, but could not answer. He must be one of the arrogant Deerslayers. There was no one else around. Robinson could settle the matter then and there, let the Orlevskys arrive and find what they would find, another credit to himself. But the rifle was in the trunk. The hunter wasn't hunting. Phyllis was present. She had a limited ability to accept the way things were. He mustn't exceed it. Maybe that meant the Deerslayers, if they existed, would have to go by the board. But not Corbett. He'd have to prepare Phyllis for a morning alone tomorrow and another on Monday.

He drove her back to Ridgeline, and they went straight to their room to watch the 6:30 news on local TV. They'd missed the ABC network news at 6:00. After some irrelevancies about Ireland, El Salvador, and the

Middle East, Deerlover was the prime subject. The usual logos behind the grim-faced anchorman. This was the first time Phyllis had watched knowing Robinson was Deerlover. They sat together on the end of the bed. He could not estimate her responses, gauge the mixture in whatever degree of sympathy and revulsion. The victim outside Prudenville had now been found. The murder was a messy one. It had been a neck shot with a large bore rifle (the Kid's .44 magnum), and yet the victim had crawled hundreds of yards to a county road before he died, draining blood along the way.

He took her hand. She didn't cringe. "That wasn't me," he said. She squeezed his hand.

All the way up in Iron Mountain, on the Wisconsin border of the Upper Peninsula, had been a shooting in the Deerlover style almost (apparently) at the same time as Prudenville hundreds of miles away.

"That wasn't me either."

This discrepancy was giving rise to a new fear: "copycat killings," or possibly murders with ordinary motives committed under cover of the Deerlover scare. Good.

The station flashed a close-up of the old composite. Massini, it seemed, had not been asked to improve the likeness. Against this they played a few sentences from his Thanksgiving tape with Cindi. "The face and voice of the killer." That was it. He switched off the set. Again, no mention of the reward garnered by the Cooper family. It hadn't been in the papers either. That bothered him for some reason.

She dressed in front of him across the bed from where he sat, changing for dinner. She'd bought panty hose at the shop in the Inn so that she could wear the English tweed suit after all, without the bruises showing. She felt sore and stiff, she said, but would be all right. Just bruises. She stepped into the skirt, adjusted it, checked the hang and flare of it in the full-length mirror on the closet door, twirling a little.

"I have some knowledge of the killer," she said. "I'm still all mixed up. I can't help thinking he's a soft touch." Her eyes went moist and she came over to him and knelt and laid her head in his lap. "If only this was over and you'd take me home. Will you really do that?"

"Yes," he said. "Please get up. Sit here on the bed." She did so and he took her hand. "Good. Listen. Tuesday we'll go. I'll drop the business in Leland. So there's only the thing south of Traverse. I'll have to, you know, check that out tomorrow morning, after breakfast. That means leaving you alone a few hours. Again on Monday. But it's safe here. He'd give up by now or he's running crazy all over the state but he won't come here. I'm certain you'll be safe. Otherwise I wouldn't leave you."

She nodded. "You must go?"

"Tomorrow morning and Monday. Then it's all over."

He escorted her down to their reserved table for two by the window in the dining room of the Inn. She looked up at him from her menu with a sudden thought: "You don't eat meat, do you?" The question hadn't come up before. He smiled and shook his head. There was no omelette or quiche. The waitress recommended the whitefish, from Lake Superior, and he allowed himself that, protein to steady and strengthen his arm for the test tomorrow. She would only have a salad, but they shared a bottle of Vouvray. The reddish sun lowered itself into Lake Michigan while they dined.

NOVEMBER

28

i

Passing through Traverse City toward Corbett's, he began to worry that he was maneuvering himself into some sort of trap. Corbett had agreed too easily to the pre-season hunt, hadn't he? Robinson had told the press that he was coming to the Michigan coast. He'd told Cindi in the interview, hadn't he? That he was practicing with bow and arrow. These things pointed to Corbett—

But this was paranoia. Wisely or not, to sound convincing and well-to-do he'd told Corbett he was at the Homestead. Then he'd decided on impulse to give his real name. The very fact there'd been no invasion of police showed Corbett not to be suspicious, didn't it? Corbett had agreed so readily because he wanted the money, the business.

He lit a cigarette with the car lighter.

He'd missed a turn and was heading toward Interlochen instead of Buckley. He retraced, made a left, and soon was on Miller. He'd forgotten the number but it was something in the six thousands, and there it was, just a frame one-story house with the sign posted in front, professionally lettered: THE WHITETAIL HUNTER. He parked in the driveway, got the compound bow and the two Easton arrows in their plastic quiver from the trunk, and rang the bell of Roger Corbett. The door opened immediately.

He recognized Corbett from the photographs in last summer's *Deer Hunting Annual.* Corbett had wild dusky hair and a bushy mustache, an open and friendly expression. Under other circumstances Robinson might have liked him.

"You're the guy that called. Jay? I'm Roger Corbett."

"Rob Jay." They shook hands. He'd given his real
name. Now he must not fail. It was existential.

Corbett did not invite him in but instead joined him
on the porch. "Let's go out back," he said. He glanced
at the bow as they started round the house. "That's a
cheap Browning."

"Yeah. I do OK with it."

"We'll see. I don't usually do this, like I said. We
have three-day hunts, advance notice to get things
scheduled. Hundred and fifty deposit. And we don't
usually guide during firearm season. And we take two
or three guys out. There is another guy, now, wants
to go along, though. And you sounded serious on the
phone. He appraised Robinson frankly, smiling pleas-
antly. "I only take out guys that are serious."

"I'm serious," said Robinson.

"I figured."

Behind the house was a large yard edging off into
fallow or harvested fields. A young oak there had a
horizontal branch maybe twelve feet off the ground
with two loops of sash cord hanging from it. It was like
a gallows. The branch, of course, was for suspending
animals dragged and trucked out of their woods so the
blood might drain from their bodies and the venison
not spoil. Up a larger tree, a maple with an eight-inch
trunk, was nailed a treestand between ten and twelve
feet high. A platform supported by two-by-sixes with
two-by-four angle bracing underneath. Nailed to the
inner side of the platform along the trunk rose a narrow
wooden ladder.

"I'd like you to climb up there and shoot my target.
Distance is twenty-two yards."

The target hung at deer shoulder height from a frame

of light pipe. It was a circular bag stuffed maybe with straw, faced with a fresh set of concentric circles on cloth or paper.

"I don't hunt from tree blinds," said Robinson. True, there might be practice in it for Texas, but he couldn't think ahead to Texas now. And now was not a time to practice. Corbett was considering this objection.

"Place I'm thinking of, the bucks will come at you from behind. You're more likely to connect out of a tree blind I rigged there."

"You have haybale blinds on the ground. I read about them."

"Yeah. But not in the best place for the animals I'm setting up and for the wind. West wind tomorrow, off the Lake again."

"Put me behind the haybales. I'll connect all right."

He stood beside the maple, laid the Easton in the new rest, caught the launching cord with the release just under the point where it engaged the slot in the arrow.

"You haven't got any peg sight," said Corbett.

"No. I sight along the arrow like an Indian. I generally connect, I tell you." He looked out toward the hung target, strangely calm and relaxed, wondering why. A few yards behind it was a broken-down plank fence and then the acres of empty field. "You said 'we'. Is the Whitetail Hunter more than just you?"

"My brother Paul."

"I sure as hell want you to guide me out. OK? Give you the hundred fifty in cash this morning. Then like I said, same price as if for three days and the bonus for the ten-point or whatever I bag. I've been out all season with my rifle and haven't had one good shot at a buck. Same all last season. It's getting embarrassing. I read about your percentages. I *want* something.

You know how it it is. Uh—you said there was another guy?''

"He called like you. I kind of put you together. Figured to take you out tomorrow. That means early, an hour before dawn. Have to get here around five."

"All right. You'll guide us in person?"

"Yes. But it's all off if you can't hit. I don't want one of those bucks I've been tracing running over half the county with an arrow in his hindquarters or his belly. Bleeding all over the foliage. Half the time you never find them at all."

The other guy was a complication Robinson would have to think about. There was an obvious means of disposing of it. Corbett stood back, folded his arms, waiting for Rob Jay to show his stuff. Robinson had nipped the string into the release just under the arrow. He stood beside the maple, left arm unsupported, for that was the hardest shot, drew the fifty pounds, sighted two inches high, and squeezed down the release with his thumb. The Easton zinged into the dead center of the target. For an instant he thought Phyllis was with him again, not the whitetail slaughterer Corbett, that he was back with her in the quiet on the lee side of the highway practicing archery, she with whom he hoped to make some kind of life together.

He shook his head to clear it and kneeled crosswise to his line of fire, looked over his left shoulder at the target and drew the bow again with the second Easton. He thought: Corbett is right here. Why not do it now, silently and efficiently? Just turn toward him, give him a second to realize, then cleave his heart in half at ten yards range. No need to abandon Phyllis again tomorrow or worry about the other guy. It would be so easy. But was there not some one else in the house behind Corbett? Some wife, or the brother Paul? He couldn't think clearly, but the moment seemed too risky. He might be trapped here and unable to return to Phyllis. And the symbolism, the impact upon the bow-and-arrow season in December, would be wrong. Corbett must die in the field, Deerlover taking the explicit credit for that, not for some backyard arrowing. He turned away from Corbett toward the target. He drew hard on the cheap Browning compound, claiming the arrow to the last possible fraction of an inch, sighting again two inches high, and squeezed the thumb release. The bow whanged and the arrow sang clear through the target right next to the first one and drove on into the rotten-looking planking of the fence six yards behind and lodged uneasily there.

He rose to his feet. "OK," said Corbett. "Not too bad. You qualify."

Corbett beckoned and led him up the steps of the back porch and into the back door of the house. Robinson set down the bow. He'd retrieve that and the two practice arrows on the way out. The kitchen was tidy and well-kept. They went through it into a sitting room with lots of glass on two sides and an inert fireplace in the corner, a roll-top desk. Robinson sat on the sofa opposite, Corbett straddling the desk chair without turning it, resting his arms on its straight back, gazing at Robinson.

"You a family man?" Robinson asked.

"No. My mother lived here. I keep it the same as it was. Housekeeper comes once a week."

Robinson wondered what day. It wouldn't do to run into her, coming back for the Aries. Tomorrow was Monday.

"About the money—"

"Oh yes." Robinson dug out his money clip and slid out three fifties for the deposit, handing it across.

"Thanks. I'll give you a receipt. Now like I told you I charge three hundred a person for a three-day hunt when I'm setting up a possible trophy. You said the three for the one day, but that's not square. I'll charge you a hundred. It's a tricky place to find, but it isn't very far in, won't take much of my time. I forget. Did I tell you about the kill fee?"

"Yes."

"Wear your camo suit. You got one?" Robinson nodded.

"Do I need waders?" He didn't own a pair but had read that Corbett sometimes took men into outlandish swampy places he knew of.

"No. It's solid ground where we're going. But the forecast is for cold, maybe rain. Warm hat, gloves, thick socks, winter underwear if you've got it. Don't eat much breakfast, don't drink much. I don't want you pissing in the area. Spoil it for a week." Robinson started to rise. "Wait. One other thing." Somehow Robinson knew what Corbett would say. "There's this freak in the state shoots hunters. You heard about him?"

"Something in the papers, yes."

Robinson looked into the frank blue eyes set in the youthful eager ruddy face with its full moustache, the long wind-blown blackish hair. Corbett was a decent man as mankind went. He honored his mother's memory. Under other circumstances . . .

Corbett hesitated an instant, smiled. "Fact is I checked you out." He swung himself off the chair and sat down again at the desk. He started to scribble the receipt. The pad looked like the kind that made a carbon copy. Yes. He tore off the original for Robinson and put the yellow carbon with the hundred fifty into a small drawer in the cubbyhole part of the old desk. The yellow copy recorded Deerlover's real name amongst the papers of a man whom (*Diane volente*) he would slay tomorrow. A telephone lay in its black cradle at the right of the desk.

"Checked me out?"

"Yeah. I called Homestead. Just to be on the safe side, you know. They rang your room. So I knew you were OK. I was going to hang up when your wife answered."

"Phyllis?" Stupid. Of course his wife was his wife.

"I guess. She said you were coming down to see me. You're the first hunter I met brought his wife. And then I see that Dodge sedan outside. I can't quite figure you, Jay, but you ain't no maniac."

"No. Maybe the other guy you mentioned is the maniac."

Corbett laughed. "Checked him out too. There's not much rifle hunting on account of that guy. Maybe that'll help you both. Keep the fields clear, if any firearm hunters could find the place. More than two good spikehorns in there for you. He don't care about bow-and-arrow hunting anyway." Corbett had not been following the news reports closely enough. "He wouldn't know how to get where I'm taking you for sure. Just thought I'd mention him."

Back in the yard Robinson retrieved his gear. Everything seemed set. Then he remembered he'd forgotten to ask about the time schedule for tomorrow. He did so.

"It's like this," Corbett replied. "I want you two guys in position a whole hour before daybreak. With the drive in, that means getting here around five, like I said. (Robinson would have to leave Phyllis at four, but she'd be asleep, sleeping in. That was best.) Course you can't shoot nothing till sun-up. And you got to stay where I put you. I don't want nobody shooting anybody else. I'll come back around eleven. Take you for some grouse hunting or some fall-run salmon, or you can just sack out here. Whatever. Don't drink. Take you back out around three-thirty or four and leave you till dark. You'll get that ten-point one time or the other, I'm pretty sure. You or the other guy will."

The other guy might be a problem. Robinson had an irrational sense that he would be somebody familiar, the nervous family man with the big pumpkin-colored pick-up in Missaukee, the hunter in camouflage from Leland, even Cooper himself, someone like that out of the past. But whether that proved to be so or not, it looked as if eleven A.M. tomorrow was the moment of truth.

ii

On the way north back to Glen Arbor, Robinson detoured into Traverse. He drove past the parked Oldsmobile wagon, still waiting there and unticketed. Then he stopped at a sporting goods store he had seen when they rented the Aries. He looked at arrows. The store carried a good supply ready for the December season. It included the Eastons he was using. He picked one from the display and studied it very closely. It was exactly the same as the four he had bought in Au Gres. There were no distinguishing marks or serial numbers. A man might have bought his four here, for all anybody could tell.

Phyllis was okay, a little nervous and pale. She'd not left their room. He walked her down the hill for lunch at their table over the shimmering lake. She said that Corbett had called. "He sounded like a nice man," she said. "Very polite."

"Yes," was all he said, and they dropped the subject. But he knew what was in her mind, and it bothered him.

And she'd made herself truly complicit, accessory. With a few words she could have warned Corbett, and she had not spoken them.

The rest of his day was free, and he drove her the thirty miles up to the top of the peninsula. It was a tip, one of the tips of the world. But though the scenery on the drive was familiar (the travel time much shorter than he remembered), the failed park he and Laura had discovered had ceased to exist. There was new steel fencing with a gate, a ranger station and other white-painted buildings, aluminum trimmed, Nature completely cleaned up, well-clad tourists, a few, ambling about, no chance of a frog pond or wild animal. This change in a territory he remembered disconcerted him. They stood on the beach where—on these very pebbles, under these diminished trees?—he and Laura had camped and made love by firelight on the outspread double sleeping bag. It was the same place and a different place both at once. He wanted only to get away. "Yes," she said when he told her. "Let's go home."

When they came down to Leland it was five-thirty

or so (the Aries lacked a clock), almost dark. He wanted a look at the restaurant, the Bluebird, to their right and across from the channel road. From the highway he'd picked out lights from the hotel, but only two or three. Where was the convention of Deerslayers? He eased past darkened weirs and mills, he couldn't tell, parts of the historic site, but across the channel to their left was the restaurant, lighted and active indeed. Or was it? Lights, and three or four people moving about, but no crowd of men at tables, waiters serving them. In the lot five or six cars only. It was wrong, false. He should not have driven down here. He backed into an alley, half inclined to black out his lights till out of sight, not doing so but coming out of the alley and away from the scene as quickly as possible without being conspicuous, back south onto the highway and the shelter of The Homestead. There, after Phyllis showered and changed, dinner over the long light cast across the lake by a faint new moon.

NOVEMBER

29

i

The activities of the morning, after he'd kissed Phyllis goodbye at 4:00, happened in such cold and darkness that he gave little thought to the ultimate purpose, but only to the immediate practicalities of getting out to the Aries, holding to the right roads south, shivering up to Corbett's door despite the layers of clothing under his wool jacket. The other guy was already there, mousey-looking with big glasses in plastic frames, a blotchy beard sprawling all over his face. Greg something. Corbett offered doughnuts and allowed each of his clients a single cup of coffee, followed by an invitation to use his bathroom facilities before they set out. But he also gave each a small thermos for later. Then the jumble out to the frigid passenger compartment of Corbett's yellow truck and the bumpy drive out into further darkness as the truck warmed to a comfortable state. Robinson tried to retain the sequence of lefts and rights back in these obscure country roads but gave it up. He'd have to find his way out by directional instinct and through luck. He'd be driving this very machine. Out of Corbett's area of high-kill probability back to The Whitetail Hunter? This was hard to grasp. He glanced at the bearded man between him and Corbett at the wheel. The man's life depended on where Corbett positioned him *vis-à-vis* Robinson, did it not? Little difference either way, really.

But now they were out at the site, still in sub-freezing cold and almost utter darkness, shining patches of remnant snow under the slim moon just perched on the edge of the horizon, tilted, ironical. The time was six-thirty, maybe two hours before sunrise. Corbett veered from the dirt road and stopped the pick-up, its lights illuminating a haybale blind stacked in front of an old fence of broad horizontal boards. The hunter stationed here would expose no human silhouette against the dawn light behind him, could shoot his heart-slicer out of that light invisibly.

"Greg, this is your spot," Corbett said. "It's a good one. They come out of the woods behind me." He indicated the west. "I say forget the does and wait for your trophy buck, morning or evening, today, tomorrow. He'll come right along this road for food I've been spreading for him."

Greg, then, was sentenced to death, since Corbett would drive on, place Robinson, come back for Greg first then Robinson. It would be necessary to arrow them both. He wasn't sure he could manage it, the two men on the same occasion. But no, Corbett drove him back down the road the way they had come.

"No tree blind," he said.

"No. I have no experience shooting from trees."

"All right. This is the best I've got for you then. It's better than Greg's, but not so comfortable."

The lights of the pick-up illuminated a passage between two stacks of haybales, other hay stacked some distance behind. Again, no dawn-light silhouette, and the arrangement supplied the hunter the deadly advantage of having the light to his back, his prey peering half-blindly into it. That was in the morning. Quite likely Corbett had laid out other blinds for evening.

All this hay was not the remnant of any defunct farming operation. Corbett had trucked it in, stacked it advantageously to the movement patterns of the deer he had come to know and, as he said, to worship, to venerate.

Caveat venator.

They sat together in the warm cab of the truck.

"Remember," Corbett said, "don't take a piss or a

crap if you can help it. If you have to, go as far as you can back there so's not to spook these animals I've spent the whole fucking year developing. They'll come out of those woods from the west. Like I told Greg, forget the antlerless ones, right? There's two bucks anyway come right along this road most days, one of 'em the ten-point. You'll get first crack at him, I figure. You wait for him, Rob."

Robinson said he would and stepped down from the cab. Corbett backed out and pulled away, leaving him the channel between haystacks to crouch in or retreat back into.

"Good hunting," came Corbett's voice out of the darkness.

"Thank you, Roger. I'll see you round eleven."

Robinson waited the two hours that brought the cold dawn, excluded the lifeless moon, spreading a meaningless light over the expanse of uncultivated field before him stretching into its fringe of undifferentiated woods westward. Indeed, the deer appeared on that remote fringe, does identifiable by their triangular image, fawns among them. Then, suddenly, out of nowhere, the two bucks on the very road just before him, one much larger than the other but both fine animals. Corbett had done his research well. Robinson slipped out of the side opening in the hayblind and angled quickly toward the road ahead of the deer so that they would not bolt in the direction of the hunter Greg. When he reached the road they had raised their heads from their grazing and were watching him. He wanted to try feeding them from his pack of cigarettes. Instead he said in a soft voice, "Shoo. Leave here." The high ears cocked toward him, showing their lining of white. No, this was not doing it right. "Go," he yelled, suddenly waving his arms and rushing toward them, "Get the hell out, damn you." For an instant they stared, then, simultaneously, shied and bounded away, jagging towards the far woods, bodies see-sawing with each bunching and driving of the hind legs, tails raised and switching, white flags of alarm. Still he ran after them though far outdistanced, waving and yelling. "No!" he called out, almost laughing yet for some reason feeling tears well in his eyes, "Bless you!" The bouncing white rumps vanished among the trees. At the very top of his lungs he called after them, "Bless you!"

After he caught his breath he reconnoitred the area, making a wide circle around the hayblind, partly to keep warm from the exercise, partly to contaminate the area with human smell as thoroughly as he could. The field was flat with little grass but clumps of tall brush, brown now and crinkly. There were patches of gray sand and some sheets of exposed rock. Maybe it had been too rocky for farming. Yet there had once been trees here, for he found widely spaced stumps, big ones, first-growth. It seemed an ideal habitat for deer except that he didn't see much for them to eat, only patches of grass beside and on what had once been the dirt road. When he had finished his circuit he returned to the road near the blind, unzipped his fly and urinated.

Just across the road was a run of brush almost thick enough to hide him if he crouched low. He pulled up some other strands of brush and used it to thicken this makeshift blind. He put the bow behind it, thinking about things that might go wrong and what he would do about them. He sipped from the thermos Corbett had supplied him. The black coffee tasted alcoholic. Corbett had spiked it with bourbon. Robinson only sipped it. He would finish it afterwards. It was good against the cold.

He decided to practice, so as to stay warm, double-check his equipment and discover the right allowances for distance and wind drift. The distance all the way to the hayblind was too far, almost out of range. He'd paced it at thirty-seven yards. Corbett would presumably stop on the road. When Robinson did not appear, he'd step down from the truck and walk over toward the blind within the twenty-yard range. If he'd picked up Greg first? But he wouldn't. He'd have to drive past Robinson's hayblind to collect Greg, then pick up Robinson on the return. Not likely. What if, for some reason, it was necessary to shoot all the way to the hayblind? That was what Robinson practiced. He found that he could not conveniently shoot around the right edge of his stand of brush but had to force an opening in the middle of it to aim through. He was visible, after all, behind this thin flimsy screen, but Corbett would not see him because he would not be looking for him. He took the squatting position that was his steadiest and that offered the lowest profile and aimed for the center of the square end of a bale of hay on the left side of the blind, four inches high and two to the right to allow for the slight breeze he felt out of the north on his right cheek. The practice arrow plunged into the bale centered but far—maybe eight or ten inches— too low. The arrow disappeared into the straw, but he had seen the moment and place of impact. He drew again, aiming this time a foot high and two inches right, and the arrow whirred across the thirty-seven yards and vanished into the geometric center of the end of the bale. He was just rising, to try to retrieve the practice arrows, when he heard the sound of a motor in the distance. It couldn't be after ten-thirty. Either Corbett was early or this was another hunter penetrating the territory. He squinted southward down the road. It was Corbett's yellow pick-up. Fifty yards south of the hayblind, the truck pulled a little off the roadway and went past the blind behind it and Corbett got out. He left the motor running. Robinson knew from experience that deer, even in remote areas like this, were not much disturbed by the sound of motors. They reacted and dispersed, rather, when the motor was cut off. That meant a human invasion. Corbett wanted to contact Robinson without queering a possible shot. He approached the hayblind from the back, went out of sight, slipping into it from the opening on the south side. A moment's hiatus, then he walked out the front, puzzled obviously, trying to figure out what had happened to this special hunter. He did not walk forward toward the road, within range. Robinson drew back the bow on his first reserve arrow. It was the shot he had just accomplished. He knew how. But the pleasant young face, the frank slate eyes. He liked the man. Maybe.

The instant's hesitation was too long. Corbett looked right into the brush blind, comprehension flashed across his face. He darted back into the strawblind and then appeared running out of it toward the truck. What to do? Robinson rose brainlessly and rushed after him past the blind. If Corbett should get away . . .

Corbett reached the truck still the fifty yards ahead. He should have leapt inside, slammed the door behind him and taken off. But he didn't. He was leaning forward into the passenger compartment, fumbling for something behind the seat. It was a rifle. Robinson saw the butt in his hand. The range was thirty-five or forty feet. The wind was behind now, wasnt' it? No allowance for drift, aim a little lower than before? Robinson drew while standing. Back hard, the fifty pounds easy now. He felt the backs of the blades of the heart-slicer dig into the gloved knuckle of his left hand. He aimed at the left shoulder, into the air just over its juncture with the neck, squeezed the release. The shot was low, below the heart he thought, but not much, not much.

Corbett stood hunched, as if thinking what to do, half turned away, holding the gun in his hands as if he still might use it. Then it fell and he started to run away, north, parallel with the road, maybe thinking he might find Greg, who would save him. Robinson went to the truck, its motor still humming evenly, and placed the bow and quiver with its remaining arrow on the passenger side of the front seat. He walked back to his blind and fetched the thermos. He'd drive out of this. But no, he had to be sure. He cut the engine, leaving the key in place, and followed the direction of Corbett's flight. He took the gun with him, which was not a rifle after all but a single-barrel shotgun. At first, the tracking was difficult. There was no blood trace on the ground, and the brush was so sparse that it did not record Corbett's progress. But here and there, above ground level, he did find blood traces, mixed with spungey matter. It had been a lung shot, messy but in the end almost certainly mortal. Then in a shallow clear dip in the ground, he found a huge pool of blood. Corbett had fallen here, should have died, but somehow rose and staggered away. He could not be very far. There were some bloody foot tracks heading north where he had tracked in his own blood, but then no spoor evidence. Robinson began an expanding spiral from the last bloody track. Seventy or eighty yards beyond it he found Corbett's booted legs extending from under some dried scrub. He was spread-armed, still clutching the rooted brush by which he had tried to pull himself from sight. The arrow stuck up from the left side of his back. Robinson felt around under it. Nothing. Corbett was dead. Greg was stationed not far away now, but it seemed best to leave him to make his harmless composite and offer his testimony to the press. What did he know? The name Rob maybe– Nothing more.

Back at the truck, Robinson finished the spiked coffee. It was still hot, and very good against the cold.

He did not try to retrace the series of turns by which Corbett had driven in. Time and efficiency were not important, just so he go out and back to Corbett's and the Aries. He kept eastward, cutting left or right when necessary, backing off from a couple of dead ends, until he hit a numbered and paved county road and knew where he was. At The Whitetail Hunter, he pried open the roll-top desk with a crow-bar he found in the basement and retrieved his hundred-fifty dollar deposit and the copy of his receipt. On Corbett's phone, he dialed Cindi Mayer at the *Detroit News*. A man's voice answered. She was away apparently.

"This is Deerlover," he said. "You know about me?"

"Yes, my God, yes."

"I have just killed a man named Corbett who called his business The Whitetail Hunter. I killed him with an arrow such as he used himself. His body will turn up in the country northwest of here. The point is that I may remain active during the rest of the bow-and-arrow season. Do you understand that? Through December."

"Yes. I think so."

"I'll confirm with Cindi Mayer later. I am calling from Corbett's former address."

"I see. Would you mind giving me the phone number and the address?"

"Not at all." Robinson gave the requested information, as polite as his interlocutor, but hung up on the next time-buying question with a curt "I'm civil, not stupid." Went out to the rented Aries and drove back at moderate speed to Phyllis at The Homestead. He left Corbett's empty thermos in the kitchen sink, next to a neat pile of unwashed plates.

On the way back, he tuned into the hourly news on radio. Nothing about Corbett. Too soon. Again, virtually no hunters seemed to be afield. State and federal authorities continued to urge that hunters stay out of the woods and fields these last two days of the firearm season. Four killings of hunters in the Deerlover-style had been confirmed after dawn this morning at widely separated points in the northern lower peninsula—one of them just ahead of him, in Leelanau County where he and Phyllis had reconnoitred. These were practically simultaneous. They could not be the work of the one man. Copycat killings or murders in disguise. Any hunter seen afield would be interrogated.

What would the news have to say about the coming month of bow-and-arrow season after the blood-drained body of Corbett was discovered sprawled under those dry bushes? At the reception center of The Homestead he signed the Visa slip for their bill through tomorrow, drove on down to the lot before the little row of condominiums on Ridgeline.

No response when he tapped on their upstairs door. For fear of frightening her he didn't just let himself in with his key. But of couse she was frightened by the knock too.

"Phyllis," he called. "It's me, Robinson."

She opened the door at once and stepped forward to embrace him. He hugged her to him. She was trembling. He looked across the room and out the patio doors to the west and the falling sun. It lit the cloud cover from below in an incredible display of pinks and greys.

NOVEMBER

30

i

They walked the nature trails of The Homestead and made love in the afternoon, sleeping afterwards until dinner time.

He said he'd like to pack up everything and put it in the Aries, so that after the relaxing elegance of the dinner they could just leave for Traverse City and the exchange of cars and the long sweet way home. She helped him pack all her new things in the suitcase they'd bought in Traverse except the English suit which she wore with the new blouse and the London Fog coat.

He was tempted to watch the 5:30 local coverage from Saginaw-Bay City for the story of Corbett and the other slayings in his style. But no, it was predictable. He didn't want Phyllis to see the body of Roger Corbett, especially not in color.

He walked her down the wooded slope to the inn. She wanted to report to the ladies' room though they had hardly left the apartment. As he waited in the lobby, he sensed someone approaching him and raised his eyes. It was—of all people—collegiate outfit but with a white felt sombrero.

"What in hell are you doing here?"

The Kid showed a surprise equal to Robinson's own. He had not, then, been following him again. It was some coincidence.

"You! I'll be damned. Sorry. I came up to check on those Deerslayers in Leland. This is the only place to stay. I couldn't find the Deerslayers. Place is nutty as hell but no Deerslayers."

"Nutty?"

"Few guys around not doing anything. They started

274

to rough me up then quit. I couldn't figure the place."

"Me either, Kid."

"Buy you a drink?" The Kid indicated the cocktail lounge adjacent to the dining room.

"Can't. We shouldn't."

"OK."

Just then Phyllis came out of the ladies' room and the Kid said goodbye and went into the lounge.

The receptionist escorted them in to the host, who sat them at their regular table. The falling sun was still a few degrees above Lake Michigan, underlighting the clouds more redly than before. The sunlit room was half filled this early hour, the candles on the tables not yet lit. Robinson noted with irritation a man dressed wholly in buckskin, incongruous here, in bad taste surely, his back to them, seated at a round table with several other men in sports clothes and two women. No matter now. Forget him. One of the men looked vaguely familiar.

He ordered their usual drinks, her daquiri, his Scotch on ice. Time to unwind. He took her hand across the table. She said, "You've saved my life." He squeezed her hand. The drinks came. He touched the rim of hers with his glass and they sipped together.

He leaned back against his chair. It was all over for the year. He'd completed his mission and could relax. And next year . . . His mind raced. Why just Texas? Why not criss-cross the whole country by jet, even the planet? The old image of the warden in Africa, no, himself, blasting the horrid blacks one by one who had poisoned thousands of elephants, the old chief last, who never even rose from his seat but nodded as if to say, Yes, it is right. Or else . . . amidst the smiters of baby seals in Canada, the sun low on the edge of the southern horizon, suddenly (for they were armed so as to kill when necessary the barking mothers of their prey) uncovering his tiny submachine gun and raking the whole hideous area free of men. Seeming to be everywhere (as he had long ago told Cindi Mayer), *being* everywhere as no man of this earth could be.

They had the fettucini and salad. While they ate, he told her more about the house in Aurora, half-isolated on its little hill surrounded by the glade, the animals, the finches, their brilliant yellow plumage darkening for winter.

For some reason as he spoke his eyes fixed on the back of the man in buckskin. Something about the shape of his head, the crewcut. And as if he felt Robinson's eyes upon him the man turned suddenly around and looked squarely at him.

Cooper.

ii

It was impossible to tell whether Cooper had recognized him. He stared blankly into Robinson's face for a moment, then turned back to his company, gesturing, speaking softly. The familiar-looking man across the round table looked up toward Robinson. He was—wasn't he?—the man Phyllis and he had talked to outside the shut-down hotel in Leland, the man in camo clothes? These were the Deerslayers, Cooper one of them? He needed time to think. But there was no time. Cooper rose, and without looking again in the direction of Robinson and Phyllis, walked out of the dining room. He was going to the security people of the inn, or to a telephone. It was all up, if Robinson did not act swiftly.

Phyllis took his hand across the table top. "Is something wrong?"

He looked at the pretty face, the wide brown eyes, whitish strip of scar tissue over the right one and the partly-healed welt.

"Yes, I'm afraid so. The man who just walked out, in deerskin? He knows who I am. I shot his brother on the first day of the season. He may be calling the authorities. Don't look. But the other men at the round table behind you may be part of a trap for me. We have to get away from here."

"Robinson." She squeezed his hand, dipped her head, closing her eyes for a moment, nodding.

"Look: you leave first, as if you were going to the ladies' room. Walk through the woods up to Ridgeline and bring around the car." He pressed the keys into her palm.

"What if they—"

"Sssh . . . I'll join you in ten or twelve minutes. If I'm longer, just get away. Leave the car in Traverse. Take the Olds or get a cab to the airport. No. You'll have to take the Olds. Get everything out of the Dodge: glove compartment, back seat, trunk. The cash is in the glove compartment. Clean it out, Phyllis. Drive to Aurora. You know where. But I'll be with you in ten minutes."

Her face was very pale. She rose and left. He watched the group at the round table. They paid not the slightest attention. How could that be? Phyllis was gone, out of sight.

How should he get away? If worse came to worst, he'd wait the ten minutes, start out of the room, bolt for the front entrance. Then he realized—it was a mistake to have asked her to bring the car down to the inn at all. Much better if he had fled into the woods, no one knowing his destination, and joined her in the car up at Ridgeline. They could have slipped quietly away, no one knowing the Aries was theirs. Too late.

Again he glanced toward the group of Deerslayers at the round table. They were talking, drinking, paying no attention to him. If they knew who he was, it was an uncannily good performance. What was happening? The whole thing had been organized for the purpose of drawing him in, hadn't it? Now they had him, and they paid no attention? But if he got up to leave . . . He looked out the paned window to his right. The huge globe of the red sun was lowering into the lake. He laid the back of his hand, the four fingers, against one of the panes, cool, it was framed in bronze. There was a bronze latch just above his hand. He looked up. The window section rose upward to the ceiling, thermal glass. There was a second higher latch that he could reach if he stood up. The bottom of the section was maybe eighteen inches from the floor. It could not be frozen in. The temperature was freezing or a little above outside, and the warmth of the dining room must have penetrated the bronze and glass. If he stood and opened the higher latch, bent and pulled the lower one, pushed open the window, he could step out of the room, dash round to Phyllis and the car and be away from here before they knew what had happened. He drank down the last of his Scotch, snuffed out his cigarette, looked up to the upper latch. Something told him no. Too conspicuous and bizarre. He would never make it.

On instinct, he simply rose. No reaction whatever from the round table. They were not even watching. He moved toward the exit, the back of his neck tingling, reflexes ready for the dash, but nothing happened. This was incomprehensible. Somehow he had it wrong.

Her London Fog was gone from the coatrack in the foyer leading to the lobby. Maybe he could still get out the main door, rush round and intercept her coming down in the car, clamber in and the two of them home free. Cooper was probably at one of the telephones ahead in the lobby, maybe with his back to the door. Or he was at the receptionist's desk.

Just then the Kid came out of the cocktail lounge. Not a flicker of recognition from him this time. He walked past toward the dining room. Robinson hesitated, called softly, "Kid." The boy stopped, turned back. "I'm in trouble. If you would stay around here a minute, maybe you could help."

The Kid nodded and stood where he was. As Robinson faced towards the lobby, from around a corner to his right stepped Cooper. The men's room was back there. He had simply gone to the men's room. He did not notice Robinson. But before he could start to return to the foyer to rejoin his friends, something outside the main entrance to the inn caught his eye. He walked over to the glass door and gazed out, studying. Robinson moved a little so as to get partly behind him and see also. It was the white Aries waiting there. Cooper watched a long while. He was putting it together. Surely he was. His friend at the table had recognized Robinson as the guy with the wife and the family car who had come by the hotel. He had mentioned the event to Cooper. That was why Cooper had turned and looked at him. He had not recognized him from the first day of the season, not then. He'd chatted with his friends for a while and then merely gone out to the bathroom. Now his eyes had caught the white sedan waiting. You could see him thinking, recalling now the face he'd tried to reconstruct with the aid of a police artist. He wheeled and strode to one of the phone stalls along the right hand wall of the lobby. He punched a short—very short—number into the touch tone receiver, glanced again out over the browned, snow-stained grass behind the inn to Phyllis in the Aries, and began to talk, impatiently, apparently having to wait to be connected to various speakers. Then he hung up and returned to his vigil at the glass doors. If he went back to enlist his friends, the car might vanish. If Robinson appeared and got away in the car, or if the woman driver suddenly pulled away, Cooper would catch the number on the rear plate, and that was all that was necessary. That would lead to the killer of his brother. Didn't he realize that all he needed was that number? Why didn't he go outside and take it down? He just stood there, maddeningly, watching.

The police were coming. And if Robinson delayed much longer, Phyllis would follow his instructions and go off on her own. He looked back at the Kid, joined him.

"The guy there at the doorway has figured out who I am," he said. "I killed his brother. I have to get away."

"I'm not physical. I couldn't take him, a guy like that. And if I tried . . ." Of course the boy could not get involved in that way. "I'll try to distract him, and you can slip past. Robinson shook his head. It wouldn't work. "Wait. I've got a handgun in the car. Right across in the lot. It was grandfather's, like the rifle. I've been using it, you know, to administer the *coup de grace*. I'll get it and . . ."

"Get it for me, son. Quick."

The Kid walked right past Cooper and away across the patch of stricken grass and the access road to the lot. He had not, thought Robinson, delivered the *coup de grace* to the farmer near Prudenville who had crawled so far bleeding from that misplaced hit to his throat. Maybe the man's wife had come running from the house and the Kid perforce had fled.

He returned at once, passing Cooper again without a glance. The gun he pulled from out his belt under his sports jacket was a long-barreled revolver out of the old-West movies. A six-shooter loaded with cartridges of dubious antiquity. Still, if the Kid had really been using it . . . He thrust the long muzzle into his own belt.

"See you," said the Kid and returned to the lounge.

Robinson approached Cooper from behind. Two or three people in the periphery of his vision stood at the desk. Others sat in chairs and sofas about the lobby. He drew the revolver under cover of his jacket and pressed it sharply into the region of Cooper's left kidney. Cooper started, tensed.

"It's me," he said. "This gun is silenced. I can waste you here and walk out to the car and leave, and no one will know what happened. I'll do that if I have to. Don't cry out. Don't do anything. Just walk ahead of me to the car and get in the back seat."

"You got it, bud, God damn you."

Robinson reached around Cooper with his left hand and twisted open the brass handle of the paned door and prodded him forward. Cooper walked toward the car. The door swung and clicked shut behind them. Robinson didn't dare look back to see whether anyone had noticed anything. If Cooper broke and ran, Robinson would drop him in his tracks and they, he and Phyllis, would get out of this. It might be simpler that way. There could be established no connection between that and Mr. and Mrs. Robinson Jay of Aurora, Ohio, with the Visa card, could there? Or could there?

Cooper stopped at the rear door to the Aries, waiting for instructions.

"Open it. Don't get in yet."

Cooper obeyed. Robinson opened the passenger door next to Phyllis.

"All right. Slide in. Yank the door shut behind you. Sit in the middle." Cooper did so. Robinson slipped in beside Phyllis and poked the long muzzle of the revolver between the bucket seats. It glinted blackly in the light from the inn and the overhead illumination of the pick-up area. "Hands in your lap. Where I can see them." Cooper complied.

Phyllis, without having spoken, eased the car away from the inn and took the turn toward M-22. Just then one of the blue State Police cars passed them going in the opposite direction, no siren or flashing lights, but moving very rapidly. They reached the intersection with the highway. A black limousine coming northward swerved around in front of them, tires squealing, and vanished past the lighted reception center into the darkness toward the inn.

Phyllis pulled up at the gateway and turned toward him. She was very pale.

"Turn right, Phyllis," he said quickly. "Drive down to where I practiced with the bow. It's four and a half or five miles. Pull across the road there if you can and park on the shoulder. I'll tell you where. Don't fret, darling." Her eyes widened. "Please. We can get clear."

He looked into Cooper's face. Fear there as well as hatred. He remembered talking with Cindi about Nazis and lampshades.

"Where'd you get that suit?"

"It was my brother's. I wanted to kill you wearing it."

The shadows were long outside, the sun out of sight, maybe set, behind some trees, radiating still in pinks against gray from the low cloud cover. A line of cars was forming behind them, headlights weaving, the drivers seeking to pass.

"Dusk," Cooper said. "The season is over."

Just a couple of minutes before they would reach the place where he knew the terrain and could manage even in the semi-dark. Maybe, after all, he could spare Cooper. He didn't want to involve Phyllis directly in a killing. The Deerslayers.

"Those men in Leland, those people at the table with you?"

"To hell with you."

"I'm trying to decide whether I have to kill you or not. I'd just as soon. But you'll bloody up my car. And my wife isn't used to—"

"Fuck your wife."

The whole thing had been a scheme to draw Robinson into the open, hadn't it? The offer of the reward hadn't worked. No one could claim it. So Cooper had fabricated the convention of the Deerslayers, published it, somehow gained use of the Leland Hotel and the restaurant when normally they'd be closed.

"Your man at the hotel didn't realize it was me," he said. Cooper looked up from his hands, trying it seemed to connect with Robinson's line of thought. "You were down at the restaurant or you were asleep. You knew I'd come hunting you. Maybe you wouldn't have recognized me yourself in these clothes, wife along, family style car. Then tonight."

"I gave up."

"Right. Rightly so. I wouldn't have come back to Leland. I had bad vibes about it."

Cooper merely glared, but there was fear behind the defiance.

It was vital now to think clearly. For him and Phyllis, their relationship, it would be best to let Cooper go. What, after all, did Cooper know more than he had known before? He could not have seen the number on the rear plate. He knew this was a white sedan. He might have the make and model. He might not. If he did, would the authorities check the registration of every such car in Michigan, surrounding states, all the states? Robinson did not know what was possible in this computer age. Would they think of checking the local rental agencies? He had paid by Visa, which gave the Aurora address, for the car as well as for the stay at The Homestead. And the table by the window had been reserved in the name of Jay. Why had he been so careless?

Ah, but that was not the point. It all came down to whether the couple at the window-side table could be connected with Deerlover. And Cooper's failure to recognize him in the dining room—in the very presence of the Deerslayers and their women—specifically exempted Mr. and Mrs. Jay from all suspicion. So long as Cooper died now. Therefore he must.

Cooper was bent over in the center of the back seat, low over his clenched hands, his cropped head only inches from the tip of the revolver. Robinson kept the gun nestled between the bucket seats. Cooper could not take a sudden swipe at it. He might go for the door, hope Robinson's nerve would fail the necessary instant, take his chances hitting the roadway, people behind to help him. Probably he suspected too much about Robinson's nerve to try that. Robinson shifted the revolver to his left hand and reached behind Phyllis to push down the left rear door lock. Now Cooper would have to fumble with that and the latch to get out. One less option.

Sleeping Bear loomed as a shadow to their right, then began to level and pull away. "There," he said

to Phyllis. "Just ahead, the wide space to the left."
She nodded, started the left turn signal. No oncoming
traffic. She crossed over and skidded the Aries to a
stop in the sand. The line of cars from behind them
swept past, eight or ten of them. She looked troubled.
He didn't know what to say to her now, Cooper with
them in the back seat. He squeezed her arm. "I'll lose
him," he said. "I'll be back in a few minutes. We'll be
in the clear. We'll talk then. OK?" She nodded but did
not look across at him. He added: "Cut the motor.
Lock all the doors till I get back."

Of course he should have gotten in the back with
Cooper in the first place. Now he had to be careful to
get him out without letting him bolt. He opened his
own door, slid his left hand past his seat and unlatched
the rear door on his side, pushed it open a little and
swung out onto the sandy shoulder, switching the aim
of the revolver across the door post so that it still covered Cooper. "Come on, Cooper." He stepped out,
straightened up in full buckskin, looked around as if
weighing his chances. "No. Walk, ahead of me. We'll
take a ramble in the woods."

Cooper moved slowly down the small slope of the
shoulder and away from the roadway into the area of
grassland and marshland that Robinson knew spread
between them and a stand of birch, beyond which, he
thought, lay drained open fields. Where, precisely, from
this point were the oblong swampy areas, where was
the stretch of solid terrain where he had practiced with
the bow and arrows? He followed Cooper closely, trying
at the same time to orient himself in this virtual darkness. But before they got into the grasses, the lights of
a car coming toward them from the south caught in
his peripheral vision, the car crossing onto the left-hand
shoulder as Phyllis had done, cutting its lights before
it had even come to a stop, the dying lights yellow,

orange, red, nothing, as the car still moved. Whitish, not State Police.

A blow to the jaw sent him reeling backward, his head and neck jolting painfully into packed sand. He lay for an instant staring up into gray overcast then lurched to his feet, the revolver still clutched in his right hand. Cooper was gone. He'd be racing back to the highway, flagging down the next car that could take him out of this. But where? Robinson scanned the whole area back to Phyllis in the Aries, the stretch of highway north and south. Nothing. Cooper had to have gone for the stand of birch. Probably he'd flounder in one of the swampy bogs, but he might make it through. Robinson dashed after, trusting the thoughtless memory, the mind-map drawn from having been here before. There was nearly no light. Then before him he saw the tawny flash of Cooper's buckskin cutting across *lacunae* between dry brush, making for the stand of birch, then Cooper imaged in a coppery light, mired in mud, staggering back, around, and through the trees. Robinson followed, staying by his mind-map to dry ground. Cooper out there, racing full tilt across a stubble field but jagging like a deer, left and right, to present the most difficult target. He was fifty, sixty yards away. A miracle if the revolver could drop him. Robinson had no idea of its characteristics. He squatted anyway, outstretched arms on his knees, gun held in both hands, aimed way high and a yard to the right where Cooper would cut next. If the shot failed, nothing else but to try to run him down out there and shoot him through the head, or lose him and to hell with it.

The thud of a heavy rifle shot somewhere to his left, behind him, and Cooper pitched forward, slid on the furrowed earth and lay still. A magnum charge, certainly.

The Kid struggled through the adjacent brush and

glanced out across the field. He held the .44 across his chest, his grandfather's gun. Robinson handed him the ancient six-shooter.

"Thanks."

"Yeah. What about next year?"

"I've been thinking of something in Texas and around."

"I'll finish it," the Kid said. He walked out onto the scraggly field. Robinson started back. After a moment there was a muffled shot. The *coup de grace*.

The line of the highway, coming into sight up the slope past the birch stand, showed the Aries right away. A car flashed behind it, going southward. Another coming far to the north, to his right.

His feet were wet and cold in the canvas shoes from stumbling into the mini-swamps. He was dead-tired.

He deviated from the straight path to the car to avoid a bog that he remembered and found himself on hard ground. It was the clearing where last Saturday (it seemed a month ago) he had practiced with the bow and arrow. The log at the far end where Phyllis had sat—he remembered it just in time, approached with short tentative steps, toed it and stepped over. Otherwise he'd have fallen.

She wasn't in the car. He'd realized that even before he finished clambering up the sandy incline to the shoulder of the road. The front passenger door was locked. He glanced into the back seat in the foolish hope that maybe she was napping. No. He looked quickly up and down the road. She was gone.

The front door on the driver's side was unlocked as he'd known it would be. He sat behind the wheel, felt for the ignition key on the steering column. Missing. He didn't worry about that either. She would no more strand him without the key than she would have driven away in the car. It wasn't on the padded dash. He felt under the seat beneath him then punched open the glove compartment. The key lay there on top of a note scrawled on the back of one of the rental papers. He read by the light from the glove compartment.

I heard the shot. I'm taking $500. I'll send it to you somehow. Sorry I can't live with you. You are kind. No time.

He started the motor, made a U-turn, and drove slowly northward, unsure whether to try to find her or to start home. She would not betray him. She, now, to be sure, was the living link between Deerlover and that couple by the window. She could turn him in for the reward offered by the Cooper family. She could testify about Corbett and tonight. She would never do it. That was not why he wanted to find her. He just wanted to have her with him. Yet she did not want to be with him, obviously, unless he abandoned his mission, as he could not. And Rod? No likelihood that Rod could catch her now. She'd be all right. Maybe the price was always to be alone.

Two patrol cars flanked the entrance to The Homestead up ahead. Now he must go on past. He drove by. An officer was interrogating the driver of a sedan headed toward the highway. A pretty woman sat beside the driver, other people in the rear. They must be stopping every car that came out. Cooper had called for them and Cooper could not be found. There was no danger. Yet as he cruised away a tingle went up the back of his neck.

In Leland he bought a six-pack of beer at the market on the hotel side of the highway and a half-tank of gas at the station next to it. He looked around, but he did not ask the elderly attendant whether a young lady had been there seeking help with her disabled car. She did not want to be with him.

The six-pack was to show on the off chance that the police noticed that he had driven by just before. He'd left his motel only to buy the nearest beer. He accelerated up close behind a truck, and a car pulled up behind him just before they passed The Homestead. The squad cars and officers were still there. Of course they paid no attention.

He drove on southward. More likely she had fled him in this direction, where the traffic was headed, toward the bus station or the airport. She might even have got a ride from the Kid. He could check out those places with a chance of finding her. He would not.

In Traverse he cruised the back residential street to check out the Oldsmobile. There it stood, in its antiquated immensity, no one around, friendly lights in the houses beside it. He drove past. No ticket. He drove around the block. This was the kind of connection he was nervous about. Somehow, for some inconceivable reason, the authorities might have it under surveillance. He pulled in front of the Oldsmobile and backed up close to it. Nothing happened. He switched off the engine of the Aries, killed the lights, stepped out onto the street. He began to transfer everything to the Oldsmobile: the .308 in its case (which he placed on the back seat within reach of the driver), the two bags behind the rear seat. So he had her new clothes, except the English skirt suit she'd been wearing. He would keep them. It might be she'd send her address with the money and then he could explain that he had not killed Cooper, that, again, she need never be involved any more in his mission. His red one-gallon gas can was missing from the trunk of the Aries. She must have taken it to help her flag down a motorist.

Everything transferred, he stood back and tried to

recall the history of this car. It reminded him of the canoe, the whole adventure in Missaukee. But actually it had come onto the scene after that, to return the canoe, participate in the snow adventure at Lost Lake, get him and Phyllis from Au Gres to Traverse. The Kid knew of it, no one else, not Rod, nobody. The Kid had the reliability of any disciple, any fanatic. This car was safe.

He drove the Aries back to the rental lot and dropped the key into the slot outside the office. He walked back to the Oldsmobile. There he felt once again his cold and discomfiture. He unlocked and raised the rear door, unzipped his canvas case, took out his boots and a pair of socks. These he pulled on in the driver's seat, throwing the wet things into the back. He ground the starter. The engine failed, caught, failed again, then started reluctantly, complaining against having been left these four days, but it coughed and started. He wound slowly about the unfamiliar streets, came out on a southbound road that led to Michigan 10 eastward across half the state to I-75, which would take him all the hundred seventy miles down to Toledo.

On the curved entrance ramp to I-75, his lights picked up a car pulled off to the side, a deer, stiff and white in his lights, a doe roped slantwise to its hood. The car had stalled or run out of gas. The driver stood behind it, trying to wave him down. A flick of the wheel and a light touch on the brakes and he'd crush the hunter against the trunk of his own car, not too violently, just enough, back away and get clear without involvement. He nearly did so, jerked left at the absolute last instant. Rolled down the right window. The man, a typical Neanderthal, was apparently frightened but unaware that the close call had not been accidental. Robinson reached back and unclasped the two latches of the case of the .308. He flipped up the lid. The rifle lay there loaded, though uncocked, gun metal gleaming faintly. He laid his hand on the stock. The man was saying something, failure of distributor, carburetor— he wasn't sure. He caught Robinson's eyes, stepped back a little. Robinson tightened his grip on the stock. But no. Cooper was right. The season was over.

He screeched away, burning rubber. Good to get back to Aurora. He lit a cigarette. He badly wanted a Scotch. He drew on the cigarette.

Trees flashing by like soldiers.

The general terror was beginning to edge in.